CHASING THE WIND

NORMA BEISHIR
COLLIN BEISHIR

Copyright (C) 2008, 2012, 2019 Norma Beishir and Collin Beishir

Layout design and Copyright (C) 2019 by Next Chapter

Published 2019 by Terminal Velocity – A Next Chapter Imprint

Edited by D.S. Williams

Cover art by Cover Mint

This book is a work of fiction. Names, characters, places, and incidents are the product of the author's imagination or are used fictitiously. Any resemblance to actual events, locales, or persons, living or dead, is purely coincidental.

All rights reserved. No part of this book may be reproduced or transmitted in any form or by any means, electronic or mechanical, including photocopying, recording, or by any information storage and retrieval system, without the author's permission.

Scripture taken from THE MESSAGE, copyright 1993, 1994, 1995, 1996, 2000, 2001, 2002. Used by permission of NavPress Publishing Group. All rights reserved.

Scripture taken from THE HOLY BIBLE, NEW INTERNATIONAL VERSION, copyright 1973, 1978, 1984 by the International Bible Society. Used by permission of Zondervan Publishing House. All rights reserved.

Is tric a bheothaich srad bheag teinne mòr.

A small spark has often kindled a great fire.

GAELIC SAYING

No matter how much we see, we are never satisfied;
    No matter how much we hear, we are not content.
    History merely repeats itself; nothing is truly new;
    It has all been done or said before....
    It is all foolishness, chasing the wind.
    What is wrong cannot be righted; it is water over the dam,
    And there is no use in thinking of what might have been....
    Everything is appropriate in its own time.
    But though God has planted eternity in the hearts of men,
    Even so, many cannot see the whole scope of God's work
    From beginning to end....
    All things are decided by Fate; it was known long ago
    What each man would be....

ECCLESIASTES 1:8-6:10

In order to be a realist you must
 believe in miracles.

DAVID BEN GURION

To the Father, the Son, and the Holy Spirit.
We committed this tale to you when it was still a
work-in-progress, and we commit it to you again now.
May it bring you glory.

AUTHOR'S NOTE:

Writing a novel is like childbirth. Some are easy and over in no time; others are long, painful labors that seem to take forever and are plagued by complications. This baby had to fight its way into the world, and we are deeply and forever grateful to the many "midwives" who assisted, in one way or another, to the birthing process: our fellow authors at the Writers of Mass Distraction—especially William Kendall, Mike Saxton, April Morone, Eve Gaal, Lorelei Bell, Mark Hunter and Linton Robinson; our two guardian angels, Carolyn Crowe and Kathie Chambers, and their husbands, Bob and Lee, respectively; our pastors at the South Side Church of God, Brandon Hunter and his wife Carly and John Morden and his wife Carole; Cathy Smith, Martin Rus, Nicole Tuberty and Kyle Tuberty from our writing group; Pearl Wilson, who watched us both grow up and became our surrogate family when we had none left; Maria Carvainis and Damaris Rowland, who once whipped a green writer into printworthy shape; Sabra Elliott, from whom I learned a great deal about "the biz"; Jim Moses and the rest of the staff at the Buder branch of the St. Louis Public Library (thanks for coming in early to get things going by the time we charged through your doors at precisely 9 am every morning!); Dr. Ferris N. Pitts, Jr, MD, who, many years ago, looked at a bad-tempered, out-of-control teenager and saw potential few could have imagined back then; Pastors Keith and Penny Holste and Susan Hunt, Christ Lutheran Church of Webster Groves; Edward Magee of St. Joan of Arc Parish, St. Louis; Joyce Moran, Annunciation Catholic Church, Webster Groves; Julia Finnegan of the now-defunct Chapter One bookstore—thanks for everything; Michael Kahn, who's both a brilliant writer and a brilliant attorney; the late Donna Julian, onetime partner in crime, who would never have believed the route we now follow—you're sorely missed, dear friend; and to the many other friends, associates, and professionals who saw us through the storms: Dr. Taylor Bear, MD, Washington University School of Medicine, Department of Neurology; Dr. Robert A. Zink, MD, South Side Family Practice; Bob Powell; Jim Wolf; Carol McGrael; Debbie Henderson; Josephine Roe; Karen Alexander; Sue Easterby; Jim Hux; Charlie Kingston; Mike Dickerson; Katie Alexander Greer; Steph Duran; and the gang at the Quality Inn Southwest, St. Louis. We had the benefit of several resources for research, but the ones that proved most beneficial were Daniel B. Davis' *Muses, Madmen and Prophets: Rethinking the History, Science and Meaning of Auditory Hallucinations*, as well as *The Creating Brain: the Neuroscience of Genius*, by Nancy C. Andreasen, MD, PhD; *Clone* by Gina Kolata; and *The Blood and the Shroud* by Ian Wilson. Of course, we take all the blame for any factual errors.

And to Jake and Lolly Beishir, our parents/grandparents. You were right. We *did* need you and we *do* miss you.

Norma & Collin Beishir

1

CAITLIN HAMMOND

The woman was hysterical.

Her husband wasn't in much better shape. He could barely talk, struggling to answer my questions in fragmented sentences. Their six-year-old daughter had been abducted from their backyard. There were no witnesses, and an exhaustive search of the neighborhood turned up nothing.

"I don't understand how this could have happened," the child's father said, choking on every other word. "She only let Mandy out of her sight for a minute."

He looked over his shoulder at his inconsolable wife, being tended by a neighbor. "She's always been an overprotective mother," he said, lowering his voice. "Mandy's our miracle baby."

"How so?" I asked, taking notes. In the years I'd been with the FBI, I'd found child abduction cases to be the biggest test of my objectivity. If somebody took my kid, I'd probably hunt them down and kill them. Kidnappers and pedophiles should always be turned over to the parents. The courts might let them go. But you didn't hear that from me.

"We'd been trying to have children for years, almost as long as we've been married," the distraught father went on. "We both come from big families and wanted kids of our own, but it just wasn't happening."

"Is your daughter adopted?" my partner, Jack Farlow, asked.

He shook his head. "No, no," he said. "She's ours. We went to a fertility clinic when we couldn't conceive. It took everything we had, all of our savings, but Mandy's worth it."

"You had difficulty in having a child," Jack said slowly. "Who was at fault?"

The man was at first puzzled, then angry. "What kind of question is that?" he asked. "What has it to do with Mandy being missing?"

"Probably nothing, maybe everything, depending on the circumstances of her birth, sir," Jack said. "Did you use an egg or sperm donor?"

The man shook his head. "No," he said. "Mandy's ours, one hundred percent. She was conceived by in vitro, but we used our own...you know."

"We have to ask," I apologized. "If your daughter were not biologically yours, then we would have to consider the possibility that the biological parent might have taken her."

"We're her parents, no one else," the man insisted. His face reflected his deep fear for his child's safety. "Please bring our baby home. Please."

"I ONLY TURNED my back for a moment," the distraught teacher repeated over and over. "I never left the schoolyard!"

A six-year-old boy had been abducted outside a prestigious Seattle school for gifted children. No one saw it happen, even though there were several children in the schoolyard, being picked up by their own parents. Everyone was being questioned.

"We understand, Mrs. Harwood," I said in an attempt to calm her.

"*I don't understand!*" The emotional outburst came from the child's mother. "You were responsible for him! You were supposed to be watching him!"

"I *was* watching him!" the teacher attempted to defend herself. "I was watching all of them! I only turned away for a moment!"

"Long enough for someone to take my son!" the angry mother shot back at her.

"Easy, Mrs. Wyndham," Jack urged. "She won't be able to remember anything if you keep attacking her."

Charlotte Wyndham turned to the window, hugging herself tightly as if trying to shield herself from the chill of fear that consumed her. Tears streamed down her cheeks. She'd said her husband was in Paris on business. He'd booked a flight as soon as she called him, but he could not be there before the next morning.

"We only had each other, until Noah was born," she said. "Neither of us have any other family, and we both wanted children. When we couldn't get pregnant on our own, we sought out the experts. It took us three years and thousands of dollars to have Noah, but he's worth every penny. If anything happens to him...."

THE WOMAN's body was found in her car, parked in the driveway outside her Florida home. She was still in the driver's seat, her seatbelt still in place. She'd been shot in the head at close range. Her five-year-old son was missing, presumably taken from his car seat.

We questioned her husband at length. He was frustrated by the endless probing. "My wife is dead, my child is missing. Why are you wasting time questioning me?" he demanded.

"You found her, sir," I said. "We have to start there. With you."

"She had no enemies," he said irritably. "None. She got along with everybody. I always envied that about her. She was the peacemaker. I was the loose cannon."

"Were you a loose cannon with her, Mr. Reynolds?" Jack asked.

"No, of course not." Roger Reynolds didn't miss the implication. "What are you asking me?"

"Only if there were any problems between the two of you."

"You think I killed her?" Reynolds asked incredulously.

"Did you?"

"No, of course not!"

"What about your son?"

"What about him?"

"Were there any problems regarding the child?" I asked.

"Don't be ridiculous!" Reynolds snapped. "Our son was perfect. Perfect."

2

LYNNE RAVEN

Dear God, how long has it been? As I stood at the window in my hotel room in London, looking at the city below, I found myself feeling like I'd just landed on another planet.

I should probably explain. I'm a field archaeologist. Home is wherever I happen to be excavating—at that time, "home" was Egypt. The only people I see on a daily basis are the members of my team. Restaurants, theaters, shopping—all are rare luxuries. My wardrobe is simple and functional, much like everything else in my life.

As I looked at the royal blue tunic I'd planned to wear that night, I realized I hadn't worn it in months. It didn't fit my normal lifestyle. Too feminine for a dig. Thinking about it, I couldn't remember the last time I'd made the effort to be feminine, to actually look like a woman. I couldn't remember the last time I'd felt like a woman, the last time I'd wanted to feel like a woman. Feeling and acting like a woman always seemed to get me into trouble. I had discovered long ago that I got on better with people who'd been dead for a thousand years than I did with the living.

I'm not one to spend a lot of time worrying about my looks. For what? I've been divorced over a decade and can't remember the last time I was on a date. I turned forty that summer, but on the good days, I could still pass for thirty. I had fine lines around my eyes—"archaeologist's squint", an occupational hazard more than a sign of aging. I haven't changed my hairstyle since college—it's long, dark and threaded with strands of copper from being out in the sun all day, every day. I know I don't look my age. But there are times I feel it acutely. I got good genes from my parents. Genes that I haven't been able to pass on to any children of my own. The thought of the children I'd never have and the family I hadn't seen in a year brought a wave of unexpected sadness I couldn't shake. It was Thanksgiving in the States. How many years had it been since I'd gone home for Thanksgiving or any other holiday? I told my parents I was too busy, but the truth was that it was too painful to see my three sisters with their children. Seeing what I'd been missing.

I always believed this was the path God had chosen for me. I could never have been satisfied with the life my sisters led back in Missouri. Taking the easy route had never been my style. We all have a purpose. I believed without doubt that mine was to find evidence that would prove the events described in the Bible had actually happened.

As for why I was in London, I hadn't planned on being here. Three weeks before, I'd been minding my own business, working on my dig in Egypt when that call came, asking me to do a series of lectures in London, to replace a colleague who'd been injured in an earthquake in China. The request surprised the hell out of me, since it came from someone I not only didn't know well personally, but had been at odds with professionally. What was it Dr. McCallum had called me? Too much of a dreamer to ever be a serious archaeologist. Whatever the reason, I wasn't about to debate the merits of his request. It had been so long since I'd taken any time off from my work, for any reason...and as much as I loved it, I'd been feeling the need for a break for a long time now. It was a feeling I'd never had before, one I was at a loss to explain, even to myself. Work had been my whole life for...how long? Ever since the divorce.

I was giving serious consideration to adopting a child, maybe two. Not babies. Older kids. Kids who could live the way I live and actually enjoy it. There are lots of kids in the world needing parents. It doesn't matter if I give birth to my kids or not.

Being in London would hopefully also provide me with an opportunity to seek the funding I needed to continue the dig. Time was running out and I'd already been rejected by the three private foundations that had funded my previous digs. *God, I need a miracle*, I silently prayed. *That's what it's going to take if I'm to continue my work—your work.*

———

I saw him enter the crowded lecture hall. He was hard to miss. He looked so out of place in the sea of conservatively dressed attendees—but it didn't seem to bother him. He wore faded jeans and a beat-up black leather jacket. He was with a young woman, a petite brunette who looked as aristocratic as he was scruffy. His light brown hair was in desperate need of a comb. His boredom was evident in his body language, the way he shoved his hands down into the pockets of his jacket. I decided I'd lost my audience before I even got to the podium.

"I fail to see why you couldn't have come to this event alone, Sarah," he said, annoyed. "You know quite well that I've no interest in spending the evening listening to a decrepit old man talk about life in some desolate outpost of Hades, digging up the pathetic remains of people who lived in another millennium."

The woman shook her head disapprovingly. "If you had even bothered to read the brochure I gave you, you would know that Dr. Raven is a woman," she told him.

"No difference," he said with an offhanded shrug. "Frumpy, gray hair in a schoolmarm's bun, sensible shoes, no doubt." He looked at his watch. "I'm going to need a pint—or two—to get me through this evening. I'll be back. Eventually." He turned to leave the lecture hall and we were face-to-face. He smiled, and his whole face seemed transformed by it. His eyes, blue and intense, instantly softened. "Hello," he said in a low voice.

The woman came up behind him. "This is Dr. Raven," she told him.

He extended his hand to me. "Connor Mackenzie," he introduced himself. His Scottish brogue was unmistakable. I noticed that he didn't introduce his date.

"Lynne Raven." I shook his hand. "I left my sensible shoes back at the hotel," I said, feigning regret.

He looked embarrassed. "You heard that?"

I nodded. "I'm afraid so."

"I'm sorry—"

"Don't be." I smiled. "I get it all the time." It was the truth. People are always surprised when they discover I'm an archaeologist. They always expect us to look and act like Indiana Jones. I do have the hat and the leather jacket, but no bullwhip. I used to wish I'd had one when I was still married. My ex could have benefited from a good whipping.

"I'm not surprised," he said. "You certainly don't look like an archaeologist."

He wasn't expecting Indiana Jones. He was expecting a fossil as old as some of my finds.

I laughed. "Having heard your description, I'm relieved to hear I don't look like one to you."

He looked me in the eye, which was a little unnerving. "I think you're quite beautiful," he said.

I could feel my cheeks flush. I couldn't remember the last time a man had made me blush. Maybe my ex-husband, but that was another lifetime—one I preferred not to remember. "Good save," I said, a bit unnerved by the intensity of his stare.

"Are you enjoying your stay in London?" he asked in an awkward attempt at small talk.

"Very much," I answered, grateful for the change of subject. "I spend most of my time on excavations. This has been heavenly."

"Where will you go when you leave?" he asked.

"Egypt," I said. "We're digging in the Sinai, near the mountain where Moses received the Ten Commandments from God."

He looked amused. "You don't really expect to find stone tablets —" he started.

I shook my head. "The tablets were taken to Israel in the Ark of the Covenant," I explained. "They were still in the Ark when it disappeared from Solomon's Temple in Jerusalem. It's been rumored that the Ark's now somewhere in Ethiopia, but no one's been able to prove it. Much as I would love to be the one to find the Ark, we don't expect to find it in Egypt. We *are* searching for evidence of the Exodus in general."

He laughed. "Have you found the secret to parting the Red Sea?" he wanted to know.

I didn't hesitate. "Yes. It's called faith."

"I've heard archaeologists are now using modern technology to aid their work," he recalled. "Computers, satellites—"

"We do." I drew in a deep breath, thinking of the equipment I still needed to continue my work. "Unfortunately, it hasn't helped in this case. We haven't found anything significant yet. This has turned out to be a long-term project, which means it's been costly. My funding's been cut off, and other sources I've used in the past have already turned me down. I have to find a new source of funding ASAP. Time is running out, if I'm going to continue my field work." Why was I dumping this on him? I glanced toward his female companion, who was watching us intently. "I think your girlfriend's getting the wrong idea."

"She's not my girlfriend," he said. "She's my sister."

Only then did I realize that he was still holding my hand. I withdrew it slowly.

"Have you eaten?" Connor asked.

I shook my head. "I'm beat. I thought I'd just get some Chinese takeout after I'm finished here and call it a night."

He laughed. "A rare trip to the civilized world and you plan to spend the evening in your hotel room? That's unacceptable." he said. "Come have dinner with me."

"I don't think so—" I started.

"I may be able to save your project," he suggested.

I was more than a little skeptical. "How?" He didn't look like he had enough cash to pay for dinner. Except for the watch. The watch he wore looked very expensive. He probably stole it. Or so I thought at the time.

He winked, lowering his voice to a conspiratorial whisper. "My trust fund," he told me.

I nodded slowly. "Right."

He wasn't about to give up. "I could surprise you. What have you to lose by hearing me out?" he asked.

I hesitated for only a moment. "All right," I said finally. Even if he didn't have the means to save the excavation, there was something so compelling about him, I couldn't refuse. I didn't want to refuse.

God help me, I was thinking.

———

HE CAME up to the podium while I was talking to a small group of academics after the presentation. He edged his way into the group and leaned in close enough to whisper in my ear, "I'll be waiting for you outside."

I nodded. "I'll only be a few minutes."

He strode off with a swagger that inspired thoughts I didn't want to be having, especially about a man I'd just met. I watched him leave the lecture hall, only half-listening to the aging paleontologist from Oxford who was rambling on in a monotone that would have put me to sleep, had my thoughts not been elsewhere. As soon as I could graciously extract myself, I grabbed my coat and headed for the exit.

I had no trouble finding him outside. He was standing next to a Harley Davidson, two helmets in hand. "Here," he said, tossing one to me. "Put this on."

I was speechless for a moment. "I don't think so," I finally managed to say.

He laughed. "Chicken?" he asked.

"I beg your pardon?" I was indignant.

What did he have in mind? I wasn't about to ride off on a motorbike with some man I'd just met, not even this one.

"I said, are you afraid to ride with me?" His blue eyes were taunting. "You needn't be. I'm quite a safe biker. At least I am when I have a passenger aboard."

"Oh, I'm sure you are." I wasn't unconvinced.

There was a chill in the air. I stood there, hugging myself. I could see my breath. How long was I going to allow the debate to continue? Finally, I slipped my coat on. As I did so, I glanced toward the security guard near the doors. The man regarded me with a look that left no doubt in my mind that he'd gotten the wrong idea about what was going on between myself and Connor.

"Get that bloody helmet on and come on." Connor was growing impatient. He put on his own helmet and gestured to me again to get on the bike.

The man was challenging me! He had nerve, I'd give him that. Impulsively and against my better judgment, I rose to the challenge, I tucked my hair behind my ears and pulled on the helmet. I climbed aboard the bike with him.

"Where's your sister?" I asked, remembering he hadn't come alone.

"Sarah? She brought her car. She had to go back to the station."

"Station?" I asked.

"She's a television journalist."

"Do you really have the means to help me get funding?" I asked then. "Or are you just coming on to me?"

"Both." He started the engine. He said something else, but I couldn't hear him above the Harley's roar. I hung onto him as he raced the bike through the streets of London, wondering what I'd gotten myself into.

I felt like a moth who'd flown dangerously close to a flame...

WE ENDED UP AT A SMALL, casual Chinese restaurant near Regent's Park. "You mentioned getting takeout," he said, holding the door for me. "I hope not being able to eat out of the cartons won't be too much of a disappointment."

"I think I can live with it," I said. We took a booth at the back of the dining room that came as close to privacy as the restaurant afforded. He slid into the booth across from me and picked up two menus. I took the menu he offered me and scanned it quickly.

"Do you know what you want?" he asked.

I could feel my cheeks flush. *He's talking about food, you idiot*, I mentally scolded myself. "Yes," I said, keeping my eyes fixed on the menu. "I'll have the cashew chicken."

I noticed a folded newspaper lying on the seat next to me. I picked it up. It was folded, a story on stem cell research facing out. I shook my head. I may be, as an archaeologist, considered a scientist, but I'm also a Christian, a pastor's daughter. And no matter what my parents think, my faith remains strong. Some things are just morally wrong.

Connor regarded me with curiosity. "What is it?" he asked.

I showed him the newspaper. "You're opposed to medical research?" he asked, surprised.

"Not at all—but they won't be satisfied with that," I predicted. "They'll want to clone human beings. Man has always had a yearning to play God."

"Do you not think it's possible that this could *benefit* mankind?" he asked. "Science is on the brink of eradicating illness, improving mental ability and physical prowess. Is that not a good thing?"

"No," I answered without reservation. "We don't have the power or the right to artificially create life."

"Obviously, we do," he disagreed, taking the paper from me. "Science is going to change the world, you know."

I disagreed. "Then maybe we need to change the scientists," I suggested.

I could tell he was trying not to laugh. "Change the scientists?"

I nodded. "They may be able to create the physical body, but they can't create a soul," I maintained. "Are you at all familiar with any of the ancient religions?"

He pursed his lips as if considering the question. "No. Can't say that I am."

"According to the ancient Jewish mystics, the Guf—the Hall of Souls—holds a finite number of souls," I explained, toying with a bottle of soy sauce absently. "When a child is born, the soul descends from Heaven to enter the physical body. In the case of a stillbirth, no soul comes. The mystics believed when the Guf is emptied, the Messiah will come. Each birth would bring the Messiah's arrival closer."

He looked amused. "And do you believe this also?" he wanted to know.

"I believe there's some truth to it," I acknowledged. "I believe the Messiah will return when the Hall is emptied."

"Perhaps your God intended us to create bodies for those souls waiting in the well," Connor suggested in a mocking tone. "Heaven could be outsourcing."

I held my tongue, just in case he could help me secure funding for the dig.

He waved to the waitress, who came with water and took our order, then made a quick exit. I took a deep breath and approached the topic I really wanted to discuss with him. "How can you help me get my funding?" I asked.

He smiled. "You get right to the point, don't you?"

"I can't afford not to," I said honestly. "The clock is ticking. I don't have much time. If I'm to stay in Egypt, I have to do something yesterday. If you've been putting me on—"

"I haven't," he assured me. "My stepfather is founder and chairman of Icarus International. Ever heard of it?"

I nodded. I was vaguely aware of it. "Pharmaceuticals, medical research..."

"The Phoenix Foundation, our philanthropic division, gives millions to various worthwhile projects every year. We can fund your work for the next five years."

"Why?" I wanted to know. There had to be a catch.

He leaned forward and grinned. "Why not?" he countered.

I took a drink, stalling while I searched for a diplomatic way to say what I was thinking, just in case he really was sincere. "You don't give me the impression you even believe in what I'm doing in the Sinai," I said finally. "Why would you care if I can continue my work or not?"

"Consider it a challenge," he said. "You believe, I don't. Prove me wrong."

I was almost amused. "You'd be willing to risk all that capital to be proven wrong?"

He shrugged. "For one thing, it's not my money. And for another, I think this might prove a most interesting experience."

A rich man looking for a diversion, I decided. Well, if he was willing to provide it, I was willing to take it. I couldn't afford to be proud. It wasn't like I had any other options. Aloud I said, "Right. You just surprised me, that's all. I need to submit a proposal—"

"That's not necessary," he said. "You have me to present your case."

"It can't be that easy," I said, unable to believe I could leave London with funding for the next five years, just like that.

"It is. Edward will do this if I ask him." He put his hand on mine. His touch made me feel odd, but not in a bad way. There was something strangely familiar about it. I withdrew my hand slowly.

"Why?" I asked again. "Of course, I'm grateful—"

"Grateful enough to put up with me for a time?" he asked, his eyes meeting mine.

"Put up with you?" I asked, immediately suspicious. There it was. I knew there would be strings attached. "What, exactly, does that mean?"

He leaned back and regarded me in a way that made me feel as though I was being appraised. "I'm interested in what you do. I'd like to see it firsthand. Is that so hard to believe?" he wanted to know.

"Would you be coming along to oversee your stepfather's investment, then?" I asked, bracing myself for an ultimatum I was pretty sure I wasn't going to want to hear.

"Not at all," he said. "Call it curiosity. It would only be for a brief time."

I hesitated momentarily. Confession time. "The Supreme Council of Antiquities in Egypt doesn't know why we're really there," I reluctantly revealed. "The Exodus is a touchy subject. To prove that it actually happened would be to reinforce Israel's claims in the territory."

"Are their suspicions not aroused by the location of your site?" he asked.

"No." I took a deep breath and went on. "You see, the reason no proof has been found so far is that the so-called experts have the dates and locations all wrong. Traditionally, it's been believed that Moses' royal adversary was Ramses II—but I'm part of a very small minority that believes the Pharaoh the Bible actually refers to is Ahmose I—who reigned two hundred years earlier. I've been studying the Exodus for most of my professional life, and all of my research points to Ahmose. I believe I'm on the right track. My benefactors think otherwise. So when we failed to make a find, they pulled the plug on me."

Connor lit a cigarette. "But the mountain, surely."

"They had the wrong mountain," I said, confident in my theory. "I believe that the actual mountain of God is the *Jebel Hashem al Tarif*—it's right on the main Sinai highway, forty-five kilometers from Taba. It fits all the information provided in Scripture much more closely than does the *Jebel Musa*."

"And the Red Sea?" he asked.

"Mistranslated. *Yam Suf* in Hebrew means reed sea, not Red Sea." I paused. "So we got our permits to dig under false pretenses. We told them we were looking for artifacts relating to Ahmose's reign. Even then, it took us a year to obtain them. We've had to be cautious. There's a military installation close to the mountain. I feel like they're always looking over our shoulders."

"I see." He was silent for a moment. "Well, I'm still willing to secure your funding, if you agree to my terms."

I still had reservations, but he was my only hope of saving the dig now. "You have a deal, Mr. Mackenzie," I agreed.

"It's Connor," he said as the waitress returned and placed our plates in front of us. He reached for one of the two cellophane-wrapped fortune cookies. "Let's see what the future holds, shall we?" He removed the wrapper and broke the cookie in half. He stared at the small slip of paper for a moment, then started to laugh. "It looks as if I have no future."

I took it from him. It was blank. "Maybe," I started, "it means your future can't be revealed to you yet."

3

CONNOR MACKENZIE

"Egypt?" my stepfather asked, unable to believe what I'd done. I shook my head. "We're realists, Edward, you and I," I said calmly. "We both know if I stay here, it's only a matter of time before they find me. If you don't want to provide the funding, I'm perfectly willing to do it myself. But it will look more legitimate if it comes from the Foundation."

"It's not that, Andrew."

"It's Connor now, Edward," I reminded him. "We have to be careful about this."

"That identity was only created to bring you safely home."

"Perhaps, but you knew I'd have to use it again." I stood at the window in Edward's office, not really paying attention to the view. I was preoccupied with planning my next move. I believed Dr. Raven's need for funding was the answer to my own problem as well as hers. "This is the perfect solution," I insisted.

My stepfather wasn't yet sold on my proposal. "I suppose," he conceded. "But to leave now, to go off and live in some desolate place, far removed from civilization—"

"They, too, are staying beneath the radar. Out of necessity," I revealed. "Dr. Raven got her permits from the Egyptian authorities under false pretenses. Apparently, the last thing the Egyptians want is proof that Moses actually did outwit their ruler."

Edward still looked unconvinced.

"I'm doing what I have to do," I maintained. "It will be the last place anyone will be looking."

"How long?" Edward asked. "How long will you stay there?"

"As long as is necessary." I picked up a news magazine lying on his desk. It was opened to a story on a racetrack scandal involving a genetically engineered horse. Our horse. I waved it at him for emphasis. "It's become a witch hunt, Edward. A bloody witch hunt! If they've become this fired up over a horse, can you imagine what they'd do if they knew *everything* we've accomplished?" I asked, throwing the paper back down on the desk. "If anyone were to find out about me—"

"Sarah rang me up earlier. She seems to think you have certain ideas regarding the archaeologist," Edward commented with mild amusement.

I wasn't going to deny it. I did find her quite attractive. The idea of getting her into bed had indeed crossed my mind. "I may need to stay for some time. I might as well make the best of a difficult situation." I couldn't help smiling at the thought of the possibilities.

"Are you sure that's all there is to it?"

"Have you ever known me to lose my head over a woman, Edward?" I asked, feeling a bit insulted.

"Leave it to you to find a way to mix business with pleasure," Edward observed, lighting his pipe. The scent of his expensive imported tobacco filled the room.

"You're not going to fight me on this, are you?" I asked, turning again to face him. "If you have a better solution, I'm willing to listen."

"No. I don't," Edward reluctantly conceded as he drew his pipe from between his lips.

"What about the funding?" I wanted to know.

"Whatever you want. I'll give you a blank check," Edward surrendered.

I nodded. "Thank you."

"You'll stay in touch?" he asked. "We do have deadlines, people to answer to, you know."

"Of course," I said.

"And you'll put everything on hold?"

I nodded. "For now," I said. "Can't have anyone uncovering the truth before we're ready now, can we?"

4

CAITLIN

"What are you two looking at?" I asked the two gawking idiots following my every move in the corridors of the FBI's J. Edgar Hoover Building in DC.

I'm used to men staring at me. I don't do anything to invite it, but they stare anyway. They always have. I may look like a runway model to them, but I'm not hesitant to remind them that I'm a special agent with the FBI. Before that, I was a New York City cop, like my father. But that was a lifetime ago...before 9/11.

I'd like to be able to remember my dad as he looked that sunny Tuesday morning at home. He was smiling, laughing, talking about the family reunion I'd missed that weekend because I was on duty. But the truth is that the last mental image I have of him, the one that will always be burned into my memory, is of the way he looked as we were separated by falling debris trying to get people out of the north tower of the World Trade Center. I went ahead, herding the others outside to safety. I was about to go back for him when I heard a loud roar. The earth shuddered violently seconds before the tower collapsed...

I realized as I stood there, watching it fall, that my father was dead. There was no way he could have survived that.

It was six months before I was deemed psychologically fit to return to duty by the FBI's designated shrink, who I came to affectionately refer to as Dr. Douchebag. Yeah, I'm being sarcastic. I hated the SOB. He'd held my future in his hands, and I hated it. I hated not being in control of my own life. Not being in control was frightening. Not being in control had prevented me from saving my father's life.

I've had to work twice as hard as anybody else since then, had to work my ass off to prove myself. I was damaged goods. I had to prove I wasn't going to cave in if placed in another situation like that on 9/11.

"All of the children in question were conceived by in vitro fertilization," Jack was saying.

"Coincidence," I stated more than asked.

"Too many so-called coincidences," Jack maintained.

"They didn't all conceive through the same clinic," I reminded him. "What makes you think they're connected?" I wanted to know.

Jack sucked in a deep breath. "Think about it, Caitlin. It's too much of a coincidence for all of those kids to be test-tube babies."

"You're talking about three abductions in three states at three different clinics here." I reminded him. "It doesn't make any sense. Even if you're right, even if there had been some kind of tampering with the embryos, what reason could there be for all of the kids to be abducted?"

"Destroying evidence, perhaps?"

I was surprised by the suggestion. "You think these kids were taken so there would be no proof of illegal tampering?" I asked. "What do you suggest they've done with them—you think they're dead?"

"Desperate measures," Jack reasoned. Out of habit, he reached for the cigarettes he'd given up a month earlier, frustrated when he found his pocket empty.

"I don't know, Goober—murder to cover something that would be in itself a much lesser charge?" I still wasn't convinced.

He gave up trying—for the moment. "C'mon. Let's go grab some lunch. I'll buy."

I looked at him, my expression sober. "You'll buy? Is the world about to end or something?" I had to get out of there.

He laughed. "Insulting me won't get you fed, pardner," he drawled.

"Let me guess." I stood up, anxious to go. "The hot dog stand again?" I asked.

"I like hot dogs," he defended himself.

"You live on hot dogs, Goober."

"C'mon, it's a beautiful day. And you look like you could use some fresh air."

He had no idea.

———

"If you believe in God, boy, how can you say you also believe in UFOs?" An old man challenged a young preacher in a group discussion on the Mall. It was unseasonably warm for November, and the people gathered had shed their coats.

The young preacher grinned. He looked more like a hippie than a man of the cloth, with his long hair and worn-out jeans. "What makes you think the two are exclusive of each other?" he wanted to know.

"The Bible says nothin' about little green men!"

"Means nothing," the preacher maintained. "The Bible is God's word to the people of this planet. If he created life here, then who is to say he didn't create life on some other world? How are we to know there isn't a race of men—men, not little green creatures—somewhere out there? And how are we to know God didn't create them millions of years before he created us?"

"You're talkin' weird, boy," the old man scoffed.

"How do you account for the dinosaurs on this planet?" a disbeliever in the group wanted to know.

The young preacher smiled patiently. "Like I said, the Bible only accounts for human history and man's interaction with God," he said. "There's nothing to say the earth wasn't around long before man—in fact, we know that it was—or that God didn't play around with his design before he got around to creating us. There's a passage in the Bible about the Tower of Babel—how God created different languages so we couldn't communicate with each other. Has it ever occurred to anyone that he might have been doing so to separate people of different planets as well as those of different nations?"

"The Bible says six days! The world was created in six days!"

"Six days in God's time is probably like six billion years in ours," the preacher said. "God is infinite, remember? He always was and always will be."

"What makes you think you know so much?" a young woman challenged.

"I don't claim to have the answers," the young preacher defended himself. "These are only my personal theories. I don't happen to believe faith and science have to be exclusive of each other."

"Makes sense."

"You're sure not like other preachers I've heard, boy."

"Are you listening to this crap?" I asked, parking myself on a bench as Jack paid the vendor for the hot dogs and drinks. "Now I've heard everything."

Jack sat down on the bench next to me and unwrapped his hot dog, inhaling it at length before taking a bite. "I don't know what it is about eating hot dogs cooked outdoors, but they taste so much better," he observed.

"Can't you think of anything but your stomach?" I brushed my hair out of my face and continued to watch the group. "That preacher—he looks more like a hippie than a real preacher."

"I didn't think you considered preachers to be real." Jack popped the ring on his soda can.

"You know what I mean," I said, annoyed. The breeze kept blowing my hair in my face, making it difficult to eat. I got hair with every bite I took. Of all days for him to want to eat outdoors. "This guy's claiming God made aliens and sent them here to populate the planet."

Jack shrugged. "Maybe God is a Scientologist."

I finished my hot dog. "Or maybe he's a fraud."

"God didn't kill your father, Blondie," Jack said, watching the young preacher continue to mesmerize the crowd.

"How could he?" I asked. "He doesn't exist."

Jack turned to look at me, puzzled. "How can you be so angry at someone you don't believe exists?" he asked.

I took a deep breath and let it out forcefully. "I'm angry at the lunatics who kill in His name," I said, crushing my soda can in my hand. The remaining soda inside gushed out, spilling over my hand and my new white slacks. I muttered an expletive and slammed it to the sidewalk in frustration.

Jack said nothing as he picked up the crushed can and tossed it into a trashcan. He knew who I really blamed for my father's death. I blamed myself.

5

CONNOR

"Have you ever been here before?" Lynne asked as we stood in line in Customs at the Cairo International Airport.

It was late afternoon and the terminal was crowded. I wondered how long we'd be kept there. I shook my head. "Never. How far is the excavation site?" I asked, handing my passport to the customs agent.

"A little over two hundred kilometers—on the eastern side of the Sinai peninsula," she said. "We're just south of the Jebel Hashem al-Tarif."

I opened my carry-on, waiting while the agent inspected the contents. My passport was stamped and I was allowed to move on. Lynne took out her passport and presented it, automatically unzipping her small carry-on for inspection.

"We're not going to be living in tents, are we?" I asked, in an attempt at humor.

Lynne shook her head. "Nothing that luxurious," she deadpanned.

I looked at her, not sure if she was joking or not.

Once we were finished, we made our way to the baggage carousel to retrieve our checked luggage. Again, there was a large crowd. It was at least fifteen minutes before the bags from our flight started to appear. "That one's mine," Lynne told me, pointing to a large bag coming our way on the conveyor.

As I reached for it, my hand collided with that of another traveler, a young woman who appeared to be in her mid-twenties, attractive, casually dressed. I recoiled, my eyes meeting hers. What I saw there unnerved me. My pulse was racing.

"Sorry," I said uneasily.

"I am sorry also," she responded in heavily accented English.

Lynne saw the look on my face. "What's wrong?" she asked as I passed her bag to her and scanned the carousel for my own.

I shook my head. "Nothing." I retrieved my bags. "Which way to the taxi stand?"

I couldn't tell her. I couldn't tell anyone what I had just discovered...or how. I couldn't call attention to myself, couldn't risk exposure....

―――

WE CHECKED INTO A SMALL, seedy hotel in the heart of the city for the night. It was deplorable. I took one look at the yellowed, peeling wallpaper and stained carpet and said, "You should have let me make the hotel reservations."

"I've been on a nonexistent budget," she reminded me.

"Not anymore."

When she suggested we have dinner at a pizza parlor on Tahir Square, I thought she was joking at first. "Pizza—in Egypt?" I asked.

"Egyptian pizza," she said. "Much better than the American knock-offs you might find here." She looked at her watch. "I have some calls to make. We can meet in the lobby in an hour."

"Sure."

I went to my own room, not bothering to unpack. Normally, I would have made sure everything was on hangers in the closet or neatly folded in the drawers before I'd even go to dinner—but here I didn't want to remove anything from my luggage unless it was absolutely necessary. I wondered if we might be better off with sleeping bags out in the square.

The bugs I killed in the tiny, antiquated bathroom were bigger than any I'd ever seen before. The bed linens were threadbare, and the wallpaper splotched with brown stains. Room service was nonexistent. It was a far cry from the accommodations to which I was accustomed.

Things were getting off to a questionable start. I shook dust from a battered pillow, one of two on the bed that were nearly flattened and smelled of sweat. I was nearly choked by the stench. I didn't care to imagine who might have previously slept there.

I rang up Edward and told him about the incident at the airport. "You have to alert the authorities," I insisted.

"And tell them what?" Edward asked impatiently. "That I know there's a bomb on that plane but I can't tell them how I know? Do you have any idea how they'll respond?"

"If that plane takes off, two hundred people will die when it begins its descent to JFK," I reminded him.

"There's nothing we can do," my stepfather, always the isolationist, maintained.

"You think I'm having seizures again, don't you?" I asked, frustrated.

"How else would you explain it?"

"And if I'm right?" I demanded.

"Let's hope you're not."

6

LYNNE

I was waiting for Connor in the lobby when I was approached by a well-dressed, middle-aged Egyptian man unwilling to take no for an answer. I tried to ignore him, but when that didn't work, I took a firm stance. "*La-a*," I kept repeating, to no avail.

"*Imshee!*"

I turned to see Connor coming toward me. "Sorry I'm late, darling—the overseas telephone service is deplorable," he said, slipping an arm around my waist. What was he doing? He kissed me deeply, taking me completely by surprise. I couldn't say anything, couldn't pull away with the other man watching us. Was Connor out of his mind?

Finally, the man turned and left us alone. Connor released me, smiling. "Think he got the message?"

"I'm sure he did," I said, "but you goofed. Big time."

"How?"

"You've mastered the language, but you've got a lot to learn about the culture," I told him. "That sort of intimacy in public is considered immoral in Arab countries."

"At least it got rid of him," Connor pointed out. "How was I, by the way?"

He was clearly enjoying my discomfort. I rolled my eyes heavenward, determined not to let him see that he'd gotten to me.

"Convincing. Let's leave it at that."

"It's called *fatir*," I explained over dinner. The Egyptian pizza, made of sauce, cheese, vegetables and meat on a flatbread that resembled filo dough, was delicious and filling. "Tim—my partner—will send someone to pick us up around noon tomorrow," I went on.

"Partner?" Connor asked, suddenly concerned.

"Professional partner," I said. "He's also an archaeologist."

Connor nodded. He seemed relieved by that bit of information, though I wasn't quite sure why.

"We all currently live in Taba," I explained. "Tim and his wife, Isabella, have three kids, so space is at a premium at their place. You can get a hotel room at Taba Heights, or you're welcome to use my spare room." Even as I made the offer, I wondered if it was a bad idea. *He's saving the dig*, I reminded myself. *Whatever his reasons, we need him.*

"How long have you been there?" he wanted to know.

I took a bite. "A little over three years."

Connor took a drink. I wondered what he was thinking. Then he asked, "Think you'll want dessert?"

"I don't know," I admitted. "I *want* it, but I'm not sure I should *have* it."

He looked at me oddly for a moment. "Are you always in the habit of denying yourself the things you really want?" he asked with an easy smile.

"I'm used to deprivation," I said, taking a bite. "I live on excavation sites."

"Do you ever miss not having a normal life?" he wanted to know. He took his cigarettes from his pocket and lit one.

"I have my moments," I confessed, "especially when I start thinking about things like family holidays, vacations, having kids—but I love my work, in spite of the obvious disadvantages. It's hot, dirty work in remote locations, living in cultures vastly different from our own. It's extreme climates, often primitive living conditions, and all too often, spiders, scorpions and snakes."

"Sounds charming."

I watched him with curiosity. "It's not for everybody."

"You mention regret at not having had children," he said, plucking an errant piece of crust from his shirt. "Another of those things you wanted but denied yourself—or was it beyond your control?"

I frowned. "My only real regret," I admitted. "I'm forty now and I've been divorced for almost fourteen years. A biological child is not in the cards at this point. I've accepted that. I'm considering adoption—older kids, kids who could more easily adapt to my rather atypical lifestyle."

"It's not uncommon for a woman to have a child at forty or later these days," he pointed out. "And it was never all that rare for a single woman to have a baby. My mum wasn't married when she gave birth to me. The husband came later."

The waiter interrupted us, bringing Connor the coffee he'd ordered. I was grateful for the interruption. "Takes a bit of getting used to," he commented after tasting it.

"You can always get western coffee here," I said, "but if you order the Arab version, be forewarned, it comes in three degrees of sweetness: no sugar, just right, and *sukkar ziyaada*, which comes with a year's sugar cane harvest in every cup."

He grimaced. "Sounds delightful."

"It could put a diabetic in a coma, Merlin."

"Merlin?" He laughed at that.

"It fits," I said, taking another bite. "You seem to be something of a wizard."

"How so?"

"You got me funding I'd been unable to find no matter how much I'd begged. You managed to get on my flight at the last minute, and got us upgraded to first class," I recalled. "We didn't have to share a taxi from the airport after your little chat with the driver—who actually took our bags from the trunk and carried them into the hotel for us. Normally, I'm lucky if the taxi stays at the curb long enough to let me remove them myself. You bribed them, right?"

"I'm not going to tell you," he answered. "I prefer to make myself indispensable to you."

"You've already done that."

Connor only smiled.

"Last chance to bail out before we enter no man's land," I half-joked when we returned to the hotel that night. I fished my room key from my pocket.

He took the key from me and leaned past me to unlock the door. "I'll check your room, make sure it's safe," he insisted.

"You don't have to—" But before I could finish, he was in the room, checking the closet and bathroom.

"Everything seems to be secure," he said, depositing the key in my hand.

"Thanks—and good night," I said. "I would say don't let the bedbugs bite, but given the size of the bugs in this place, I doubt they'll bother with biting. They'll probably just move you to another location to eat you."

He laughed. "They might, at that."

I turned to put the key on the dresser. When I turned back, Connor's face was only a few inches from mine. I took a step back. "I just need room to maneuver in case I have to shove my knee into your groin," I said.

"I'll take my chances." With his fingertips, he raised my face to his. He nuzzled my mouth lazily, then kissed me. "Are you sure you'll be all right here alone?" he whispered in my ear, his lips lightly tugging on my earlobe. "I could stay—"

"No," I said quickly, nervously. "You're going to be trouble, aren't you?"

"That would depend upon your definition of trouble, I think." He released me and walked out, not looking back.

If records are being kept for this sort of thing, we must have broken several here tonight, I thought as I locked the door behind him. *The ink's not even dry on the check, and already he's hitting on me.*

Yep, he's definitely going to be trouble.

7

CONNOR

I was still wide awake at three a.m. I tried to tell myself it was simply a matter of the time difference between London and Cairo, that my body was still on London time, but I knew that wasn't the case at all. I stood at the window, staring into the night. I wasn't alone. I was never alone. There were the voices, and they never left me, always there, always trying to control me. They'd been with me since childhood, for as long as I could remember. Some good, some evil, always warring for control.

Feeling the need to relax, I reached for my cigarettes. "You knew, didn't you?"

"*Knew what?*"

"You knew about the explosives that girl was carrying. You know what's going to happen."

"*Of course. It was my idea. Brilliant, don't you think?*"

"Brilliant?" I asked. "Two hundred people are going to die!"

"*You could always warn them.*"

"And they'd arrest me," I predicted. "Is that your idea as well?"

"*We all have choices to make. Your freedom or the lives of those people you don't even know. What's it going to be?*"

"You know bloody well I can't come out of hiding!"

"*I didn't think you'd be so noble. You'd never risk your life, your freedom for anyone....*"

―――――

An airliner en route to New York City from Cairo went down over the Atlantic Ocean less than ten miles from JFK International Airport. Reports from ships in the area at the time indicated an explosion had taken place aboard the aircraft. Coast Guard ships searching the debris field held out little hope that any of the twelve crewmembers or one hundred eighty-eight passengers could have survived. According to worldwide media reports, Al Qaeda was taking credit for the disaster.

I hadn't been hallucinating, as Edward had suggested.

8

CONNOR

Traveling from Cairo to the Sinai was like arriving on another planet. It was the most barren place on earth, desolate, much like photographs I had seen of the surface of Mars. The first thing I noticed about the desert was the brilliant white light that seemed to bleach out the horizon as it bounced off the quartz in the sand. Bushes bent in the wind as it blew across the ground. As far as I could see there was only barrenness: rocks, sand and mountains. As we traveled further into the interior, the only signs of life I could detect were the occasional black tents of the Bedouin camps amid jagged rocks, drifting sand and a wind-scoured landscape that seemed to stretch on forever.

No one would be looking for me there. I knew that with certainty.

It was a five-hour drive from Cairo to Taba, and by the time we arrived, it was late evening. I was fighting off sleep. I hadn't slept the night before, and I wanted nothing more than a shower and a soft bed.

Lynne's home was larger than I had expected. There were three bedrooms. One had been converted into a small office. The only furnishings in the room were a long table and two standard office chairs. There were two computers, a printer and a scanner/fax on the table. The phone and internet service was obtained via satellite. Stacks of books lined one wall, and the open closet held miscellaneous equipment.

"And this is your room," she was saying. I turned. The door across the hall was open. It was small, simply furnished, and looked reasonably comfortable. "Your bathroom's through that door," Lynne said, pointing to the closed door on the other side of the bed. "There are towels and sheets in the linen closet, and we send someone into town a couple of times a week, so if there's anything you need, just make a list."

I put my bags down next to the bed. "It seems almost civilized," I observed.

She laughed, leaning against the door frame. "The bakery in town is decent. So are the restaurants. There's a bank, a post office, even a small hospital. We get most of what we need here, but we still have to go all the way to Cairo a couple of times a month."

I unzipped my garment bag and started hanging clothes in the closet. "Tell me about the excavation site," I urged.

"We do have a trailer there—sometimes I or Tim will stay overnight." She paused, a look of concern on her face. "This has been an expensive project, I'm afraid. Had you not come along with your very generous offer, we'd be closing up shop and heading back to the States in another few weeks."

"Glad I could be of service." I opened the bureau's top drawer and started to unpack my bags.

"You must be tired," she said then, glancing at her watch. "I'll leave you to settle in. If you're hungry, I can make some sandwiches."

I shook my head. "I think I'd just like to get some sleep," I said. "Didn't get much last night, and it's catching up with me. I'm afraid I'm still on London time."

She nodded. "See you in the morning, then." She started to walk away, then came back to the doorway. "Anything in particular you'd like for breakfast?"

I gave her a dismissive wave. "I don't expect you to look after me."

"I'm going to be cooking anyway," she said. "Besides, I'm guessing you've never set foot in a kitchen."

"As it happens, I have had occasion to learn to cook," I said, amused by her assumption. "My stepfather has servants. I've never had any myself. I dislike having employees in my home. And since we're already on the subject, I thought we might share household responsibilities as long as we're going to be roommates."

Lynne looked unconvinced. "This should be interesting." She stifled a yawn. "Good night, Merlin."

I smiled. "You too."

I waited until I heard her go into her own bedroom and close the door. Then I retrieved a small leather zippered case from the bottom of the carry-on. I glanced toward the door before I opened it and took out two prescription bottles. I paused again, listening. I could hear her shower running. Satisfied she would not be coming back, I took a pill from each bottle, then went into the bathroom and filled a paper cup with water. I popped the pills into my mouth and chased them down with the water.

I took a deep breath, went back into the bedroom, tucked the prescription bottles in the carry-on again and stashed it at the back of the closet.

"*Go to the mountain. Hear the voice of God. You are here to find your destiny—embrace it. Find God. Find yourself. Go to the mountain.*"

"Leave me alone," I grumbled as I continued to unpack.

"*Go to the mountain and you will find the truth....*"

I tried to shut out the voice in my head, but it refused to be silenced. "I'm not climbing any damned mountain!" I snapped, unable to take it any longer.

9

LYNNE

I rolled over in bed and opened my eyes, vaguely aware of an unexpected aroma in the air. As I emerged from the fog of sleep, I realized what I was smelling. Food. I got out of bed, padding barefoot to the kitchen.

I found Connor standing at the stove, wearing jeans and a blue work shirt. He had a dishtowel draped over one shoulder and a frying pan in hand. He was heaping scrambled eggs onto two plates that already held bacon and fried potatoes.

He glanced over his shoulder when he realized I was there. "Good morning, Raven," he greeted me cheerfully.

"What are you doing?" I asked.

"Proving I can cook." He put down the frying pan and moved the plates to the table. "Toast?"

I shrugged. "Sure. Why not?" So he hadn't been kidding. He really could cook.

He popped four slices of bread into the toaster. "Juice?"

I nodded. "We have orange and grape—but I can do that."

He shook his head. "This is my show. You sit." Then, turning to face me, he smiled appreciatively. "On second thought, don't sit. Nice legs."

That's when I realized I wore only the three-sizes-too-big St. Louis Blues jersey I'd slept in. Living with a man platonically was going to require a major adjustment on my part. "Enjoy the view all you like," I said. "Just so you know the trail never goes any further north."

He looked amused. "Not even for special tours?"

"There are no special tours in this country," I assured him, seating myself at the table. I tucked my legs beneath it in a way that shielded them from his view, then changed the subject. "If you like, after breakfast we can drive out to the site and I'll give you a tour."

He nodded. "I would indeed like that." He sat down across the table from me. "Do you have a working lab?"

"We have a lab here in Taba, but it's in need of equipment," I admitted. "One more thing we haven't been able to afford."

"Take me there this afternoon and we'll see what we can do about that," he said promptly. "I should mention that I've arranged to have one of my motorbikes shipped here. I'd be lost without it."

"Ride a lot, do you?" I asked.

He gave a deep sigh. "My bikes are my therapy," he said. "I'm not good at talking out my issues, so when I need to deal with things, I just go off on my bike for a time."

"Does it really help?" I asked.

"For the most part. Some things have no resolution."

"You'll want to stick to the paved roads here," I cautioned. "There are still land mines out in the Peninsula. I wouldn't want to see you get blown up."

10

LYNNE

"We have fourteen graduate students and at least sixty volunteers working on the site at all times," I told Connor as I gave him a tour of the site.

"Where do you get your volunteers?" he asked.

"Mostly people who sign up to work here as part of their vacation, students looking for extra credit, Indiana Jones wannabes."

Two Egyptian fighter jets flew directly overhead as we continued the tour. "This is a military zone," I told him. "I feel like they're always watching us, waiting for us to expose our true intentions." I shoved my hands into the pockets of my faded jeans. I wore a tan fedora that shielded my face from the sun. Too bad it couldn't shield me from his gaze. He had the most seductive eyes...

"What would they do if they did find out?" Connor put on his sunglasses.

"Kick us out of here," I answered. "They've managed to keep us off the mountain for the past three years."

"And you would like to climb that mountain," he concluded.

"Of course."

"Because it's there, I presume." He looked toward the mountain.

I shook my head. "Because Moses climbed that mountain. Because he saw the face of God there."

"So...you really do believe in all the hocus pocus, do you?" Connor was intrigued. "You're not just looking for a prize?"

"If I didn't believe, I wouldn't be here," I said. "In archaeological circles, I'm what's called a maximalist."

Connor cocked an eyebrow. "A maximalist?"

I nodded. "An archaeologist who uses the Bible, literally, as a guidebook," I explained. "I walk this land and I can imagine Moses leading the Hebrews across this same spot. I can see Joseph and Mary with the infant Jesus, fleeing Herod's death warrant as clearly as I can see you now."

"But you've been here three years and haven't found anything." He stepped past a volunteer, a woman in a wide-brimmed hat, sifting soil.

"Whatever is here has been lost to us for over three thousand years," I pointed out. "Eventually, we'll find it."

"You sure about that?" he asked.

"Tim and I did our first dig ten years ago in Megiddo," I told him. "I'll never forget how I felt when I unearthed artifacts confirming King Solomon's reign. I knew then that was my calling, to verify events in the Bible with independent archaeological evidence."

"You and Tim—you've known each other a long time?" There it was again. He seemed concerned about the nature of my relationship with my partner.

"Since college," I said with a nod. "We're like siblings."

"You've never been involved?"

I laughed at the suggestion. "No, he's been with Isabella since high school. They decided they wanted to get married when they were still kids. He and I, we're best friends. We never saw each other in any other way."

"What made you decide to become an archaeologist?" Connor asked as we paused at a cooler to pick up two bottles of water.

"My uncle, my father's brother," I said. "He was an archaeologist.

I was just a kid, and I thought he had the most interesting life. He seemed to have been everywhere. I was completely infatuated with it."

He looked around, taking it all in. "If you believe God is real, then you must also believe Satan is real," he said then.

I was surprised by his statement. "Unfortunately, he is," I said. "Satan's strength lies in the fact that most people either don't believe he's real, or they believe he is but think they can stand up to him on their own."

"You don't believe that's possible?"

I frowned. "You can't fight a supernatural war with the weapons of this world," I said. "It would be like taking on Godzilla with a pea shooter."

Connor chuckled at the mental image that prompted. "So you don't believe bad things just happen, that we're programmed either by DNA or by our environment to do wrong?" he asked.

"No. We all sin—that's one thing. It's quite another to look into the face of true evil," I answered. "To forgive, we have to be able to understand what we're expected to forgive. How do we begin to understand true, absolute evil?"

"And how would one define absolute evil?" he challenged me.

I gave the question some thought. "9/11. The Holocaust. Darfur," I said. "Mothers who murder their children, but afterward can't explain why they did it. Actions that are indefensible. Satan is a real charmer, a master manipulator. He whispers in your ear, enticing. Evil is easier than good. More fun, some would say."

"Do you believe Satan—or God, for that matter—speaks to the individual?" he asked then.

"Sure, absolutely," I answered without hesitation.

"In an audible voice?"

I removed the cap from my water bottle and took a long swallow. "Sometimes," I said, "but usually it's a voice that comes from within."

"Like schizophrenia?"

I shook my head. "Throughout recorded history, those who heard and saw what others couldn't were automatically labeled mentally ill," I said. "Sure, there are some who actually are, but consider what made them ill."

"The voices," Connor said. "But who decides what's true evil? Does one get labeled evil simply by being different, outside the established norm? Wasn't that how Hitler justified the killing of millions of Jews? Isn't that bin Laden's excuse for turning commercial airliners into weapons to commit mass murder? He claimed, I believe, that the West is decadent, populated by evil individuals?"

I gave a little laugh. "You should be a sociologist," I said. "What did your father—your biological father—do?"

Connor's mood turned abruptly dark. "I have no idea who my father was."

"So, am I going to have to call him sir?"

This came from my longtime partner, Tim O'Halloran, a tall, thin, bespectacled African-American who had a habit of introducing himself to newcomers at the site by saying, "I know, I don't look Irish."

Yes, he had a warped sense of humor.

Tim and I had been friends since our days at the University of Utah, and partners for the past ten years. Ours was the kind of friendship that allowed us to be totally uncensored with each other, as Tim was now.

"No," I assured him, wiping my face with a handkerchief.

He wasn't convinced. "Is there going to be a problem?" he pursued as he reached for his toolbox. "Is he going to override every decision we make? Do we have to consult him on everything?"

I rolled my eyes. "He's not going to pull rank," I said, checking the fixed GPS receiver. I decided it was probably best not to admit that I'd initially had the same reservations. "When I met him, he sure didn't look like a billionaire's stepson. I don't think money means all that much to him."

Tim adjusted the harness on the GPS rover unit worn by one of the team members. Using global positioning, which relies on US military satellites, we were able to map out the site and create a contour map of the area. He grinned at me. "It sounds like you spent a lot of time looking at him," he said.

"Tim!" His wife scolded him gently. Isabella was a photographer who documented their work on film. She was tall, reed-thin, with a mass of tight black curls framing her heart-shaped face. I used to tell him she was far too beautiful to have wound up married to a nerd like him.

"There wouldn't be anything wrong with it if she did, babe," Tim defended himself. "She's been alone way too long. It's about time she met somebody who can make her see all men aren't like that jackass she married."

"For the record, Connor and I are strictly business," I cut in. "Mixing business and pleasure would be a very bad idea."

Tim made another adjustment in the harness before sending the rover out. "Yeah," he said, unconvinced. "That's why you let him move in with you. Talk about sending out serious mixed signals."

"He needed a place to stay," I said with a shrug. Again, I'd had the same reservations. "He won't be staying very long."

Tim turned to Isabella with a look that suggested they had been speculating about just how I'd managed to obtain the funding so easily. Then he turned back to me. "I say go for it. You deserve to be happy."

"You just met Connor. For that matter, I just met him," I said, parking my butt on a large wooden crate. I wiped my hands on my jeans. "How would you know if he could make me happy or not?"

"I don't," Tim conceded. "But I've been there with you through David Masters and that bonehead Darcy. I watched you get kicked to the curb by both of them. This is the first time since the divorce I've seen you look at a man like you gave a rat's ass. Maybe it'll happen, maybe it won't--but you won't know if you don't take the chance. You like the guy. Why don't you want to admit it?"

Isabella spoke up. "It's possible she doesn't want you sticking your nose where it doesn't belong," she guessed, looking around to make sure all of her kids were within her range of vision.

"Funding for five years, and you didn't even have to submit a proposal," Tim reminded me. "Even if you don't have ideas about him, I think it's pretty clear he's got ideas about you."

"You cannot seriously believe he'd put out that kind of money for —" I couldn't even say the words. It was ridiculous. Connor wasn't the kind of man who had trouble finding women who'd be willing to share his bed.

"He's not here for the ambiance," Tim reasoned, pulling a bottle of water from a nearby cooler.

I shook my head. "There's nothing between Connor and me and there's not going to be," I said firmly. I'd learned my lesson when it came to men. "And for the record, Connor is not interested in any woman beyond a roll in the hay. He's been completely honest about that."

Tim grinned. "How long do you plan to maintain that vow of celibacy?" he wanted to know.

Pam Hill, the team's botanist, spoke up then. "He can move in with me," she volunteered.

"You only have one bedroom," Isabella pointed out.

Pam put down the tools she'd been digging with and wiped her brow with the back of her hand. Her blond hair escaped the cloth headband she wore, spilling across her forehead. "We'd only need one," she said. "If I had a man who looked like him under my roof, I'd be all over him like a bad rash."

"If you got all over him, he'd probably end up with a bad rash," Tim said, only half-joking. Pam had a reputation for promiscuity. It didn't matter if the men were married or single. A wedding ring didn't stop her.

"Hey, Connor!" Isabella called out. He was heading toward us. She raised her camera to get a shot of him.

"No photographs!" he shouted, waving her off.

"This is just for—"

"*No photographs!*" This time, there was anger in his voice.

Isabella lowered her camera. She and Tim both looked at me, perplexed. I shrugged. "He's very private." But I wondered if that was really the case, or if there were more to it than that.

11

LYNNE

"What do you think of the changes I've made?" Connor asked as he escorted me into the lab.

I looked around, amazed. The equipment he'd ordered had arrived, and the place looked like something out of *Star Trek*. There were half a dozen lab techs in white coats, checking over everything.

"I barely recognize it," I said. "This is so high-tech—what are we going to do with all of this?"

He smiled. "That's up to you."

"Me?"

"We're going to need something to work with. Find us something." He regarded me with amusement. "Consider this a challenge."

I walked around, taking it all in. "I don't even recognize some of this equipment." I turned back to face Connor again. "You could always create Frankenstein's monster if you get bored."

He leaned back against one of the counters, folding his arms across his chest. "You're used to operating on a shoestring," he observed. "That's now at an end. If you want to make history, you have to gamble."

"Are you planning to make history?" I asked.

"As a matter of fact, I am."

I didn't believe for a moment that he was joking.

12

CONNOR

I was on my laptop, ordering equipment for the lab, when Lynne came in with a small cardboard box with holes poked in the lid. "What have you there?" I asked, nodding toward the box, hoping it was not a snake. I'd always had a bit of a fear of them, though I was not quick to admit to that.

She sat down next to me. "My patient." She lifted the lid so that I could see what was inside. Huddled in one corner of the box was a tiny bird with one wing askew. "He's injured his wing," she explained.

I looked up at her. "What are you going to do, put a splint on it?" I asked, amused.

"Hardly. I just have to keep him quiet and make sure he gets enough nourishment until he heals. Then I send him on his way."

"And how will you know when he's well enough to be set free?" I asked.

"I won't. But he will." She placed the box on the table in front of me.

I studied the tiny creature for a long moment. It brought back a sudden rush of memories from the distant past, of all the injured creatures my mum and I tended when I was a wee lad. *"They're God's creatures, just as we are,"* she would tell me. *"We are responsible for them. We must take care of them. We have been given stewardship over all the creatures of the earth."*

"Then why do we eat them, Mummy?" I asked. It didn't make sense.

She smiled patiently. "We're allowed to kill only for food," she explained. "One day you will understand. But you—you have a gift, and a responsibility to use that gift to make this world a better place."

"What gift, Mummy?" I wanted to know.

"You're a healer," she told me, extending her hand to me. She was holding a bird that had crashed into our kitchen window. It looked to be near death.

"He's dying," I remembered her saying. The pitiful creature was barely breathing. My heart broke for it.

She shook her head. "He's hurt, but he's still alive. You can heal him."

"But how?" I didn't understand. "What can I do?"

"Touch him. Stroke him," she instructed.

I did as she said. I always obeyed my mum without question. I stroked the bird's tiny body with my fingers, and almost immediately, its wings started to flutter. Mum released her hold on it, and it flew away as if it had never been injured.

"If I can heal animals and birds, Mummy, why can I not heal you?" I asked.

She looked surprised. "Why would I need healing?" she asked.

"You're hurting," I observed solemnly. "I can see it in your eyes."

She hesitated. "There are different kinds of hurting," she tried to explain. "Some hurts only God himself can heal."

"Why doesn't he, then?" I challenged.

"In his time, he will," she assured me. "There are things we must accept without question." She hugged me tightly.

But there were things I had never been able to accept.

I WAS UP EARLY the next morning, working on my laptop again. Almost as an afterthought, I decided to check on the bird. I lifted the lid on the box slowly, trying not to startle it or allow it to escape. Not that it could, weak as it was.

It wasn't moving. It lay on one side, its tiny legs stiff. It was dead, or so I thought. I decided to dispose of it, but when I reached down to pick it up, it jerked as if startled and hopped to its feet, its feathers ruffled. It looked up at me, as surprised as I was.

"Little bugger," I growled. "You sure as hell looked dead."

"That's odd," Lynne said, coming up behind me.

"What?" I asked, still baffled by what had just happened.

"The bird," she said. "Last night, he wasn't doing very well. I was starting to think he might not make it."

"They may look fragile, but the little bastards are actually quite resilient," I said with an offhanded shrug.

"I think he wants to go home," Lynne said, observing the bird for a long moment. It looked up at her expectantly. She took the box and went over to the door. I followed, watching as she opened the door, then lifted the lid from the box. The bird didn't move. It seemed to be waiting for instructions.

"Well, what are you waiting for?" I asked. "You've worn out your welcome. Go!"

The bird took off, flying confidently westward until we could no longer see it. I put an arm around Lynne. She didn't push me away.

She turned to look at me. "Did you ever have a pet as a child?" she asked.

I thought about it. "When I was very young, I had many pets. All of them temporary," I said. "Hungry strays, injured creatures. Mum had a soft heart."

"I think I would have liked her," Lynne said.

"My mum used to say animals had the ability to see evil. She said they could predict the weather, foresee disasters and see demon spirits."

"They can," Lynne said quietly.

"Any stray that came to our door was fed what crumbs we could manage, no matter how little we had," I remembered. "The lost tend to stick together, it would seem.

THE NIGHTS in the Sinai could be surprisingly cold. Most evenings, I would return from the lab, Lynne would come in from the site, and whoever got home first made dinner. Afterward, we'd finish up our paperwork, then settle down with coffee or hot cocoa and unwind. I found, to my surprise, that I genuinely enjoyed being with her. I was comfortable with her in ways I'd never been with anyone else.

I was going to miss her when the time came to leave this last outpost of hell and return to London. A shame, really. If circumstances were different, I'd take her with me.

"You want whipped cream?" she asked as she took the mugs from the cabinet.

"Sounds good. Need any help?"

"To make cocoa?" She laughed. "I'm not *that* pathetic in the kitchen."

I sat on the couch. I noticed a photo album lying atop a stack of books on the floor and picked it up, leafing through the pages. I saw that most of the photographs were of children. Boys, girls, all ages and sizes. Some were recent, while others appeared to be old photographs. I found it interesting that she kept a traditional photo album, rather than putting all of her photos on her computer. A bow to traditionalism? I wondered.

"Family photos," Lynne said as she came into the room, carrying our mugs. "I don't get home very often, so I bring all of them with me."

I looked up at her. "The black-and-white shots—you and your sisters?" I asked.

She settled down beside me, handing me one of the mugs. "'Fraid so," she said. She pointed to one of the group shots. "That's me at seven. I looked like an ugly little bird."

I smiled, sipping my cocoa. "I find it hard to believe you could ever have been ugly."

She tapped the photo lightly with the tip of her index finger. "The evidence speaks for itself," she told me. "I had to grow into this face."

I looked at her for a moment, resisting the urge to touch that face. "You've succeeded." I turned back to the photo album. "Your sisters are all in dresses. But not you," I noticed.

"I was always a tomboy," she said, "as different from my sisters as I could be. Mom said I was nothing but trouble, right from the start. I surprised her and arrived three weeks early. She and Dad were at a prayer retreat near Kansas City, and she went into labor right in the middle of morning prayers. Twenty-one hours later, I arrived—red-faced and screaming, or so I'm told."

"Prayer retreat?" I asked.

She nodded. "My father's a preacher. He has a small church near St. Louis," she said.

I chuckled at the thought. "I warn you now, you'll not make a convert of me," I said. "I'm a lost cause."

"There's no such thing," she said with certainty.

"Says the eternal optimist." I continued to look at the photographs.

"That's how I was brought up," she said, turning her attention back to the photo album. "My sisters were all sweet, calm babies. I, on the other hand, was a difficult child who wanted to walk before I could crawl and had a temper, even in the crib. My mother said I would become frustrated and scream until my face turned red when I was unable to do anything I wanted, even minor stuff."

Her expression changed. "I was always the odd one. I was the only one to leave Missouri, even to attend college. My sisters all married local men and stayed there. They all managed to stay married and have families. I'm the only one who failed as a wife."

I finished my cocoa and set the mug aside. "You're quite a paradox, Dr. Raven," I told her. "You're an accomplished professional, an independent woman, but you want the fairy tale. You want what your siblings have, but you took great pains to distance yourself from that lifestyle. You want children, yet you've put yourself in a position that makes motherhood an unlikely prospect."

Lynne didn't respond.

"Could it be your expectations are unrealistic?" I asked then.

"Meaning?" she asked carefully.

"That perhaps you need to rethink your priorities, reconsider what's most important to you," I suggested. "Bearing children doesn't require a husband. My mum didn't even know who my father was."

Lynne put her mug down. "I was brought up to believe you had the husband first, then the kids," she said, avoiding his eyes. "I had the husband, he didn't want kids. I left him, end of story."

It was well past midnight when I logged onto my laptop in the privacy of my bedroom. I stared at the monitor for a long moment, ambivalent, rereading the e-mail I had just completed.

SHE WANTS A CHILD BUT HAS LOST HOPE. WE DISCUSSED ALL OPTIONS. SHE HAS ACTIVELY PURSUED THIS. SHE IS QUITE SERIOUS ABOUT IT. I HAVE OFFERED MY ASSISTANCE. SHE

IS RELUCTANT, BUT I BELIEVE SHE WILL
EVENTUALLY ACCEPT.

I took a deep breath, then hit "Send".

13

CAITLIN

"The child was a girl, two weeks shy of her sixth birthday," Jack said, reading the information from his notebook computer. "Name, Samantha Peterson. Parents, Catherine and James Peterson. They'd been trying to conceive for almost eight years when they opted for the in vitro route. The OB-GYN's name, Dr. Peter Feinberg. The in vitro was performed at the Small Miracles clinic in Palo Alto, California."

"Did you cross reference the other missing children?" I asked. For the past three months, we'd been hitting dead ends, and my frustration was growing with each passing day. I was a perfectionist. I didn't take failure well.

Jack nodded. "And that's the weird part."

I perked up. "Weird how?"

"There were ten child abductions in that area in the past year," he started. "Of the ten, only three were in vitro babies, and those three were all age six or younger. All of them were conceived at the Small Miracles Clinic."

"What have we got on Small Miracles?" I asked.

He shook his head. "Nothing yet, but I'm working on it," he said.

"Work faster," I ordered.

"I REALIZE this is difficult for you, Mrs. Peterson," Jack said patiently, "but we really do have to ask these questions."

Clarice Peterson was visibly upset. "I don't understand," she said, dabbing at her eyes with a ball of used tissues. "We've been through this so many times already. How is this going to help us find our baby?"

"We have to explore every possibility," he explained.

"Mrs. Peterson, why did you choose to use the Valleyview Clinic?" I asked.

The question seemed to surprise the other woman. "What has that to do with Samantha's kidnapping?" she asked.

I was impatient. "Please, just answer the question, Mrs. Peterson," I said sharply. Jack regarded me with annoyance. "I'm sorry," I said in a low voice.

Clarice Peterson nodded slowly. "It wasn't our choice. It was our doctor's," she recalled. "He said he sent all of his patients there."

Jack and I exchanged a look. "Was the birth normal?"

Clarice Ryan nodded. "No complications at all. She was a beautiful baby—beautiful, healthy. Perfect in every way." She paused. "Really perfect. She was amazing."

"Amazing in what way?" I wanted to know.

"She never had any of the usual childhood ailments," Clarice remembered. "Not even colic. She was so beautiful, and so bright. She walked at nine months, talked at eight. She could read when she was barely two. My husband used to joke about it. He'd ask when the mothership was coming back for her. He said she was too perfect to be ours."

"Mr. and Mrs. Anders, I'm Agent Caitlin Hammond and this is Agent Jack Farlow," I told the parents of the second missing child.

"Have you found Randy?" the woman asked anxiously.

"No, ma'am, I'm sorry, we haven't," Jack said apologetically.

"That's why we're here," I said. "We need to ask you some questions about your son."

"We'll tell you anything we can," Ross Anders said.

"Did your son have any medical issues?" I asked.

The couple looked puzzled by the question. "No," Ross Anders said after giving it a moment's thought. "As a matter of fact, Randy was never sick."

"What about developmentally?" Jack questioned. "Normal?"

Linda Anders shook her head. "No."

Jack and I exchanged looks.

"He was far above average. That's why he was attending a school for the gifted," she went on. "He walked and talked early. He had superb coordination, even when he was just starting to walk. Ross had hopes he'd become a professional athlete." She started to cry.

Her husband comforted her. "It's been almost seven months since he disappeared. Do we dare hope he'll be found alive?" he implored.

"Mr. Reynolds, we realize this is difficult for you," I said as we all sat down, "but if we're to find your wife's killer and locate your son, we have to have as much information as possible."

He nodded numbly. "I understand." Then: "It's been months. Do you believe he'll be found alive?"

"We're doing everything we can," Jack assured him. "What can you tell us about the procedure your wife underwent?"

"The *in vitro*?" He was obviously puzzled by the question. "We had been warned that it could take a long time. We could spend thousands of dollars and still not have a baby in the end—but Linda conceived on the third try."

"Your wife's doctor sent you to the Humboldt Clinic?" I asked.

He nodded. "He said it was the best in the country."

"Were there any complications in the pregnancy?"

Roger Reynolds shook his head. "She had an uneventful pregnancy," he recalled, "but even so, she was so closely monitored, she complained that she felt suffocated by the clinic staff."

"Suffocated?" Jack asked.

"The nurses were what my wife called dictatorial," he said. "She had to write down everything she ate or drank. They read her the riot act if she ate anything not on her diet. That was rough on Linda—she had cravings for burritos and pasta. Exercise was also restricted. She could do yoga, nothing else. She was ordered to get at least ten hours sleep every night." His smile was sad. "That was the one thing she didn't mind."

"Seems unusual," I said.

He sucked in his breath. "Yeah. Her two sisters both had kids, and neither of them had to go through that shit when they were pregnant. When she mentioned this to her doctor at the clinic, he brushed it off—said her pregnancy was different because of the in vitro. She had to be careful and all that. And now she's dead and our son is gone."

"BINGO!"

"You have something?" I asked, looking up from the notes I'd been making on my smartphone.

"The common denominator." Jack was staring at the images on his notebook computer. "All of the fertility clinics in question are connected to GenTech Laboratories. It's a research facility in Massachusetts. All of its funding comes from the private sector."

He had my attention. "Do tell," I urged, perching on one corner of his desk.

"All of the clinics' success rates for helping infertile couples are impressive. GenTech's cutting-edge research has supposedly made that possible. No previous record of any problems with any of them—no malpractice suits, not even a red flag. Just a lot of satisfied customers."

"Not all of them are satisfied," I disagreed.

Jack pursed his lips and rubbed his chin as he turned the thought over in his mind. "As for GenTech, there's very little information available on them," he started, going for the keyboard again. "They're more secretive than the NSA."

I nodded. "Are they international?" I wondered aloud.

He raised an eyebrow.

"I ran our missing child cases through Interpol," I said, waving the file in my hand. "They have twenty missing kids in seven countries, all *in vitro* babies, all the same age, all considered gifted kids."

Jack turned his attention back to the computer for several minutes. "Okay, GenTech's based in Boston," he said. "Genetic research. The facility used to be run by a hotshot geneticist named—are you ready for this—Joseph Sadowski."

"Sadowski?" I asked. "Wasn't he—"

"The mad scientist who dropped dead as the FDA was about to bust his ass. The same Sadowski who got caught tampering with a racehorse. He claimed he didn't do it, of course, but that's what they all say."

I thought about it for a moment. "I wonder what else he tampered with?" I speculated.

Jack's laugh was tinged with sarcasm. "This whole thing is so fishy you could serve it with fries and hushpuppies."

14

LYNNE

"You know, sometimes I wonder where a skinny guy like you puts all that food," I chided Connor as I cleared the dinner dishes from the table. "Think you'll have room for the cake?"

"Cake?" he asked.

"Um-hmm." I removed the cover from a cake plate, revealing a lopsided cake topped with six mismatched candles I'd gotten from Isabella, who had leftovers from her three kids birthdays. I placed it in front of him and lit the candles. "Happy birthday, Merlin."

He looked up at me, puzzled. "How did you know—"

"Your birthdate's on your passport, remember?" I reminded him. "I saw your passport when we were in Customs."

"You didn't have to sneak a peek. I'll show you any part of me you wish to see," he said with a wink.

I gave his shoulder a little slap. "Get your mind out of the gutter, Mackenzie, and blow out the candles sometime before your *next* birthday."

He looked at the cake again. "There are only six candles," he observed.

"I thought if I put all of them on, we might risk starting a fire," I said. "Besides, you might have trouble blowing them all out, and then you wouldn't get your wish."

He leaned forward and blew, taking out all six in one attempt, then looked up at me again. "As for my wish, you tell me—am I going to get it?"

I turned away for a moment, pointedly ignoring his question. He had no idea how much I wanted to grant that wish, and I wasn't about to tell him. "I have something for you," I told him, taking a brown paper bag off the counter. From it I took a small, wrapped gift and handed it to him. "I wasn't sure what you'd like, so I went for symbolic. After all, what does one get the man who already has everything?"

He opened the box and drew out the gold chain and medallion. "A religious medallion?" he asked, perplexed.

I nodded. "St. Jude," I said. "Patron saint of lost causes."

"You're trying to tell me something here," he guessed, amused.

"You say you're a lost cause. I say you're not," I said.

He looked at me for a moment. "Maybe you should practice what you preach, Raven."

"Your birthday, your gift, your hang-up," I said tightly.

He tried to put the medallion around his neck. "Would you give me a hand with this?" he asked when he couldn't manage it on his own.

I took the chain and drew it around his neck, fastening it. The movement put my arms around his neck and my face too close to his. He kissed me. I didn't resist. I didn't really want to. Truth be told, I liked it. He kissed me again, his arms enveloping me. After a few minutes, I broke the embrace. "Cake," I said, moving away quickly. "We should eat the cake."

"I'd rather have you," he said honestly.

I busied myself with cutting the cake, not responding to his comment. My pulse was racing. I was trembling. I didn't want him to see it.

"This has been the best birthday I've had since my mother met Edward," he confided.

I was surprised by his statement. "I would have thought you'd have had some pretty impressive birthday parties."

"Quite impressive," he acknowledged. "Large, elegant affairs, best caterers in town, a hundred or so people I didn't even know, gifts that meant nothing to me. Most of the time I'd go off, feeling lonelier that ever, wondering why I was even there. Tonight, you went to the trouble of baking a cake yourself, picking a personal gift. I'm touched. I am."

"I'd planned a party with the whole team, but then, you don't really mingle," I said.

"I prefer this," he admitted.

"You don't care that the cake's a little lopsided, then."

"I like that the cake is lopsided."

I shook my head. "You're a tough nut to crack," I told him.

He dipped his finger into the icing on the cake and swiped it across my lips, then slowly licked it off. "Are you going to grant my wish or not?" he whispered.

I slowly extracted myself. "Stick to the cake, Merlin," I told him.

I watched Connor with concern. "I don't know why he's so determined to do this."

"He's trying to impress you," Tim said with a grin. "Haven't you ever watched any of those documentaries on animal mating rituals?"

I rolled my eyes. "Are you going to start that again?"

"If you can't see how hot he is for you, you're the only one," Tim insisted. "Give the man a break before he drops from heatstroke."

Connor didn't tolerate the blazing sun and intense heat well and today was no exception. As he peeled off his perspiration-soaked T-shirt, I could tell it did nothing to alleviate his discomfort.

Though the lab was his priority, in recent weeks he'd begun to take a more active role in the dig. I almost believed he was enjoying it. Almost.

His hair, bleached out by the sun, had grown longer, curling around his face and neck, resembling a lion's mane. He now sported a neatly trimmed beard. Physically, he seemed to have matured overnight. He was even more attractive to me than he had been that night we met in London. *Big mistake*, I warned myself. *Got to keep a lid on those feelings.*

"Big mistake there, Merlin," I said aloud.

"Just trying to cool off," he said, using the shirt to wipe his face.

"With that pale skin, you'll be sorry," I called out to him.

I was laying out the grid for the dig. Our team's geophysicist, Elliot Cooper, was making some notations on his PDA. Tim instructed the latest group of volunteers who had arrived that morning. Pam, who used her skills in identifying ancient botanical specimens to date our finds, was digging in the dirt several yards away. When she saw Connor look her way, she smiled seductively. He immediately turned away. Pam never made any secret of her interest in Connor, and I found myself wondering if he would eventually turn to her for sexual gratification.

I stifled a wave of jealousy at the thought of him with Pam. *You don't have the right to be jealous*, I told myself. *He's free to do whatever he wants with whomever he wants. You won't give him what he wants, so why shouldn't he get it elsewhere?*

I realized he was watching me, smiling. Smiling as if he knew what I was thinking. But that wasn't possible, was it? With Connor, I was never quite sure. I felt as if he could read my mind sometimes.

The thought made me intensely uncomfortable.

———

"I warned you, didn't I?" I asked. "You look like a lobster—a fully-cooked lobster."

He lay face down on his bed while I applied a cooling lotion to his sunburned skin. He was so red, I was certain he was going to blister. "You're too pale to be baring your skin out here," I told him. "It takes some getting used to—sunblock with an industrial strength SPF is a necessity."

"Now the rookie finds out," he groaned. "Hard to see anything out there, the sun is so brilliant. Tell me, where do the vultures wait for their dinner to die?"

"We haven't lost anyone yet," I assured him. "If there are vultures, they're starving."

I continued to massage the lotion into his skin. He had a good body, lean and hard, a swimmer's body. I found my thoughts going places they shouldn't be going. "Ah, that feels good," he said as my hands moved down to the waistband of his jeans. "A bit lower, please."

I was tempted, but no. I wasn't going there. "Don't move until it dries, Merlin." I replaced the cap on the tube and placed it on the nightstand.

He twisted his neck so that he could look at me from an awkward angle. "Tell me—how is it that a good Christian girl like you would call me by such an obviously pagan nickname?" he asked, curious.

"Unfortunately, you *are* a pagan of sorts," I pointed out, leaning across his back to retrieve a towel. "Hopefully, what you experience here will change that." I blew an errant strand of hair out of my face as I wiped my hands on the towel.

"Right. We suffer to such an extent that we beg God to take us, is that it?"

"Very funny." I recapped the lotion and set it aside.

"You know, Merlin the name means 'falcon', but it's actually derived from a title given to the so-called wizards on whom the fictional Merlin was based," he told me. "The title means, loosely translated, 'mad prophet'."

"Then it's more appropriate than I realized," I decided.

"Don't you ever get tired of sleeping alone?" he asked then.

"It beats the alternative."

"Pleasure?" he asked.

"Pain."

"For the record, I am *not* into anything kinky," he said.

"That's not the kind of pain I was talking about."

He rolled over on his back, not bothering to wait for the lotion to dry. "Do you think no one has speculated about us?" he asked. "After all, we do live together. You'd be hard pressed to find a normal, healthy man willing to live with a woman and not be boffing her."

"Let them think whatever they want," I said, getting off the bed.

He looked up at me. "You've never thought about it?"

"No. I haven't."

"Overkill," he said, folding his arms behind his head.

"What are you talking about?"

"Overkill," he repeated. "You stress over and over what you don't want, but I think you're trying to convince yourself, not me."

I didn't respond and tried not to look him in the eye. He knew. He could tell how attracted I was to him.

"You're trying so hard to be who you think you should be, you're denying who you really are," he said. "You want to be a good girl, like your sisters. You want your father's approval. But the truth is that you're a strong, passionate woman. You need to give your passions free rein."

"Thanks for the psychoanalysis, Dr. Freud."

He looked at me, frowning. "You do deny yourself the things you really want, don't you?" he asked.

15

CONNOR

I stood at the bathroom sink the next morning, taking my medication and wondering what it was going to take to get Lynne to finally say yes. I knew she had feelings for me—strong feelings. I sensed it every time I was near her. I knew she wanted me as much as I wanted her. Past experience, however, was proving to be an effective barrier.

To my surprise, I found myself reluctant to be one more man to leave her emotionally scarred. For the first time in my life, I was concerned with someone other than myself. But in the end, I wanted what I wanted...and she was what I wanted.

"You have feelings for her."

The voices...again. "I don't know how to feel," I insisted.

"You don't want to feel. There's a difference. You want to be able to have a physical relationship with her and still be able to walk away. You wish to prove to yourself that you're still in control."

"I am in control." I capped the prescription bottles and put them back in the leather case in which I always stashed them.

"Are you, now?"

"Yes."

"What, then, do you feel for her?"

"Horny."

"If that were true, you could be with anyone."

"She turned me down. No woman's ever said no to me before," I rationalized as I combed my hair.

"And that is all?"

"Of course."

I caught sight of my bare back in the bathroom mirror as I was putting on my shirt and stopped short.

The sunburn was gone.

16

CAITLIN

"This is nuts," Jack said.

"What?" I asked, distracted.

"Sadowski." He stared at the computer's monitor, having spent the past three days searching for a possible connection between the late scientist's bizarre experiments and the missing children. What he'd discovered was the last thing we expected to find. "He apparently got himself into hot water and lost his tenure just before his death for claiming he could clone Jesus Christ."

I looked up. "Whaaat?" I thought he was joking.

"Yeah. He said he if he could obtain enough DNA, from the Shroud of Turin, for example, he could clone Christ and prove, once and for all, whether or not he was really divine."

"Might have been interesting," I conceded.

"Yeah, in a *Prozac Nation* kind of way."

"They caught two of Sadowski's people," I said, looking over his shoulder at the computer. "One in Mexico, the other in the Caymans. Maybe we can ask them if he ever tried."

"So how many are still out there?"

"Six—but the one who would be most likely to know Sadowski's deepest, darkest secrets would be his former second-in-command, a Dr. Stewart. Then there's Sadowski's ex-wife Dorothea, and their son." I continued to stare at the screen.

"What do we have on Stewart?" he asked.

"Not much. The guy was as low profile as it gets. To be any lower, he'd have to be a mole," I said. "Probably a good thing, working with a man whose ego was as big as Sadowski's."

"Anybody looking for the ex-wife and son?" he wanted to know.

"Nobody's seen or heard from the son in at least two years," I said. "He just dropped off the face of the earth. The ex-wife was last known to be living somewhere in Italy. No address that I could find. The divorce shocked everybody who knew them, partly—and this is the interesting part—because Mrs. Sadowski was such a devout Catholic."

He laughed. "A devout Catholic, married to the man who wanted to clone Jesus Christ. There's irony in that." Then he posed another question. "Do you think they actually did it, Blondie?"

"Did what?" I asked.

"Cloned a human being."

"We know they did. The guys from the FDA found the embryos, remember?"

"I'm not talking about embryos," he said. "I'm talking about a living, breathing, fully developed human being."

I frowned. "Get real, Goober. Cloning is still in its infancy. If there *were* a living clone, he or she would be a small child at best."

"You sure about that?"

"What are you getting at?"

"Sadowski and company were into a lot of different things. Accelerated growth hormones, for one thing. Suppose they did successfully clone a human and used that to age him—or her?"

"You've been reading too many sci-fi novels, Goob." I dismissed the possibility.

He reached for his root beer. "Look what they did with the Bionic Racehorse."

"Right. They've created a superhuman who can leap tall buildings in a single bound. Get real, Farlow."

He dug into his carton of Chinese takeout. He handled the chopsticks easily, while I, having given up the fight after a few failed attempts, fished a plastic fork from the previous meal's takeout bag. It always bugged me that he could eat with chopsticks, but I couldn't. That's why he ordered Chinese takeout whenever we worked late. He did it to irritate me.

"Nothing about Sadowski's family life adds up," I said then.

"What do you mean?"

"I've been doing some personal background research on him," I started. "His marriage wasn't exactly a great love match. In fact, it's been confirmed, supposedly by Mrs. Sadowski herself, that the marriage was never even consummated."

He was surprised. "Hard to believe, unless he was a eunuch or something. So did they adopt the kid?" he asked.

I shook my head. "Listen to this. According to sources, he was a young Polish immigrant with brains and ambition but no resources," I began. "He'd come to the States with a plan that didn't materialize, and he was about to be deported. Dorothea Wilhite was the plain, mousy only child of wealthy parents who desired an heir to the family fortune, a legacy for the family's future. They were desperate to find a suitable husband for this girl who'd never even had a date. They decided they'd have to buy her a husband. They paid for Sadowski's education and financed a solid start in the marriage for the young couple. In return, he had to be a dutiful husband and produce an heir."

"Yeah, so?"

"He was not in the least attracted to her. Never touched her, according to my sources. There were rumors that he had a thing for young women, beautiful, well-endowed young women."

"The guy looked like a toad. How could he get hot babes to put out for him?" he wanted to know.

"He supposedly targeted his female students—girls who were

failing his classes and couldn't graduate without a passing grade from him."

"So one of those girls gave him a baby?"

"Nope. The deal was that the heir had to be a legitimate blood heir." I shook my head. "Mrs. Sadowski gave birth, all right."

"And how did he get her pregnant?"

"In vitro fertilization."

He laughed. "Are you saying the Sadowskis' only child was a virgin birth?"

"Exactly."

"This man who claimed he could clone Jesus Christ? Talk about irony!" he hooted with laughter. "Did he really have a coronary—or did lightning strike him?"

"They were married what—thirty years? She was obviously willing to be married to a man who didn't love her, who had never been attracted to her, never touched her. So why, after all those years in a loveless marriage, did the devoutly Catholic Mrs. Sadowski risk excommunication by the Church by divorcing her husband? And why did she walk out on her own child?"

He finished the contents of his carton and put it aside. "Maybe she found out the kid wasn't hers," he suggested, only half-joking.

I rolled my eyes. "Be serious, Goober."

"I am serious," he insisted. "Think about it. Can you picture Dr. Toady jerking off to porn in some fertility clinic's bathroom? The man was a scientist. This was his area of expertise. If the rumors are true, and he was getting it from all those young women, maybe he knocked one of them up and transferred the fertilized egg from a girl he couldn't afford to have pregnant, to his wife, whose pregnancy would net him a fortune. How would the Mrs. have any way of knowing the embryo wasn't her own?"

I shook my head. "What must it have been like for her—Dorothea, I mean? Knowing she was so undesirable, her parents had to buy her a husband—one who wanted no part of her sexually? If your theory is correct, and she gave birth to a baby that wasn't even hers—"

He grinned. "You'll never know how she felt, Blondie," he said. "Men would line up to marry you. For free."

"Interesting coincidence," I said thoughtfully, ignoring his comment.

"What?"

"This e-mail from Lambert," I said. "If Sadowski did ever seriously plan to clone the Almighty, he had the opportunity. Seems he was part of the STURP team back in '78."

"The—what?" He stopped eating.

"STURP—the American Shroud of Turin Research Project," I explained. "A group of scientists went to Italy back in 1978 to test the Shroud, to find out what had made the image on the cloth. Joseph Sadowski was on that team. They extracted blood samples from the Shroud at that time. If he wanted samples for cloning purposes, he could have obtained them then."

He raised an eyebrow. "The question is—*did* he?"

17

CONNOR

I woke abruptly, at first unsure where I was. I sat up in the darkness, gasping, struggling to catch my breath. I was shaking uncontrollably.

It was the dream. Again.

I'd had it countless times over the past fifteen years. The first time was when I was fifteen. It was always the same: I was drowning. The sea was dark, turbulent. There was a storm, a violent storm. I was exhausted, struggling against the undertow. It was cold—I felt as though a thousand knives were lashing into my flesh. I was barely able to keep my head above water. There was a light. A boat. It was several hundred yards away. If I could swim to it, I'd be all right. I summoned up every ounce of strength I could manage and pushed forward.

I could still see the light. I was getting closer. There was a woman on the deck. She was leaning over the railing, calling to me, reaching out to me. I tried to call out to her. I saw her face in the flashing light, just for a moment, before the current pulled me under.

It was Lynne....

It didn't make sense. I'd had this same dream for years. Years before I'd even met her. I'd seen her face a thousand times, always assuming, until now, that the face of the woman I saw on the boat was simply a product of my subconscious. A psychiatrist would no doubt have made something significant of a fifteen-year recurring nightmare, had I consulted one. I pulled on my clothes and went outside, breathing in the cool night air. My heart rate slowly returned to normal. *This is insane*, I thought. *How could I have been dreaming all these years about a woman I hadn't yet met?*

"Your mother never told you anything at all about your biological father?" Lynne asked. I wished she'd just drop it, but that was unlikely.

"No."

"How did she meet your stepfather?"

"She worked for him," I recalled. "She was a student at the time. He'd been interested in her from the start, but it wasn't mutual. He was old enough to be her father. He offered her a better position—but then she got pregnant."

"It's not possible he's your father?" she asked.

"I wondered about that myself," I confessed as I opened my bottle and took a drink. "But several years ago, I ran a paternity test. Edward and I are in no way biologically connected."

"Did he love her, or—"

I shook my head. "My mother was quite beautiful. Edward had been widowed for a number of years, and was feeling the need for a woman."

Lynne was silent, waiting for me to continue.

"He wanted my mum. Like most rich men, he was used to getting what he wanted. She didn't love him, mind you. He didn't love her. He bought her. I received a rather large, irrevocable trust fund the day my mother became his wife," I said. "I'm a very wealthy man today because my mother was such a hot piece of arse."

"Not something I would do," she admitted, "but I'm sure she did what she did because she wanted the best for you."

"I didn't care about the money," I said, the old, pent-up anger surging to the surface along with the unpleasant memories. "I needed my mum. The day she died, I stopped needing anyone."

"You resented her for dying?" Lynne asked.

"I resented her for leaving me!" I snapped.

"What about your stepfather? Have you ever had a good relationship with him?"

I was pragmatic when it came to that relationship. "Edward gave me a good education and that fat trust fund, and in time I grew to understand that most marriages are nothing more than business deals anyway. From that viewpoint, my mother had made quite a good deal for us."

"You sound pretty down on marriage," Lynne said, sounding somewhat disappointed.

"I don't believe love and marriage go hand in hand, if that's what you're suggesting. Marriage is a business arrangement. Sex is currency."

"What about love?" she asked.

I shrugged. "I'm not sure I even know what love is."

Lynne was quiet. I could tell this entire conversation was making her acutely uncomfortable, even though she'd started it.

"Love's a word that gets tossed around far too easily," I continued. "I haven't said it to anyone since Mum died, and I won't, unless I mean it."

"That automatically puts you ten rungs higher on the food chain than most of the men I've known," Lynne said, looking down at the floor.

I looked at her, filled with an unexpected sadness. "He really did a number on you, didn't he?" I asked. "Your ex, I mean."

She didn't answer immediately. "It's exes. Plural," she said finally. "There have been two men in my life—two I was serious about—and both relationships ended badly. The first was my archaeology professor, my mentor. His name was David Masters. He was older, a worldly man, larger-than-life. I was innocent compared to my female friends. David singled me out from the start. He chose me to go with him on a dig in Jordan, my first dig. The week before we left, he seduced me. We were lovers that entire summer. Then I discovered I wasn't his first and wouldn't be his last. He chose a different girl every summer."

"And your ex-husband?" I asked.

"I met Phillip Darcy when I was working on my PhD. I should have known better—not only because of what I'd been through with David, but because this man had already been married and divorced twice. Darcy had grown children he never saw or heard from. Trouble was, I was feeling pretty inadequate by that time. He pulled out all the stops, romanced me in a big way. He wanted me, and I wanted to be wanted."

"And?"

"The romance died the moment the ring was on my finger. Darcy and I never argued. I tried, but he was never around long enough for that. He's a photojournalist. He was away most of the time—his career always came first," she said. "When he *was* home, he only wanted one thing from me."

"Sex," I guessed.

"When I left him, I promised myself I'd never go through that again."

I tried to smile but didn't quite succeed. "It would seem you and I are actually quite a bit alike. We're both damaged goods. Perhaps that makes us a match, after all."

"How do you figure?"

"You want a child. I want sex," I stated bluntly. "We can accommodate each other's needs without unrealistic expectations. No illusions. If you don't want anyone to know I knocked you up, you can just tell them to look for three blokes on camels and a bright star in the east."

She made a face. "I don't think so."

I regarded her intently. "Some years back, a group of climbers set off to conquer Everest," I began. "They encountered one obstacle after another until they could not go any further. Totally discouraged, they turned back. Only after they returned to their base camp did they find they had been only a hundred feet from the summit when they gave up. Would you want to give up if you were so close to getting what you wanted?"

"Do you have a photo of your mother?" Lynne asked, curious.

"This is the only one I have with me," I said, pulling my wallet from my pocket. I removed a small photograph and gave it to her.

The picture was my favorite of Mum, taken when she was young—she was smiling, with long, unrestrained red hair. Lynne looked at the photo, then at me. "She was beautiful," she said. "You have her eyes."

"That was taken just before she married Edward," I recalled. "After they got married, I never saw her smile again."

"Most mothers will sacrifice their own happiness for their children," Lynne said.

"I would rather have made my own opportunities than have her prostitute herself as she did." I stared wistfully at the photograph. "She used to tell me an angel gave me to her, that God had sent me into the world for a special purpose. Can you believe that?"

"Actually, I can," Lynne answered honestly.

"I've always suspected I was the product of rape," I confided. "If not Edward, then someone else."

"Angry or not, you still love her," Lynne said.

"I loved her, perhaps too much," I said. "I was never able to love anyone else after she left me."

"What about your sister?" she asked. "You love her, don't you?"

"I was always protective of Sarah," I told her. "As children, we only had each other. Edward was too busy to be a real father to either of us. He was too busy changing the world."

"It's good that you and she were close."

I smiled. "I used to drive her quite mad by telling her the labels on her designer dresses should be on the outside so everyone could tell who had designed them—otherwise, it was pointless to wear them at all."

"I don't even own a dress," Lynne admitted then. "I haven't worn one in maybe ten years."

"A pity," I said, smiling at the thought. "You have lovely legs. I do enjoy looking at them."

"Glad you like the view." She stood up and started clearing the table.

"In fact, you're quite nice all over," I went on, getting up to help her. "I like to look at you when you're out at the site in shorts and a T-shirt, and the humidity makes the shirt cling to your—"

She laughed. "Is sex all you ever think about?"

"It is when I'm not getting any."

She rolled her eyes. "I think I'd better get started on those dishes." She threw me a dishtowel. "I'll wash, you dry."

I nodded. "Fair enough."

She focused her attention on the sink, trying not to let me see her smiling. "It never fails," she said.

"What?"

"My nose itches," she said, wrinkling it up in a vain attempt to relieve the problem.

"Turn around, I'll scratch it for you," I offered. As she turned to face me, I dipped my fingers into the soapsuds before scratching the tip of her nose, leaving bubbles in my wake.

"Thanks, that was a big help." In retaliation, she scooped up a handful of suds and swiped her hand across my face. I spit bubbles, then, laughing, stuck my hand down into the sink and pulled up a large cup full of soapy water.

"You wouldn't!" she laughed.

"Wouldn't I?" I advanced on her menacingly, about to dump it down the front of her shirt, when we were interrupted by a knock at the door.

"*Oh, bloody hell!*" I dropped the cup back into the sink, threw down the towel and stormed off to my bedroom, slamming the door. Would we ever have enough privacy?

I BROUGHT my motorbike to a stop and sat there in the darkness for a bit, getting my bearings. I wasn't sure how far I'd gone from the site, and I'd left my watch on the kitchen table.

I knew it had to be late. I'd had to get away, to cool off. Every time I found myself getting close to Lynne, about to make my move, we inevitably were interrupted by someone or something. It was unbearably frustrating. I wanted to take our relationship to the next level, but I was no longer sure what that next level should be.

I was also still thinking of my mother. I took out my wallet and removed the small photograph I'd shown Lynne earlier. There were times I was still so angry with Anne, I couldn't bear to look at it, and other times I couldn't take my eyes off it. Lynne was right. I loved my mother and I hated her, sometimes simultaneously.

Lynne reminded me of Anne in so many ways—her stubborn devotion to her faith, her principles, her simple, natural manner. Like Anne, Lynne seldom wore makeup, and when she did, it was minimal. The only jewelry I'd ever seen her wear was an inexpensive wristwatch and a silver crucifix on a chain around her neck. She paid no attention to fashion and her hair was never sprayed, gelled or moussed. She eschewed manicures and pedicures and called them "silly".

Like my mother, Lynne was genuine...and her feelings for me were genuine. Those feelings drew me to her, a powerful, irresistible magnet.

For as long as I could remember, I had been able to read the thoughts and emotions of others simply by being in contact with them. I recalled one incident in particular. My mother had left Edward. She was pregnant with Sarah at the time...

We were living in Scotland, and one morning we'd encountered a neighbour outside our building. The woman had always been kind to us, and I got up on her lap to give her a hug. "That's my wee laddie," she laughed, holding me tightly. "You're such a sweetheart."

I was overcome by a strange sadness and drew back. "I'm sorry, Maddie," I told her.

"Sorry about what, Andrew?" she asked, puzzled.

"I'm sorry you have cancer. I don't want you to be sick."

"Andrew!" my mum hushed me.

Maddie looked at Mum. "How could the lad know?" she asked. "I only just found out myself yesterday."

Mummy was surprised. "You do have—"

"Colon cancer," Maddie said with a nod.

Until that day, I had believed my ability was completely normal, that everyone could do it. That day, my mother told me about the angels...

"You are different from everyone else, my baby," she told me. "Special."

"Special...how?" I asked.

"You were a gift from God," she said, taking me in her arms. "I didn't even know I was going to have a baby. Then one day an angel, the Archangel Gabriel, came and told me I would be blessed with a special baby who would grow up to be God's messenger."

"Was the angel my daddy?" I asked.

"Yes, he was," she said. "He put you in my arms, and you were the most beautiful baby I had ever seen."

"Why did he not stay?" I challenged. "Declan's daddy is still around."

"Angels have to return to heaven," she patiently explained. "They can't just stay here."

"I want to see my daddy," I insisted.

"*One day, perhaps,*" *she said evasively.*

I'd been too young then to understand that my mother had been mentally ill. I believed my father had been an angel, until my mother left one day and didn't come back, and I stopped believing in anything or anyone...

―――

LYNNE WAS asleep when I finally returned in the early hours of the morning. I noticed her bedroom door was ajar when I entered the trailer. I wondered if she was still awake and went to find out. She wasn't. I stood in the doorway for a long time, watching her sleep. She lay on her left side, her hair a dark mass on her pillow, the jersey in which she slept hiked up over her hip. Watching her stirred feelings in me that I fought to reject. Had it been a simple matter of lust, I could have dealt with that—but I was fighting emotions I'd not experienced since childhood. I tried to tell myself it was the situation we were in, the place, the isolation, even the fact that she had said no.

But this one was different from the others. *Why?* I asked myself, believing that knowing the answer would take away the allure. I wanted to touch her. I wanted to stroke her hair, to feel her skin against mine, to taste her...all familiar responses, to be sure. But I wanted more than the physical. That was unsettling.

18

LYNNE

When I woke early the next morning, I went to see if Connor had returned. I found him in his room, fully-clothed and asleep, lying face down on the bed.

I wish I knew what's going on in that head of yours, Merlin, I thought.

Connor opened his eyes and rolled over on his back. "Have I overslept?" he asked when he saw me standing in the doorway.

I shook my head. "I was just checking to see if you had come back," I admitted. "You weren't in the best of moods when you left."

He pulled himself upright. "You're concerned about me. I'm touched," he said, scratching the back of his head. His hair was rumpled, his eyes only half open, and still I found him more appealing than any man I'd ever known.

"Hungry?" I asked, trying not to think about that.

"Now that you mention it, yes." He looked up at me. "I seem to have fallen asleep with my clothes on. I wouldn't have minded if you had elected to take them off for me, you know."

I shook my head. He was persistent, I had to give him that. "You came in so late, I didn't even know you were back until just now," I told him. "I'll go get breakfast started."

"Thank you," he said then.

I didn't get it. "For what?" I asked.

"You never question me," he said. "You never press me for details of where I've been."

I shrugged it off. "It's none of my business."

"We live together."

"Not in that way." I hesitated, wanting answers but not feeling I had the right to ask. "Connor, tell me one thing, will you?"

"If I can."

"Why did you choose to ask your stepfather to fund the dig? Really? I'm sure you didn't do it just for a one-night stand—"

He grinned. "Not for just one night, no."

"I'm serious," I insisted.

"So am I."

"I'm sure you could have had any woman you wanted back in London," I started. If I was wrong about this, I was going to end up feeling pretty foolish. "Probably had them throwing themselves at you."

"I might have. Your point?"

"I can't figure you out. You've said that you're only looking for sex, yet you left a female buffet behind in London, you ignore Pam's advances—"

"I do have the option of changing my mind, don't I?"

I nodded. "Of course."

"I want you."

"Why—because I turned you down?"

"No," he answered honestly. "Is it so hard for you to believe I could want only you?"

"Yes." That much was the truth.

"I'm not some dog out to mate with whatever happens to be in heat at the moment." He looked offended by the suggestion that this might be what I was thinking.

"Sorry," I apologized. "I didn't mean to imply you are."

"If you must know why you're so important to my needs, I'll confess," he conceded with gravity in his voice. "I'm part of a top secret experiment. I was created in a laboratory—a superior man in every way. There are only ten of my kind. We have to go out into the world and mate with normal women to produce hybrid offspring who will be of superior intelligence and physicality."

"And why is it necessary for you to mate with normal women?" I asked, amused.

He looked genuinely sad. "My kind cannot survive for long in the outside world, you see. We need women like you to help our children to thrive."

"Why can't you survive?" I asked, playing along.

"If I told you, I'd have to kill you," he said solemnly.

I almost thought he was serious.

THE MONTHS PASSED QUICKLY, and before we knew it, it was June. Connor and I were closer with each passing week, but in spite of his persistence and my fading willpower, we still had not crossed that line.

One afternoon, with the sun high in the cloudless sky, the heat was unbearable—but the hottest part of summer had yet to arrive. I wondered what we'd be dealing with in the next two months.

I went to one of the coolers, took out two bottles of water and gave one to Connor. "Take a break before you drop," I ordered.

He looked up at me for a moment, unsmiling, then opened the bottled water and took a long swallow. I watched him, concerned. He could be so stubborn sometimes. His face was red and he was perspiring heavily as he worked with a faulty GPS rover. He was dirty and sweating, dressed in old jeans that were worn at the knees and a filthy *Sturgis* T-shirt.

He swore under his breath when his attempt to adjust the rover failed. He finished the bottle and threw it down. I picked it up. "Face it, Mackenzie. You'll always be a lab rat. There's no shame in that."

We were excavating the caves at the base of the mountain, but our equipment was not cooperating. "I'm ordering all new GPS equipment tomorrow," he said, throwing a screwdriver in frustration.

"Don't let it get to you," I advised.

"Easier said than done." He muttered something that I couldn't decipher. When he was angry or upset, his brogue became so thick, he was difficult to understand. I suspected it was deliberate on his part.

Tim's Land Rover came to a stop nearby. Tim got out of the vehicle and walked around to the back to unload the supplies he'd brought back from Cairo. I left Connor to do battle with the rover and went to help Tim.

"Sorry I'm late," he told me. "Some of the items we ordered didn't come in, so I had to make substitutions." He put the box down and took from it some folded newspapers, which he handed to me. "There's some sort of mass deportation going on in Israel," he said.

"Again?" I asked. Back in 2000, there had been a pilgrimage of cults arriving in Jerusalem, expecting Jesus to appear there. The Israeli government had deported all of them.

Connor never looked up from the GPS.

"I guess it's never going to end," Tim theorized. "Now they think the Messiah could come out of some lab somewhere, that he's going to be cloned from the blood spilled at the Crucifixion."

I laughed. "That's ridiculous."

Tim took a bottle of water from the cooler, opened it and took a drink. "Takes all kinds to fill the freeway, I guess." He paused. "Remember that nutcase who claimed he could extract Holy DNA from the Shroud of Turin? I suppose it's possible."

I started to disagree, then changed my mind, remembering something. "The Shroud has Christ's blood on it."

Connor spoke up for the first time. "If DNA is available, if the

Shroud is authentic, then yes, it might be possible," he concluded, wiping his face with a dirty handkerchief.

"Doesn't cloning require preserved blood?" Tim asked. "The blood on the Shroud is two thousand years old—and dried up for more than a few centuries."

Connor shook his head. "Actually, DNA can be obtained in a number of ways—a strand of hair, nail clippings, skin scrapings, saliva," he explained. "Dried blood could be used. There would be gaps in the genetic code, to be sure, but that could be fixed with the addition of other human DNA. Gene sequencing can be done by computer—"

"I can't believe the two of you are even discussing this," I told them. "The whole idea is absurd."

"Whoever does it—and someone will, eventually—will be credited with one of the greatest scientific breakthroughs of all time," Connor reasoned.

I disagreed. "Even if the physical being of Christ could be cloned, it would prove nothing. His power didn't come from his flesh—it came from His spirit, from God."

Connor gave me a skeptical look. "If you believe in that sort of thing." He knew it would open a debate. Sometimes I thought he enjoyed those debates. The more passionate the better.

"Look around," I said, extending my arms in an expansive gesture. "What have we been doing here?"

Connor looked annoyed. "Good question."

Tim recapped his bottle. "I don't think you've convinced him," he said, noting the dispassionate expression on Connor's face. "I doubt you ever will."

I wasn't giving up. "Archaeologists have unearthed evidence that events described in the Bible actually took place," I went on. "What further proof do you need?"

"I'm not saying I don't believe He ever existed," Connor told me, pushing his hair back off his face. "In fact, I'm certain He did. I'm also certain He was executed in Jerusalem—and yes, probably by crucifixion, since that was the usual method of the time and place. The Romans did go to great lengths to squelch any hint of insurrection. I just don't believe Christ was any kind of deity."

"So, Connor—who do you think He was?" Tim asked, genuinely interested. He parked himself on a wooden crate and waited for the scientific explanation.

"He was a revolutionary," Connor answered without hesitation. "His influence was most likely political rather than spiritual. Was He not descended from the royal line of King David? He would have had a claim to the throne. At any rate, He ultimately became so powerful that He was seen as a threat and put to death to send a warning to His followers."

"In other words," Tim concluded, "a charismatic rabble rouser."

Connor nodded. "Not exactly the words I'd use but close enough."

I slam-dunked my empty water bottle into the barrel designated for trash. "You know, you two, not everything has a practical—or logical—explanation," I told them. "It's like debating which came first, the chicken or the egg."

"The egg," Tim said, laughing.

"The chicken," I disagreed. "God created the first chicken. The chicken laid the first egg."

"And you would know this—how?" Tim asked.

"I read it somewhere," I responded with sarcasm.

"I didn't say I agreed with him," Tim quickly defended himself.

I turned to Connor. "So—you really think Christ was some kind of radical?"

Connor gave it momentary thought. "One who wielded enormous power, to be sure—no one else in history has ever had that kind of following, which probably accounts for the myth," he concluded.

"Myth?"

"Legends happen when a story captures the collective imagination so that when it's passed along to subsequent generations, it's embellished with each telling," Connor offered as an explanation. "In two thousand years, He went from activist to god."

I shook my head. "I would love to get you and my father together," I said.

Connor grinned for the first time. "Anytime," he responded. "Think I could shock him?"

"I'm sure of it," I said.

"Especially if he knew you're living with his daughter," Tim said.

"We're roommates," I reminded him. "Just roommates."

"If that's what you want everyone to believe, that's quite all right with me," Connor teased.

One of the volunteers working down in the caves started yelling, bringing the entire excavation to a halt. "I've found something!" she shouted. "Dr. Raven, I've found something!"

I was already sprinting toward the cave. "Stop digging!" I ordered. "Don't go any further!"

Connor ran after me, with Tim following closely behind. By the time they caught up, I was on my knees, using my bare hands to expose the find. I pushed the dirt away to reveal an object that appeared to be a piece of some kind of clay jar. Isabella photographed it as the rest of the team looked on.

I carefully withdrew fragments from the earth as Isabella switched to a videorecorder. I spoke to the camera, explaining what had been discovered. I was overcome with excitement as I held it in my hands.

"We did it, everybody," I declared. "We did it!"

Whistles and cheers erupted as everyone started hugging and high-fiving each other. Tim took the fragments and placed them in a secure metal box to transport them to the lab for carbon dating and verification. I scrambled to my feet, wiping my hands on my jeans. I hugged Tim, Isabella and Elliott, then hesitated as I came face-to-face with Connor.

He smiled. "You did it," he told me.

I shook my head. "We did it," I said softly. "Without you, it would not have happened."

"In that case, I think I deserve a proper thank you." He pulled me into his arms, lifting me off my feet as he kissed me. I wrapped my arms around his neck, responding enthusiastically, oblivious to our audience.

"Told you," Tim said to his wife.

"Stop staring," Isabella scolded him.

"I hope she marries him," Tim said. "We'll never have to beg for funds again."

Isabella rolled her eyes skyward.

Tim only grinned. "I think they're vapor locked."

19

CONNOR

"We have to celebrate." I went to the kitchen and returned with the bottle of Dom Perignon I'd kept on hand for the day we made an important find...or the night I finally got Lynne in the sack, whichever came first. I must admit, I was hoping for the latter.

"None for me," Lynne said with a dismissive wave. "You go ahead, though."

"You don't like champagne?" I asked as I searched the cabinets for substitutes for proper glassware among the mismatched pieces Lynne owned.

"It doesn't like me," she lamented. "I don't hold any kind of alcohol well."

"One glass," I urged. "I can't celebrate alone." I tried to imagine her intoxicated and suppressed a smile. Did I want to get her drunk and have my way with her? Of course not. I wanted a willing participant.

Lynne hesitated, then relented. "All right. One." She flopped down onto the couch.

I half-filled two glasses and handed one to her. I sat beside her. "A toast," I insisted, raising my glass. "To discovery."

"I'll drink to that," she said, lightly tapping her glass to mine.

"Drink slowly. Savor it," I advised.

She followed my instruction. "This is good," she said, impressed.

I tried to kiss her, but she pushed me away gently. "You didn't mind making out with me out there with everyone watching," I reminded her. "Are you an exhibitionist? Do you require an audience? I'm a bit shy myself, but if this is what it will take, I'll go along."

"I was caught up in the moment, the discovery," she said.

"You didn't kiss Tim or Elliott," I reminded her.

"You kissed me." She reached for her glass. "Besides, out there it was safe."

"Safe?"

"You wouldn't go any further with everyone watching."

"I'm a desperate man. I could be pushed to discard my modesty."

"What modesty?" She started to laugh.

I attempted to kiss her again. This time, she didn't protest.

"You taste like champagne," she giggled, lying back against the couch. I kept kissing her. She ran her hands through my hair. I drew her closer, my touches more intimate. Finally, she pulled back. "You have the most beautiful eyes. I can see forever in your eyes," she sang off-key.

I laughed. "You really can't hold it, can you?"

"Nope." She started to giggle again.

I nuzzled her neck. She started to squirm. "Stop that. Your beard tickles."

I kept kissing her in spite of her halfhearted protests. I started nibbling at her earlobes. She was a willing, if intoxicated, participant, holding me tightly, wrapping her legs around me.

Then, abruptly, she stopped moving.

I drew back and looked down at her. She was out cold. Frustrated, I let out a loud groan and pulled myself upright.

Unbelievable.

20

LYNNE

I woke early the next morning with a splitting headache. It took me a few moments to get my bearings and realize where I was. I lay on my back on the couch, my legs across Connor's lap. He was shirtless, sleeping in an upright position.

I tried to remember what had happened the night before, but most of it was a blur. I did recall celebrating the find, drinking champagne, kissing Connor....

"Connor." I nudged him with my bare foot. "Connor, wake up." I nudged him again. When that produced no results, I kicked him. "Connor!"

He woke with a start. "What?"

"Refresh my memory," I said. "Why are we here, like this?"

He regarded me with a lazy smile. "You don't remember?"

"Obviously, no."

"We had quite a celebration last night," he said. "I'm hurt you don't remember. Most women find me unforgettable."

Was he saying we'd had sex? For a moment, I wondered. "I remember the champagne, but—"

He licked his lips. "You were delicious."

"Nice try, Merlin, but I still have my clothes on," I realized.

"Getting them off was simple," he said. "Putting them back on presented problems. I suspect I put your underwear on backwards."

I pulled at the waistband to check. He laughed. "Had you there, didn't I?"

I snatched a pillow from behind my head and hit him with it. He took it from me and threw it back. I caught it and tried to hit him again, but he blocked the blow. I sat up, throwing a mock punch. He grabbed both of my wrists. "Bit of a hellcat, aren't you?" he laughed as he twisted me around so that my back was pressed against his chest, my arms pinned to my sides.

"Let go." My tone held a warning note.

"Turn you loose so you can assault me again?" he asked, kissing my neck. "I don't think so."

"What did we do last night?" I wanted to know.

"Got off to a brilliant start," he said, still nuzzling me. "Making out, you were all over me."

"Connor!"

"The champagne rid you of all those nasty inhibitions," he told me. "Then you passed out."

"Passed out? While you were—" I couldn't finish. I was laughing too hard.

"You dealt a severe blow to my ego." He nibbled my earlobe. "Now you're going to make it up to me, aren't you?"

"In your dreams, Merlin. In your dreams."

21

CONNOR

"It's old, just not old enough to have been from the Exodus." I broke the news to Lynne. "The carbon dating shows it's approximately two thousand years old."

Lynne's expression changed from disappointment to renewed hope. "Two thousand years old? Are you sure?" she asked.

I nodded. "No doubt."

"It could be from the time of Christ, then," she said slowly, her hope restored. She looked at me. "It's possible."

"What?" I asked, not understanding.

"When Joseph and Mary left Israel with the infant Jesus, Joseph had received a vision from God, telling him to take mother and child to Egypt, to safety. They crossed the Sinai to get into Egypt," she explained. "It was a long, difficult journey. The exact route they took has never been known. They could have come this way."

"You don't see this as a total loss, then." I said.

She smiled hopefully. "It could be an important find, after all. We need to photograph all of the fragments," she said. I could tell her mind was already racing ahead to the next step in determining the degree of importance of the find. "I can work on the translation on the computer."

I raised an eyebrow. "It's written in Aramaic," I reminded her.

She nodded. "I know."

"You can read a dead language?"

She smiled, leaning back against the back of the worn couch. "Enough to know it when I see it," she told him.

I nodded, smiling. "Everyone should learn a dead language, right?"

"This might very well answer questions mankind has been asking for centuries," she said.

I grinned. "Or it could be some ancient grocery list."

I EMERGED FROM SLEEP SLOWLY. I opened my eyes and lay there for a few moments before catching sight of the thin ribbon of light under the closed door. I turned over and looked at the LED display on the alarm clock on my nightstand. Curious, I got out of bed, wearing only drawstring pajama bottoms—more than I wore in bed back home, actually—and opened the door. Across the hall, Lynne was at her computer, an image of the papyrus on the monitor.

She was unaware of my presence until I spoke. "Do you know what time it is?" I asked, rubbing the back of my head.

She didn't turn around. "Sorry if I woke you," she apologized.

"You've been at this for the past nine hours," I pointed out. "You need sleep."

She shook her head. "What I need is to complete the translation. I can't do it myself, so I just sent it to a colleague in Israel." She faced me for the first time. "Connor, this is why I became an archaeologist. This could be what I've always been searching for."

"Go to bed," I ordered. "This isn't going anywhere tonight."

She nodded. "A few hours of sleep sounds good."

"Eight. At least eight."

"I can't."

"You can, and you will. I'll pull rank if I have to," I warned.

She was too exhausted to argue with me. She stood up slowly, supporting herself by holding onto the table. "I think I was in that chair too long," she admitted. "My legs feel like overcooked spaghetti."

"Shall I carry you to your room?" I asked, taking her arm.

She managed a smile. "I can manage." She took a few wobbly steps and let out a groan. I took her by the arm and steadied her.

"Have you made any progress at all with it?" I asked.

"It says, *'the prophet shall come in advance of the Messiah's arrival'*. I'm assuming it refers to John the Baptist," she said, "but there are parts that don't make sense. It says the prophet will come forth from the island of the angels."

"What does that mean?" I asked.

"I have no idea."

22

LYNNE

"Looks like we've got a storm brewing," I told Tim, observing the ominous dark clouds approaching from the west.

"I'll make sure everything's secure," Tim told me. "Go on."

He didn't have to twist my arm. I was exhausted. Every bone and muscle in my body ached. All I wanted was a hot shower and a soft bed. *I'm glad it's Connor's night to cook,* I thought.

He was in the kitchen taking dinner from the oven when I arrived home. "Smells good," I told him as I pulled off my baseball cap and tossed it aside. "Y'know, Merlin, you'd make somebody a great wife."

He looked up and smiled. "Is that a proposal?" he wanted to know.

I sat on the couch and pulled off my shoes. "You don't believe in marriage, remember?"

He took plates from the cabinet. "I could be had for the right offer," he suggested. "Are you offering?"

I just laughed, not taking him seriously. Connor was not the marrying kind, no matter how good he was in the kitchen. "Do I have time for a shower?"

"If you make it quick. I don't want this to get cold."

"You sound like my mother."

He gave me a look that I couldn't quite read. "I won't be long," I promised.

I went into my bathroom and stripped off my dirty clothes, dropping them into the hamper. Once in the shower, I started to relax. It had been a long day. As I worked the shampoo into my hair, I was still thinking about Connor. It was getting harder and harder to resist him. The real problem was that I no longer wanted to resist him.

God help me, I love him.

Why do I always end up falling for men who are all wrong for me? Why can't I fall in love with a nice, safe, boring man who wouldn't turn my life inside out?

A psychiatrist would have a field day with me, I thought miserably. *He'd probably tell me it all goes back to my problems with Dad. I keep seeking out men as unlike my father as I can find. And I end up with men who are even more trouble for me than he's ever been.*

Connor's right. We are both damaged goods. Does that make us a match, or a disaster waiting to happen?

He thinks that in taking her own life, his mother abandoned him. I guessed he sees all women that way. Leave them before they can leave him.

CONNOR HAD dinner on the table when I emerged from the bathroom, dressed in faded denim shorts and a baggy pink T-shirt. My hair was still damp from the shower, curling around my neck and shoulders. I guess most women would have felt self-conscious about having him see them that way, but I had two failed relationships behind me in which I'd tried to be someone I wasn't. For better or worse, Connor was getting the real me. "You're not like any woman I've ever known," he commented, pouring our tea.

I seated myself at the table. "Is that good or bad?" I asked, not sure I wanted to know.

"Good, quite good," he said. "Most of them, my sister included, would never allow themselves to be seen without full makeup, hair done and just the right attire. Get them into bed, and they're more concerned with how they look than they are with pleasure. I have to say I don't care at all for the taste of mascara. And lip gloss is quite greasy, actually."

I had the fork halfway to my mouth, but that mental image made me stop short. I made a face.

"But you," he went on, "I suspect I could roll in the sheets with you for a month straight and every part of you I tasted would be completely natural."

The temperature in the room just went up thirty degrees, I thought, acutely uncomfortable. "I think we have a storm coming," I said uneasily, changing the subject.

He wasn't having any of it. "I'd like to put my theory to the test," he told me.

So would I, I was thinking. "Maybe I should seduce you and make you marry me," I said in a deceptively light tone.

"Maybe I should seduce you and make you marry me," I said in a deceptively light tone.

"Why would you want to marry me? You know me too well," he joked.

"True," I conceded. "They don't call you the Black Knight for nothing."

He laughed. "The Black Knight? Who calls me that?" he asked.

"The rest of the team," I said, taking a bite. "That's how they see you. Dark, mysterious, revealing precious little of yourself, isolating yourself from the rest of the group. Always in full armor."

"Not always," he disagreed.

"You're never completely without it," I said, getting up to get more tea. "That breastplate's always in place."

I turned and found his face inches from my own. "Breastplate?" he asked, resting his hands on my hips.

"Protecting your heart." I tried to step past him, but he wouldn't let me go.

"The food's going to get cold."

"Better it than me."

I gave him a poke. "You're so full of shit, your eyes should be brown."

"All right." Releasing me reluctantly, he took a step back and made a sweeping motion with his hands. "Remove my armor."

I shook my head. "You wish."

"I can't do it alone." He feigned helplessness. "I need your help."

I leaned back against the counter. "And if I refuse?"

"You don't want to do that."

"I don't?"

"How would you live with yourself if my poor, starving heart were to die sad and lonely because you refused to set it free?" he pleaded.

I ran my hand down the front of his shirt. "And how do I do that?" I asked. *This is a mistake. Stop now while you still can.*

He unbuttoned his shirt. "I think this needs to be out of the way. Try again."

Exhilarated, I stroked his bare chest. *I'm down for the count. No turning back now,* I thought. *I'm going to regret this.*

He kissed me. "Keep trying," he urged.

I put one arm around his neck, my free hand continuing to stroke his chest. I felt bold, sexy. "Anything happening yet?" I muttered against his mouth.

"Definitely. Keep going." He reached down and unzipped his jeans.

Then the phone rang...

———

Earthquakes are common in the Sinai. Three major fault lines converge there. We had experienced them many times in the three years we'd been there...but I never expected an earthquake to be the turning point in my life. I guess I should have. Mom always said a building had to fall on me. From her mouth to God's ear...

We were finished for the day and preparing to head for home. Unexpectedly, the trailer began to shake. Connor held onto me. "What the hell—"

"Earthquake," I said. "We've got to get outside."

"Lynne!" Tim called from outside.

I ran for the door with Connor behind me. We got outside as the quake gained in intensity. "The equipment!" Tim shouted. Isabella was herding their three children toward the Land Rovers.

Tim and I ran toward the equipment. Connor ran after us. I got there first. Large rocks began to fall from the mountainside. One came down in front of Connor as he tried to get to me. Another hit my left shoulder, knocking me to the ground.

"Lynne!" he shouted. He got to me as I was trying to get up. "Are you all right, darlin'?"

"I think so," I said, dazed, as he helped me to my feet.

More rocks showered us as the earth continued to shudder violently. It only lasted a few moments, but felt like an eternity. Connor shielded my body with his own, holding me tightly against his chest until the tremblors finally ceased.

23

CONNOR

"Take your shirt off," I told Lynne as we entered the house. "I need to examine you." I kicked off my shoes next to hers on the mat at the door.

She shook her head. "All I need is a soft bed and a good night's sleep," she insisted.

"You could have a fracture there," I argued. "If so, you'll need to go to the casualty."

"The—what?"

"I believe you Americans call it the emergency room," I clarified.

"I'm fine. No fractures, just tired and sore." Her expression softened. "Thanks for being my knight in tarnished armor out there."

"Then humor me, all right?" I wasn't going to take no for an answer. She could indeed have a fracture there. "Let me see your shoulder."

"You just want to get me to take my clothes off."

I gave her a stern look.

She hesitated for only a moment, then turned away from me and pulled the T-shirt up over her head to expose her shoulder. There was a large, purple discoloration covering her left shoulder blade.

"You've a nasty bruise there," I said, tracing it with my fingertips. "You need to have it x-rayed, just to be sure it's not fractured. I'll drive you to the hospital—"

"No," she said stubbornly. "If I'm still in pain in the morning, maybe, but not tonight."

I lowered my head, kissing her shoulder. She laughed. "What are you doing?" she asked.

"When you were a wee girl, did your mum never kiss your scratches and bruises to make them better?" I asked.

"Sure, but it never felt like that."

"I should hope not."

"I'm going to bed," she said then. She pulled her shirt into place.

"Not yet." I turned her back to face me again. "I believe we have some unfinished business."

"Unfinished business?" She gave me a blank look.

"You were about to free me from my self-imposed prison when the earth threatened to swallow us," I reminded her.

"Ah, yes. Your armor."

"You were in the process of removing it, as I recall."

She hesitated. "Oh, yeah. Now I remember," she said. "Maybe later."

I shook my head. "Now."

She resisted. "It's late."

"I just saved your life. In some cultures, that would mean your life now belongs to me." I refused to let her go.

She made a face. "You're not interested in my life, just my body." My shirt was still unbuttoned. She reached out tentatively, running her hands up my bare chest. "You said this was working, I believe."

"Oh, yeah. It's working. Don't stop." I nuzzled her neck. "Get me out of it, darlin'," I whispered. "Set me free."

She kissed me, a bold kiss that let me know she was finally ready for me. She pushed the shirt off my shoulders. It fell to the floor as I grabbed the hem of her T-shirt and pulled it over her head. "It's only fair," I said with a smile that left nothing to her imagination.

"I wasn't wearing any armor," she said, kissing my chest.

"That's a matter of opinion." I pulled her close. "At any rate, you're not wearing any now."

"Or much of anything else."

I wanted to say something important. I wanted to tell her I'd realized I loved her, but decided against it. Instead, I kissed her....

IT WAS MORNING. The storm had come and gone. The earthquake was over, but the aftershocks remained. I lay beside Lynne, staring up at the ceiling. "Did you sleep at all?" she asked.

"No."

She hesitated. "I hope I wasn't too much of a disappointment," she said.

Her comment surprised me. I turned on my side to face her. "Why would I be disappointed?" I wanted to know.

"I don't know," she said. "It's been a while since...."

I stroked her cheek. "Look at this face. This is the face of a man who's quite satisfied." I reached past her and took her phone from the nightstand. "Ring up Tim. Tell him anything to keep everyone away from our door today." I wanted—needed—to be alone with her for as long as possible.

She nodded, not even trying to argue. She punched in Tim's number. He answered almost immediately. "Can you do without me today?" she asked. "No, I'm pretty sure it's okay. Connor says I have a nasty bruise and he's insisting I have it x-rayed."

I started kissing her neck. My beard tickled her, and she tried to push me away. "As a matter of fact, he did examine me. It was my shoulder, Tim, not my—never mind. I'll talk to you later." She pushed me away again and put the phone back on the nightstand. "That was mean."

I was concerned. "You don't plan to keep us a secret, do you?" I wanted to know.

"I wasn't sure if you did."

"No, I don't," I said, kissing her again. "I'm quite territorial, darlin'. I want everyone to know you belong to me now."

She kissed the tip of my nose playfully. "Does that mean you also belong to me?" she asked.

"If you want, but I have to warn you that I require quite a lot of attention if you wish to possess me." I nibbled her earlobe. "Think you're up for it?"

"I think you're trouble. I thought you were trouble from the start," she said, "but I'll take my chances."

"Will you, now?"

"Why were you so quiet afterward?" she asked then.

"It's nothing," I said.

She didn't believe me. "If we're going to be together, we have to be honest with each other. Talk to me," she urged. "Please."

I must have seemed to be struggling. I felt like someone trying to make an important statement in a language I'd never spoken before. "I love you," I said finally.

"You don't look like a man in love," she observed. "You look terrified."

"I am terrified," I admitted. "I haven't loved anyone since I was five years old, and that was quite a different kind of love."

She took my face in her hands. "I'm scared, too," she admitted.

I tried to smile. "This is insane."

"Yeah, it is. Really crazy. We should both be locked up."

"Together. Only if we're together."

She sat up, and I couldn't believe what I was seeing. The bruise on her shoulder had completely disappeared. How...

"It was an act of God," she said.

"What?" I was still focused on the missing bruise.

"Us. Tonight. I was still on the fence...until..."

"If you want to get married, we can do that," I said then.

She gave a little laugh, then realized I wasn't joking. "You're serious?"

I didn't smile. "The paperwork doesn't mean shit to me," I acknowledged. "A legal document won't influence my commitment to you one way or the other, but if a marriage license proves to you that I love you, then so be it."

She took a deep breath as if considering it but feeling a degree of uncertainty. "Well," she said finally, "if that's a proposal, then I suppose my answer has to be yes."

I didn't hide my sense of relief. "I was starting to think for a moment there that you might actually turn me down," I said, kissing her neck.

"There's a condition," she went on.

I drew back. "Do I have to get you pregnant before you'll marry me?" I asked, feigning concern. "What will people think?"

She never got the chance to respond. My satellite phone rang, interrupting us. "Damn!" I muttered under my breath as I released her. I rolled over, snatched my jeans off the floor and fished my phone from one pocket. I knew who was calling without asking. This was the third time in the past four hours Edward had tried to reach me. I turned back to Lynne. "Don't go anywhere," I said. "This won't take long."

"Is something wrong?" she asked, pulling the sheet around herself as she rose up on one elbow, watching me collect my clothes.

"Nothing I can't fix," I assured her, bending down to kiss her. "I'll be right back."

I jerked on my jeans and stalked down the hallway to the front door, slamming it in my wake. I punched in Edward's number as I stomped down the front steps.

He picked up on the first ring. "Where have you been?" he demanded.

"None of your damned business!" I snapped. "This had better be good. Do you have any idea what time it is here?"

"If you had returned my first call—"

"If I had not been otherwise occupied, I would have!" I was anxious to be done with this. I wanted to get back to Lynne. I had just done something monumental: I'd told her I loved her. Edward was an unwelcome intrusion. "Has the world come to an end without my knowledge?"

"I realize you're annoyed with me, but—"

"The word is pissed, Edward. Pissed off. And you're damned right I'm pissed off. Your days of ordering me around like your trained pony are over. I'm not coming back to London. I've just asked Lynne to marry me."

"You can't be serious!"

"I've never been more serious in my life," I assured him.

"Your work—"

"Work was all I had before I came here," I reminded him. "I gave everything to the project. Now, I want something for myself, and you and your associates will have to accept that."

"And what will you do there?"

"Make up for all the years I've lost." I ended the call abruptly.

I should have told him to go to hell long before now, I thought, raking a hand through my hair in exasperation. *Time to cut all ties with Andrew's past. It's for the best. We'll stay here. No one will ever find me. She'll never have to know what I've done.*

24

LYNNE

I was out of bed and dressed, watching him from the kitchen window. When he didn't come back inside after fifteen minutes, I worried that something might be wrong.

He was pacing out there in the darkness. He paced when he was angry or frustrated. I knew him well enough to give him space when he was dealing with a problem, but now I wanted to go to him. I was going to be his wife. I didn't have to pretend to be indifferent. I could show concern. I could help him when he was working through a problem. *I can stick my nose right in there now.*

I went outside. "Are you all right?" I asked.

He turned to face me, forcing a smile. "Never better."

I was dubious. "Right. It shows," I said. "Merlin, if something is bothering you, I—" Before I could finish, he grabbed me, scooping me up into his arms, holding me tightly.

"Connor!" I shrieked.

"Snake—" he gasped.

"What?"

"Snake...bit me...."

"Put me down," I told him. I needed to check the bite.

"No...not sure...it's gone...."

"Put me down!" I ordered. In the dim light, I saw the creature slither away in pursuit of a small rodent. "I have to check the bite!"

Finally, he lowered me to the ground. I got on my knees. He had come out without his shoes. There was a bite on his right foot that was already beginning to swell. I dug into my pocket. My cell wasn't there. It must have fallen out when he removed my shorts. I pulled his satellite phone from the clip on his belt and called for help....

"I HAVE TO BE WITH HIM," I told the triage nurse as Connor was wheeled into the ER on a gurney, the doors swinging shut behind the EMTs who had tended him on the medivac helicopter that brought us from the local hospital in Taba to Cairo.

"We have to have some paperwork completed first," the nurse said stubbornly. "The doctor will tell you when you may see him."

"He could die!" I shouted, causing everyone in the emergency admissions area to look my way. "I have to be with him!"

"We need someone to sign consent for treatment," the nurse argued. "Since he's unconscious, we need his next of kin, someone legally responsible. Are you related?"

I thought quickly. "Yes," I lied. "I'm his wife."

The nurse shoved some papers on a clipboard at me. "Sign all of the blanks indicated."

I glared at her, scribbling my name on the forms. "I want to see my husband now," I said in a low, threatening voice. "You don't want to get in my way."

I turned and ran into the ER, leaving the stunned nurse staring after me.

THE WAIT SEEMED LIKE AN ETERNITY. I wasn't allowed to be with Connor while he was being treated, and no one was telling me anything. Tim and Isabella had stayed with me for a while, but I finally sent them away. I insisted I needed to be alone, needed to think. "Bring me some clothes, some stuff," I said, distracted. "I don't know how long we'll be here."

I could hear them talking as they departed. "I've never seen her like this," Isabella commented as they left the waiting area.

Tim frowned. "Neither have I," he admitted. "When I got out there, she was on the ground with him, with him lying across her lap. She was going nuts."

"She found the right guy, as you wanted her to," Isabella said.

"I hope he makes it. If he doesn't, that damn snake might as well have gotten both of them," Tim predicted.

"HE'S BEEN GIVEN ANTIVENIN, and we're monitoring his hematological values closely," the doctor assured me. "He is most fortunate. The bite of the desert horned viper can be fatal. He will have to stay in the hospital for a time, and even after he's released, he will not be able to resume normal activity for several weeks. But he should recover fully. He had a seizure in the casualty, but that's not unexpected, given that's he's epileptic."

I tried to hide my surprise. "Of course," I said slowly. *He's epileptic?*

We stood outside Connor's room. Through the door, I watched two nurses check Connor's vital signs and IV. I said a silent prayer of gratitude.

After the doctor left, I pulled up a chair next to Connor's bed and sat down, assuming he was still asleep. He opened his eyes and smiled at me. "I must be dead," he said. "I'm looking at an angel."

I gave a tired laugh. "Even now, after all you've been through, you're still full of it," I said. "Tell me, why did I have to hear from the doctor that you're epileptic?"

He closed his eyes for a moment. "I should have told you," he said.

"Yes, you should have," I agreed. "Why didn't you?"

"I intended to," he said. "Just never got around to it."

"Right."

"I don't have tonic-clonic seizures," he said. "What I have is temporal lobe epilepsy. Are you familiar with it?"

I nodded. "A little."

"Over the years, I've had countless EEGs, CT scans and MRIs. They've all been inconclusive, but there's been enough there to convince every doctor who's ever examined me to come to the same conclusion," he said.

"TLE has been often misdiagnosed as schizophrenia or bipolar disorder. I see things, hear things. I have blackouts. How would you have felt when I went off into the desert all those nights if you had known?"

"The same way I felt not knowing," I said. "Afraid you'd go off some night and never come back. I always worried you'd hit a land mine or be attacked."

"You never said anything."

"I didn't want to sound like a nagging wife."

He took my hand. His felt clammy and there was a heparin lock inserted into the back of it, there in case he went into cardiac arrest and had to receive medication immediately. "What does the doctor say? Am I going to live?"

"Absolutely. You're too mean to die," I said. "Your recovery's going to be a long one, though."

He grimaced. "How long are they planning to hold me prisoner here?"

"I'm not sure. I don't think the doctor even knows yet," I said, kissing his forehead. "I'm staying here with you until you're released."

"You don't have to."

"As long as you're here, so am I," I said firmly. "I won't consider you out of the woods until you walk out of this hospital. Maybe not even then."

"I never had you pegged for a worrier."

"When Tim and I were at the University of Utah, a mutual friend was in a car accident," I recalled. "The driver was killed. Our friend was the lucky one—or so we thought at the time. He only broke his leg. He seemed to be recovering, but the break had caused a blood clot. The clot made its way to his heart. His roommate found him dead in their room. No warning, nothing."

"You've made me feel so optimistic," he said, wincing in pain.

"My point is that I'm going to be here if and when you need me," I said. "I'm not going to be out there at the site, unable to get here in an emergency."

"Are there any hotels in the vicinity?" he asked.

"I've asked for a cot. I'm staying here."

"Why don't you just get in this bed with me then?" he suggested.

I gave him The Look. "I'm not sure the staff would approve."

He was quiet for a while. "There's something else I've never told you about," he started. "I've had a nightmare—the same one—since I was fifteen. It's always the same, it never changes. There's a violent storm. I'm in the water, and it's very cold. The current is overwhelming me. I'm struggling to stay afloat. I see a light, a boat, and try to swim toward it. There's someone on the deck, calling out to me, reaching for me, but I can't quite make it. I see your face, just once, before I'm pulled under."

"Mine?" I asked.

"You," Connor said. "The woman on the boat is you. I saw your face for the first time over twenty years ago. That's why you seemed so familiar to me the night we met."

"What do you think it means?" I asked. I didn't laugh, didn't question his honesty or his sanity. I believed him. "God gives us visions sometimes to lead us where we have to go."

"Visions?"

I nodded. "The ancient prophets received visions to lead them, or to lead their people. The Book of Revelation, for example, was given to St. John in a vision."

"If only prophets have visions—"

"When John the Baptist began his ministry, preparing the world for Jesus' arrival, there had not been a prophet in four hundred years. God had been silent because his people were not listening to him. And there have been no official prophets since Jesus' resurrection, though many have had visions."

"Says a lot about our society, doesn't it?" Connor said lightly. "God's kicked us to the curb."

"Hardly."

"Does my dream mean you're supposed to save me from something?"

"Possibly." I managed a smile. "Probably from yourself."

25

CONNOR

"You will be weak for some time to come," the doctor told me. "Everyday activities will be restricted—forbidden, in some instances."

I looked at Lynne, then at the doctor again. "What about sex?" I wanted to know.

The doctor shook his head. "Too strenuous."

Not what I wanted to hear. "Suppose I promise to skip the kinky stuff?" Lynne slapped my shoulder lightly.

The doctor regarded me with mild amusement.

"For how long?" I asked.

"A month, perhaps longer," the doctor answered. "It will depend upon the progress of your recovery."

"A month?"

"I'll see that he plays by the rules, Doctor," Lynne assured him. "He won't be doing anything he's not supposed to do." She gave me that look. "Anything."

After the doctor left the room, I turned to Lynne. "A month or longer?" I let out a loud groan.

"You managed without it for six months," she reminded me.

"Not willingly."

She kissed me. "We'll get through it," she assured me.

"You will. I'll go quite mad."

She stroked my hair. I felt the stirrings of arousal at her touch. "No, you won't. You'll be frustrated and cranky and an all-around pain in the ass and you'll test my patience to its limits. But you won't go mad."

I looked at her. "How can you be so bloody cheerful?" I asked.

She took my face in her hands. "Because you're alive," she said. "I'd rather have you like this than not at all."

"Even if I'm not a whole man?" I asked, frustrated.

"You are a whole man, albeit a grumpy one," she insisted. "Even if we could never have sex again, you're the only man I could ever want. Anyway, what makes you think being a whole man is contingent upon sexual performance? Is that all you think you have to offer, all you think I want from you? You've made love to me every day and night since the night we met—with your eyes, your voice, your touch."

I wasn't satisfied. "I'd rather be able to do it with my—"

She pressed her fingers to my lips. "I get it, okay?" she said. "You're impossible."

"Promise me you'll take it easy while I'm gone." Lynne was going to Cairo with Tim.

"How much trouble could I get into here alone?" I asked, trying unsuccessfully to pull off an innocent expression.

She eyed me warily. "You don't really want me to answer that, do you?"

I tried to look properly offended. "I thought I'd just listen to music or read. Or perhaps try my hand at snake charming."

"That's not funny."

"I'm going to go mad if this enforced celibacy is long term," I said then.

"Me, too," she confessed. "You're becoming a bigger pain in the ass every day."

"I think I should pose a question to the good doctor," I said. "I might ask if he feels the brief stress of lovemaking is not preferable to the long-term stress of celibacy."

"That could be a persuasive argument," she said, bending down to kiss me. "And no one knows better than I do how persuasive you can be."

I didn't smile. "If I believed in all that supernatural crap, I'd think the devil's testing me to see if I'm eligible for hell," I complained.

After she left, I took out my satellite phone and rang up Edward and informed him my solicitor would be in contact with him with regard to my legal affairs. I wanted him to know I wished to distance myself from Icarus and from GenTech as quickly as possible, that I would not be returning to London.

"Please, Andrew—don't do anything rash," Edward urged me. "Think it over."

"I have thought it over," I insisted. "I'm staying here. I'm going to marry Lynne. I'm going to have children with her."

"Are you going to tell her everything?"

"I'd rather not, but if I must, I will," I said.

"How long do you think she'll stay with you, once she knows the truth about you?" Edward wanted to know.

"I'd like to believe she'll forgive my deception."

"You're far too intelligent to believe that."

I was quiet for a moment. There was one question I'd never asked, but now I felt a need to know the answer. "Tell me, Edward—did you ever love my mother?" When he didn't respond immediately, I said, "I didn't think so."

"How long do you think you'll be satisfied, living as you do now?" Edward asked.

"I think I could be happy here indefinitely."

"Have you lost your mind?" There was panic in his voice.

"No, Edward. I've found my soul."

26

CAITLIN

"There's not much I can tell you," Audrey Mann apologized. "I was Dr. Sadowski's assistant—that is, secretary—for many years, but I'm afraid he was very tight-lipped about his work. I was only there to answer the phones and keep everyone at bay when he didn't want to be disturbed. I never had access to any of his files."

"You had no knowledge of his experiments?" I asked.

Audrey shook her head. "None, I'm sorry to say," she apologized. "Few did, actually. In fact, I'm fairly certain only Dr. Sadowski and Dr. Stewart had full access to everything."

"What can you tell us about Dr. Stewart?" I asked.

"He was Dr. Sadowski's protege," the woman said. "He was a science prodigy—graduated college at eleven years of age. He had three degrees, including his doctorate, by the time he was fifteen. He started working with Dr. Sadowski when he was only sixteen."

"Genius," I said.

"Beyond anything you might imagine," Audrey said, nodding. "He was brilliant."

"Where is he now?" Jack asked.

"No idea," the woman said. "He left Boston the week before Dr. Sadowski passed away, and I haven't seen or heard from him since."

"He didn't leave a forwarding address or anything?" I asked.

"No one did, under the circumstances."

"Do you know where he was from?" Jack pursued.

Audrey shook her head. "I knew nothing about him. To tell the truth, I rarely even saw him when he was here," she admitted. "He preferred to work alone. To be left alone. He could be very testy when he was disturbed."

I turned to Jack. "Flag his passport. If he's still in the country, he won't be able to leave," she said. "If he's left, we'll know where he went."

OLIVE OYL'S was the funkiest restaurant I'd ever seen. Located near the harbor in a low, weather-beaten building with peeling gray paint, it was a family-style seafood restaurant with decidedly nautical decor. Nets and fishing paraphernalia hung on the walls, there were benches instead of tables, and food and drink was served on tin plates and in Mason jars.

We found an empty bench near a window facing the water. Our server, a young woman with strawberry blond hair pulled back in a ponytail, was chewing gum. She blew a large bubble as she approached, then popped it and sucked the gum back into her mouth. She pulled her order book from the pocket of her apron. "Hi, I'm Melanie," she greeted us, grabbing the pencil tucked behind her ear. "Ready to order?"

"Not yet," I said, scanning the menu. "What do you recommend?"

Melanie didn't hesitate. "Getting out of here while you still can," she deadpanned.

Jack laughed. "That bad?"

She nodded. "The catch of the day was thrown back four days in a row, but it finally made the menu today," she confided. "It was the only fish in the net, I'm told."

"I'll have the tilapia," I finally decided.

Melanie wrote it down. "Tilapia with a side order of e.coli." She turned to me. "You?"

"I think I'll have the orange roughy," Jack said.

"Good choice," Melanie said with an approving nod. "We've only had three incidents with the roughy. Just a minute." She turned her attention to another customer who was headed for the door. "Hey, cheapskate—where's my tip?"

Stunned, the man scurried back to his table, dropped some bills on it, then rushed out.

Jack laughed. I shot him a disapproving look. "Hey, it was funny," he defended himself.

"Do you always chase customers for tips?" I asked.

"On the crappy wages Olive pays, I have to," she said with a shrug.

"There really is an Olive?" Jack asked.

Melanie nodded. "Her last name's not really Oyl, but yeah. No Popeye, though." She lowered her voice to a conspiratorial whisper. "That woman could sit on a dime and squeeze out nine cents. Anything to drink?"

"I'll have an Arnold Palmer," I said.

"Half iced tea and half lemonade," Melanie said as she wrote it down.

"Make it two," Jack said. He'd never had it before, but was clearly looking forward to hearing what she had to say about it.

Melanie nodded. "Two Arnolds, a roughy and a tilapia. Anything else?"

"Maybe dessert, if we survive dinner," I said.

"Dessert's safe. We don't make it here," Melanie said.

As she headed for the kitchen with the order, I turned my attention to my partner. "I keep waiting for Rod Serling's voice over," I admitted, keeping my voice low.

"Without proof, who's going to believe it?" he wondered aloud.

I stared absently toward the window overlooking the harbor. "Dorothea's parents died years ago. There are no living relatives in her family to speak with. Sadowski's, the few he had left, are all in Poland. The Sadowskis' son left Boston years ago. Nobody knows where he is now. We can talk to some of his former colleagues at the university—and I've tracked down two of the women he coerced into sex."

He picked absently at a sugar packet. It was an old habit, picking at things on the dinner table. "That should be an interesting interview," he said.

"Yeah." I continued to stare through the window at the water. "I don't think I want to hear any of the details. Not without a barf bag, anyway."

"Stewart's still in the US, according to the State Department," he said then. "Now all we have to do is find out where."

"You make it sound so simple," I said.

"At least we only have to scour one country," he reminded me.

"Interesting fellow," I commented. "He's a super genius in the truest sense of the term. Young, very attractive—according to Audrey Mann—but a real loner."

"Geniuses tend to be a little quirky," he pointed out. "Super genius, super quirky."

"If any of Sadowski's records remain, I'm betting Stewart has them," I said. Reaching for my cell phone, I called one of our colleagues. "Berkley? Hammond here. I need you to run a check for me..."

"WE KNOW that Sadowski's right-hand man, Dr. Stewart, is still somewhere here in the States," I told Randy Baker. "We know that the rumors about Sadowski's extracurricular activities with his female students are true. We don't know if he really did have a celibate relationship with the wife or if he did indeed impregnate her by in vitro. The only one who would know for sure, obviously, is Sadowski himself, and he's currently living in a timeshare in hell. It's all speculation, but given what we do know, I'm inclined to believe it's true."

"None of Sadowski's files were found," Jack put in. "Destroyed, obviously."

"We have some information regarding one of Sadowski's experiments," Baker said. "The horse, Icarus' Agenda, was bred in the UK, not here. He was brought to the US by the owner, who claimed he just wanted the horse to compete here."

"We have the name of the owner?" I asked.

Baker nodded. "A man in London by the name of Edward Rhys-Williams," he said. "He's richer than Midas, founder and chairman of a company called Icarus International."

"What do we know about him beyond that?" Jack asked.

"No previous illegal dealings or anything remotely suspicious. He's a real recluse, a widower with two adult children. Philanthropist. Gives millions to charity through his own foundation, a real do-gooder."

"And his connection to Sadowski and company?" I asked.

"He was Sadowski's chief financial backer."

———

"Sadowski knew the FDA was going to shut him down," I told FBI Special Agent Harry Lambert, speaking to him by phone in London. "Somebody warned him of what was coming down. He destroyed most of his files before their people were able to seize them. But from what we got from the staffers we interrogated, he was into some pretty bizarre experiments—genetic enhancements, accelerated growth hormones, human cloning...."

"He actually cloned human beings?" Lambert asked, amazed.

"Yeah. He did what Hitler's boys couldn't. The man was on the fast track to creating the master race—physically superior, super-geniuses," Jack put in.

"What about Rhys-Williams?" I asked then. "You talked to him. What did he have to say?"

There was a pause. "He denies knowing anything of the nature of Sadowski's experiments."

Jack and I exchanged a look. Jack shook his head.

"He poured millions into the man's research and didn't keep tabs on his activities?" My laugh was hollow. "That's hard to believe. Especially since it was his horse that got the benefit of all that work."

"He claims he hadn't seen the horse in more than a year. He bought the dam as an investment, or so he says. He'd never even watched the thing race. As for the money he gave to Sadowski's research, he says that's all done by committee. He's not even involved in the approval process."

"Yeah, right." I said, unconvinced.

"Keep us posted. If you find anything at all—"

"Count on it. And you do the same."

27

PHILLIP DARCY

It was turning out to be one of those days. How had I ended up in Israel?

I looked at my watch as I collected my bags, trying to remember if I had reset it to accommodate the time change when I arrived in Athens from Moscow. At this point, I wasn't even sure what day it was. Tel Aviv had the tightest security of any airport in the world. Not unwarranted, of course, given its history with terrorism, but it was still a pain, especially when I was in a hurry. Two terminals handled an average of 17,000 passengers daily. Each vehicle that entered the property was routinely searched. Baggage was screened thoroughly. Travelers were profiled in ways that would never be tolerated in the States. If they had been, terrorists would not have been able to take over our planes and kill thousands of our own. We won't be done in by nuclear weapons—the ACLU will be our downfall.

I spent what seemed like an eternity in Customs, and I still wasn't sure what, exactly, I was supposed to be doing here. The e-mail from the Boss Lady said only that I should take the first available flight to Tel Aviv and call the office from there. The fact that my editor was e-mailing me was an indicator that she probably wasn't in a good mood. It meant she'd tried unsuccessfully to phone me. It bugged her that I was so hard to reach sometimes—deliberately so, I might add. Ally liked direct contact.

This had better be good, I thought as I headed off to the Solan communications center to make the call. When I received the message from Alberta Ashland, I was at the airport in Athens, waiting to board a flight back to the States. I hadn't been home in six weeks and for once was actually looking forward to some down time.

So much for down time, I thought after considering deleting the offensive e-mail and claiming I never received it. Knowing Ally, she'd have my hard drive checked out to make sure.

I purchased a calling card and went to the nearest available phone. As I waited for my call to be put through, I took off my Chicago Cubs baseball cap and ran a hand through my hair. "Come on, pick up," I muttered. "If I'm here much longer, they'll charge me rent."

A female voice answered on the fourth ring. "*Viewpoint,* good afternoon."

"What's good about it?" I grumbled.

"Excuse me?"

"Sorry," I said. "Put me through to Alberta Ashland."

"Who's calling, please?"

"Tell her it's Darcy. Tell her I don't have a lot of time," I snapped.

There was a pause on the other end. "Sorry, Mr. Darcy. I didn't realize it was you. I'll put you right through," she assured me.

"You do that." My patience was wearing thin.

Moments later, Alberta came on the line. "Darcy," she greeted me with a cheerfulness that made me want to puke. "I take it you got my e-mail?"

"I got it. What's this assignment?"

"Charlie Cross is there covering the conflict," Alberta said. "He needs the best lensman I've got—and that's you."

"Yeah? When did you take up brown-nosing, Ally?"

"Much as I hate to admit it, you are the best," she responded begrudgingly.

"I'm officially on vacation, remember?"

"You'll have to postpone it. War waits for no man."

"War? Is that what they're calling it this week?"

There was a warning pause on the other end of the line. "I don't have time for this today, Darcy," she said finally.

I scratched my head. "So where is Big Thunder?" I asked.

"Tel Aviv. Leaving for Megiddo in the morning."

I laughed. "Armageddon Megiddo?" I asked. "End-of-the world Megiddo?"

"The same. There was another suicide bombing there overnight," she explained. "Six people were killed, including the bomber, seventeen injured."

"This is not news, Ally. They've been at war since Moses came down from the mountain," I pointed out.

"You're not funny, Darcy."

"I'm too tired to be funny. Funny takes effort." I paused. "I really needed this vacation, Ally."

"I'm sure. Who is she this time?"

"Who's who?" I asked.

"The woman. You're a chronic workaholic. The only time you want time off is when you've got some poor, unsuspecting woman caught in the crosshairs," Alberta laughed. "You're already paying alimony to two of your three ex-wives, but I hear you're always on the lookout for number four."

"You hear wrong," I said. "I've sworn off marriage. If there were a twelve-step program for it, I'd sign up. From here on out, I only live in sin." Hell, I couldn't afford to be stuck paying out more alimony.

"If you say so." Alberta was obviously in no mood to debate with me. "Listen, Charlie's at the Armon Ha Yarkon. I suggest you catch up with him tonight. He wants to get an early start tomorrow morning."

I took off my glasses and rubbed the bridge of my nose. "I'm glad it's not summer. By midday, it'd be hotter than hell."

Alberta didn't miss the opportunity when it presented itself. "And I'm sure you have firsthand knowledge of hell."

"As you said, I've been married three times," I said.

Alberta started to say something else, but was stopped by another incoming call. "Got to run, Darcy," she told me. "Call Charlie."

"Yeah."

I hung up, checking my watch again before leaving the communications center. So much for my vacation....

ON THE ROAD east of the Ramat David Israeli Air Force Base, Charlie Cross and I were covering another suicide bombing aboard a bus that had, only a few hours before, been filled with tourists. Now, it was a burned-out shell smoldering in spite of all attempts to extinguish the fire resulting from a homemade bomb. Charlie talked to the survivors who were able to speak, law enforcement officials on the scene, and emergency workers. I took a series of photographs. I'd been so jaded for so many years, numb to the pain and suffering that was depicted in my work—but in one day, everything had changed. Now, I found it hard to be objective about much of anything in the Middle East.

The world had changed so dramatically in such a short period of time.

"When I was in college, when I was still young and stupid and a little idealistic, I used to find it hard to believe anything like this could happen," Charlie admitted as we gratefully accepted water offered to us by one of the emergency workers. "I guess a few years in this business kind of leaves you hardened to the realities, though."

I mopped sweat from my face. "Yeah. I thought I was desensitized to it all—until a bunch of maniacs in jetliners flew right over the top of my home to take out the World Trade Center," I said. "I was having coffee and getting ready to leave for the airport. I was headed for Manila—would have been on United Flight 93 if Mia hadn't screwed up my reservation."

"Makes you think, doesn't it?" A few yards away, bodies covered in black were removed. Beyond that scene, the wreckage of the bus was about to be towed away.

"Makes me wonder why I wasn't on that plane. Really." I paused. "I've found myself wondering more than once if there was more to it than Mia's ineptitude."

Charlie grinned for the first time. "Do you believe in Fate, Darcy?"

"I'm not sure what I believe anymore." I watched as the last of the emergency vehicles pulled away. "I believe the whole world's gone nuts, that's for sure."

"I was in Washington," Charlie recalled. "On 9/11, I mean. I passed the Pentagon maybe fifteen minutes after it happened. Things seemed pretty senseless to me that day."

"Yeah."

"Makes you wonder where it's all going to end."

I thought about it. "My ex-wife would have said with Armageddon."

Charlie looked up at the road sign nearby: Megiddo, 5km. His smile was forced. "Well, it looks like we're in the right place for that."

I shot him a skeptical look. "You believe in that sort of thing?" I asked, surprised.

Charlie shook his head. "Heaven and hell and all that supernatural baloney? I'm not sure. I do believe there's such a thing as pure evil. The things that have happened in the past few years couldn't have happened if there weren't."

I remained skeptical. "You sound like my ex."

Charlie stared at me for a moment. "She's been on your mind a lot lately, hasn't she?" he finally asked.

I didn't bother to deny the obvious. "Yeah," I admitted. "After 9/11, I started thinking about all the things she'd tried to tell me while we were together—things I didn't listen to, didn't take seriously. The joke's on me, I guess. She may have been right. We may turn out to be the architects of our own downfall, after all."

"You think?"

"I'm starting to think anything is possible—"

"Hey! Stop!" Charlie broke into a run—and for a man of Charlie Cross' bulk, that was no easy feat. When anyone describes Charlie as a bear of a man, they're not exaggerating. I turned to see three young men driving off—in our rented Jeep. I ran after Charlie, but it proved useless. We finally stopped in the middle of the road, watching helplessly as the Jeep disappeared on the western horizon.

We were stranded.

28

CONNOR

"I've gone over it several times, Lynne." Dr. Moshe Biran was what one might expect of a Biblical scholar, Israeli citizenship aside: a small man with thick white hair and a neatly-trimmed beard. Lynne had studied Aramaic under him years before. We had come to Jerusalem to hopefully have him verify her suspicions regarding the papyrus.

Biran turned his computer monitor at an angle that allowed us to see it as he spoke. "You are certain it is no more than two thousand years old?"

"No question," I assured him.

"Puzzling, to say the least," he said, thoughtfully rubbing his beard.

"It's a reference to John the Baptist, isn't it?" Lynne asked.

Biran shook his head. "No, I don't believe it is," he said.

"But it doesn't fit any other Biblical reference," Lynne said.

"Perhaps not any of the books of the canonical Bible," Biran suggested.

Lynne nodded. "The Apocryphal books." She studied the monitor for a moment. "The prophet shall come forth out of the island of the angels at a time when perpetual darkness threatens to consume the earth. He must find hope himself before he can give hope to the world, and become one again under the eyes of God."

Biran nodded. I was silent. It all sounded like the premise of an apocalyptic movie to me.

"It doesn't make sense," Lynne started. "Which prophet does it refer to?"

"None," Biran said. "I believe this is a reference to a prophet yet to come."

Lynne gave him a puzzled look.

"If only we had the complete text," Biran said with a heavy sigh. "Some fragments do coincide with the prophecies of Daniel and Revelation in that it makes reference to a dark, turbulent time preceding the Second Coming."

I found that amusing. "The end of the world?" I asked.

"Theologians are divided on whether or not the prophecies describe the literal end of the world, or an ending of the world as we know it," Biran said. "My personal belief is that it is symbolic, written in a rather poetic language of the time. Dreams, visions, all symbolic."

I leaned back in my chair and regarded Biran with skepticism. "So we're not going to have our cities trashed by three-headed monsters or be overrun by insects with human faces whose stings cause such agony we're driven to insanity?"

"I do not believe so, no. Think instead of the monsters as dictators, world leaders corrupted by power," Biran suggested. "Think of the insects as disease, economic recession. Think of what the Four Horsemen of the Apocalypse represent."

"And this prophet, whoever he or she is, will have the power to stop it?" I asked, still unconvinced.

Lynne spoke up. "No. Only God can do that," she explained. "The prophet is a messenger. Whatever power he may possess comes from God working through him. He will have no control over it himself. It will come and go at God's will."

"Convenient," I said.

Lynne gave Biran an apologetic look. "He's not a believer," she explained.

Biran smiled. "Neither was I at one time."

"Island of the angels," Lynne said thoughtfully. "To my knowledge, there is no such place in the Middle East. I've never seen any references to anything even close in description."

"You're looking in the wrong direction," I said.

Lynne and Biran looked at me, both of them surprised.

"In Latin, it would be *ex insula Angelorum*," I told them. "The Angel Isle. England."

"I KNOW you wanted to be married in your father's church," I started as we headed back to our hotel, "but that may not be possible for a long time. How would you feel about getting married here?"

I could tell she was surprised...but she wasn't opposed to the idea. Jerusalem was a special place for her. "We'd have to do the paperwork—I'm not even sure what that involves here. We'd need witnesses, rings...and photos. I want wedding photos."

"Is that a yes?" I asked.

"That's a yes," she said, kissing me.

29

DARCY

"I don't believe it," I said slowly, recognizing the woman I spotted across the street.

Charlie laughed. "You look like you've seen the Ghost of Christmas Past there, buddy," he noticed.

"You're not too far off," I said, gesturing. "Over there. My ex-wife."

Charlie looked in the direction I was pointing. "Which one?"

I could have strangled the smartass. "What do you mean, which one? The woman, idiot."

"No, I mean which ex-wife," Charlie said. "You've had so many, you know."

"The third Mrs. Darcy," I said. "Over there, with that man."

Charlie grinned. "Looks like she traded up, bud," he commented. "He's a lot younger than you."

"So is she," I said, heading across the busy street. Charlie reluctantly followed, muttering something about it not being a good idea.

"Duchess!" I called out to her, waving.

She didn't look happy to see me. Not that it surprised me. I considered myself lucky we were in a public place and wondered if she might be armed.

"Darcy," she said, obviously uneasy as I joined them on the curb. "I wish I could say it's good to see you, but..."

"You were always a lousy liar." I glanced at the man with her. He was silent, but the look in his eyes said it all: possessive. He reached out and took Lynne's hand, clutching it tightly.

Lynne was looking at him, too. "Connor, this is my ex-husband, Phillip Darcy," she said. "Darcy, this is my fiancé, Connor Mackenzie."

Fiancé? She's marrying this guy? I was surprised. Finding my voice, I introduced Charlie, who finally caught up. "This is my colleague and sometimes friend, Charlie Cross. Charlie, my ex-wife, Lynne Raven, and her fiancé, Connor Mackenzie."

"Hi." Charlie shook Connor's hand.

"Duchess is an archaeologist," I told Charlie. Then, to Lynne: "Doing a dig here?"

She shook her head. "The dig's in Egypt. We just made what we believe is a major find, a two-thousand-year-old papyrus—that's why we're here. We came to consult with Moshe Biran."

I laughed. "Is that old fossil still alive?" I turned to Charlie. "This guy's so old, I suspect he was there when Moses came down from the mountain." Then, to Lynne: "Are you going to be sticking around awhile?"

She nodded. "We're going to be married while we're here," she said, smiling for the first time.

That surprised me. "You always wanted to get married in your father's church," I recalled.

"And you didn't." She paused. "We can't get away right now, so Connor and I are looking for a church here."

"There's a nice little church near Gethsemane," Charlie offered. "Perfect for an intimate wedding."

I was annoyed with my so-called friend. Lynne looked grateful. "We'll check it out, thank you."

Connor looked at his watch. "Darlin', I think we should be going," he said in a low voice.

She nodded, then turned back to me. She obviously didn't know what to say. "It's been interesting," she said finally.

I nodded. "Yeah." I looked at Connor, then back at Lynne. "I know I was an ass when we were together, Duchess," I admitted. "I can't take that back, but I do hope you're happy now."

She nodded again. "I am. Very happy."

I looked at Connor again. "Congratulations."

Connor only nodded.

"I blew it with her," I told Charlie as they walked away. "I blew it with every woman I've ever known."

Charlie chuckled. "Post that confession on the internet and the entire female population will declare a worldwide holiday," he said.

"She's something of a surprise," Charlie said as we walked back to our hotel. "Not what I would have expected. Your more recent women friends have all been of the same breed—elegant, sophisticated, cosmopolitan types. Beautiful packages, but not much going on inside."

I was too tired by that time to be insulted by Charlie's implication. "Shallow and superficial, you mean," I concluded.

"Well—yeah. This woman, she's different."

"Believe it or not, pal, I used to go for smart women—but then I discovered that beautiful and brainless had lower expectations."

"And she's wife number—what, again?"

"Three. She packed up and took off while I was on an assignment," I recalled. "I came back to find her gone. No forwarding address, no explanation, no nothing."

Charlie grinned. "As many times as you've been divorced, I wouldn't think an explanation would be necessary." He lit a cigarette and took a long drag.

I shook my head. "I didn't realize she was so unhappy until the suit showed up at my door, handed me the legal papers and told me to have a nice day," I said. The memory still pissed me off. "I really wanted to deck him."

"Shooting the messenger?" Charlie asked, amused.

"It was that smug smile of his. It was like, 'Hey, loser, you're being dumped.' It was like he knew."

"He probably did," Charlie said agreeably. "You must hold some kind of record for this sort of thing."

"Yeah."

30

LYNNE

"Why does he call you Duchess?" Connor asked.

I shrugged. The truth was that I hadn't a clue. "It's not meant as flattery, or any kind of term of endearment. I used to think he called all of his women 'Duchess'—it was easier than trying to remember all of our names. It's like the guy who names all of his dogs Rover rather than have to keep reminding himself of his new dog's name," I said.

"Do you think he still loves you?"

I laughed aloud at the thought. "Darcy wouldn't recognize love if it walked up and slapped him in the face!" I said. "Darcy knows lust. He and lust are longtime cellmates. But love? Nope—they're complete strangers."

"Did you ever love him?" Connor wanted to know.

"I thought I did when I married him. Then one morning I woke up and realized it was just a bad joke," I admitted.

"You waited fifteen years to remarry," he pointed out.

"It wasn't because no one's ever measured up to him," I said. "Darcy's the kind of man who makes a woman swear off marriage. If they're with him long enough, he can make them swear off love."

A RECENT EXPLOSION had sucked the life out of the air. The smell of burning flesh was all around us. The sounds of gunfire and sirens were suddenly everywhere. Connor shook his head. "This is what is done in the name of God," he said with disdain. "They fight for what does not exist."

"They fight for what they believe in, for the right to follow their beliefs," I told him. I loved Jerusalem, in spite of the danger, in spite of the battles raging there on a daily basis.

I had always loved walking along the streets at dusk, admiring the lavender and ruby colors of the evening sky. Sometimes the clouds look like mother of pearl. It's said that God cast the first light upon the world in Jerusalem. I've often imagined that moment and wondered if it were true.

"Must be nice for those for whom it's the last thing they see," Connor said, keeping one arm around me in a protective gesture. I've always been independent, and I like to believe strong as well, but I loved his protectiveness.

"When Tim and I had our dig in Megiddo, I'd come here on the Friday before Christmas, the last Friday of Hanukkah, to watch the monks' procession down the Via Dolorosa and the lighting of the traditional six candles at the Western Wall."

I marveled at the eerie golden gleam of the sunlight on the Dome of the Rock, wanting to share it with the man I was about to marry. "This is a sacred site for three faiths," I told him. "Jesus prayed here. Mohammed ascended to Heaven here. Solomon built the Temple here. Abraham came here to sacrifice Isaac. Legend has it God issued the first light upon the earth here, on the Rock."

"And now they all kill to claim it. They each preach peace, and then they kill in the name of God," he said. "Hypocrites, all of them."

"Where'd you get all that faith and trust?" I asked.

He didn't smile. "It's my inheritance."

Whenever I had to come to Jerusalem in the past, no matter how tense the ongoing battles around me might be, I looked forward to visiting the places I imagined Christ himself visiting. I had once retraced His footsteps. It made me feel closer to God somehow. I wished my father could understand....

"The Apocrypha?" He looked as though he were on the verge of a massive stroke. "Those books were banned from the Bible because they're blasphemous!"

"How do we know God didn't intend them to be a part of the Bible?" I questioned him.

"How do we know? These books suggest things that God would never have allowed!" he roared. "They claim Jesus had a carnal relationship with a woman! They claim he killed a man who argued with Joseph! They claim he killed another child when he was young and then brought him back to life! That's blasphemy!"

"He was wholly man and wholly God, wasn't he?" I asked, refusing to back down.

"Yes, of course, but—"

"If he was wholly man, then he would have lived as a man," I reasoned. "Dad, I didn't say I believed all of it. I said the early church had no right to censor such documents."

"They had every right!"

"It doesn't matter if Jesus was biologically God's son or Joseph's," I argued. "He was still the Son of God, indwelt with God's spirit. His power came from God, not from the human flesh. He was supposed to live on earth as a man."

"A sinless man!"

"However he lived on earth, he was the Messiah. He gave his life for us. That's the bottom line."

"Lynne?"

The sound of Connor's voice interrupted my thoughts. "Are you all right?" he asked.

I nodded. "Just thinking."

My father hadn't understood. He didn't understand that my faith was unconditional, no matter what had been written. I was simply curious. The more he'd tried to censor me, the more I'd rebelled.

Looking back, I suspected that was one of the reasons I'd had the affair with David. Older and wiser now, I wondered if I would have been as vulnerable to him if I had not been at odds with Dad. David was the antithesis of my father: bold, daring, unconventional, a true adventurer. He told me I was beautiful. He made me feel beautiful. And he taught me to take risks.

Then he betrayed my trust.

I had never been able to tell my parents what had happened. I couldn't handle the judgment I expected from them. Nor had I been able to face them immediately after the divorce from Darcy. I knew my entire family saw the failure of my marriage as my fault, my failure. I was too difficult, they would say. Too headstrong. I wasn't willing to do whatever was necessary to keep my marriage going.

I hadn't told them about Connor yet. I hadn't told them I was getting married again, much as I wanted to. As much as I would have liked to marry the love of my life in the church where I'd grown up, I hadn't been able to bring myself to even tell them about him. Not yet.

"Where is this church?" Connor asked.

"It's not far. Near Gethsemane."

He nodded.

"Getting married at the embassy just wouldn't be the same," I told him.

"That's why I suggested we get married here," he said. "I know you wanted to be married in your family's church, but since we can't go to the US, this might be the next best thing."

"Calvary isn't far from here," I said, leaning closer to him. "Jesus was crucified there, hung between two thieves—one, even in death, sought the approval of the crowd by rejecting him, mocking him. The other humbled himself before God and was promised Paradise. The Crucifixion always made me think of the concept of the whipping boy, of the animal sacrifices nonbelievers thought so cruel. Watching someone else punished for your sins was supposed to make you realize how terrible sin really was.

"The problem was that not everyone got the message."

"We tend to not see what the mirror is telling us if it's unpleasant," Connor said.

"The first dig I worked on wasn't far from here," I told him. "It was near Hebron, the epicenter of the Israeli-Muslim conflict. The road south from Jerusalem to Beer-Sheba had been nicknamed 'Blood Road' because it was a main target of both Israeli and Palestinian snipers, who bore down on the road from rival hills. I had more than one close call on that road myself.

"There's the church," I said, pointing. It was small, simple and serene, near Gethsemane. "I've always loved old churches. As a child, my father's church was my private sanctuary, a place to go whenever something was bothering me. I'd would sit alone in one of the pews and talk to God, and even if I didn't get an immediate answer, I always took comfort in the conversation."

We entered the small church and noticed a few worshippers scattered about as we made our way up the aisle and found the pastor. "May I be of assistance?" he asked.

"I hope so," I said. "My fiancé and I want to be married as soon as possible. We're far from home—Connor is from Scotland and I'm American. I want very much to be married in a Christian church."

"I see." He studied Connor for a moment. "Do you have the necessary documents?"

"Yes," Connor said confidently.

"Would you like to be married this evening?"

I was relieved. "That would be perfect."

I PICKED up the phone three times and put it down again before finally making the call. I had mixed feelings about what I was about to do, but I hadn't been able to find anyone else on such short notice. "Phillip Darcy's room, please," I told the front desk clerk.

"One moment."

I reconsidered for the fifth time and started to hang up as the call was transferred. I knew this wasn't a good idea, but I didn't have time to find someone else. Connor and I were getting married in a matter of hours.

"Darcy. Talk," said the familiar voice on the other end of the line.

"Darcy, it's Lynne," I said. "Look—I need a favor."

There was a momentary silence on the other end. "From me?" he asked, surprised.

"Connor and I are getting married this evening," I began. "It's last minute, I know, but I want you to take some photos for us."

"You couldn't get anyone else," he guessed.

"What do you think?"

"Duchess, I'm no wedding photographer," he reminded me.

"You were no husband, either, but we were still married for two years," I fired back at him. "I want photos of my wedding tonight."

"Lynne—"

"You owe me, Darcy," I repeated.

"Yeah, I guess I do, don't I?" he said. "You're the only one of my ex-wives who didn't want alimony. Where and when?"

I gave him the time and address of the church. "Don't disappoint me, Darcy."

"Like that's ever happened before," he said. "You know, we didn't have any photos of our wedding."

"If we had, I would have burned them."

31

DARCY

"You're going to do what?" Charlie asked, unable to refrain from laughing.

"She asked me to take some wedding photos for her. And she's right. I do owe her," I said. "I was a half-assed husband to her. Hell, I was a half-assed husband to all three of my wives—and every other woman I've ever known."

"How does her husband-to-be feel about it?" Charlie reached for a pastry, but I snatched it from him.

"That shit's gonna kill you," I warned.

"I take my insulin religiously," Charlie maintained.

"And then you proceed to eat everything that's not nailed down or on fire," I reminded him. "You're defeating the purpose of the insulin. You're diabetic, remember?"

"How could I forget?" Charlie changed the subject. "Doesn't her fiancé object to the ex being at the wedding?"

I shrugged. "No idea. But I can't imagine she'd even ask me without his blessing."

I was wrong...

32

CONNOR

"What are you doing here?" I asked when I saw Darcy come into the sanctuary. I couldn't believe Lynne had invited him and didn't hide my displeasure at the idea of my new wife's ex-husband being at our wedding.

"Duchess—Lynne—asked me to be your official wedding photographer," Darcy said.

I shook my head. "No photographs," I said.

"You tell her that," Darcy advised. "She bullied me into this. She wants photographs, and I'm not about to tell her no."

I was frustrated, but backed down. "Very well," I conceded, making it clear to him that I hated the idea.

Darcy was watching me, grinning. "You've never seen the Duchess lose her temper, have you?" he asked. "Be forewarned. It's measured on the Richter Scale."

"Perhaps you deserved it," I suggested.

"Yeah. I take it she's told you about us." He opened his camera bag and readied his equipment.

"She told me you saw her as little more than a concubine," I said.

Darcy nodded. "I guess I have that coming. I wasn't Husband of the Year, I'll admit that."

"I suppose I should thank you for that," I said, turning to face him. "Because of you, she was reluctant to even allow another man into her life. Otherwise, she might not have been free when I met her."

"Glad I could be of assistance," Darcy said with sarcasm.

"Mr. Mackenzie?" The pastor emerged from his office and gestured to me to join him at the altar.

I took my place there as Lynne emerged from the bridal chamber. She wore a white silk dress, a simple halter design, with her silver crucifix resting on her collarbone, and a single Stargazer lily pinned in her long hair. As she joined me, I whispered, "You are beautiful, you know."

She smiled, her lips trembling a little. "You clean up pretty good yourself, Mr. Mackenzie." I wore a dark blue suit and silk tie.

"Do you have the rings?" the pastor asked.

Lynne's eyes widened. "We forgot—"

"I didn't," I said softly. I took the rings from my pocket and gave them to the pastor, who said a brief prayer over them, then gave us each other's ring. Lynne looked at the ring in her hand. Platinum, with an infinity symbol engraved on it. On the inside of the band were the words *Forever...no beginning, no end*.

"Where did you get them?" she asked in a low voice.

I winked. "I'm a wizard, remember?" I'd bought them when I first asked her to marry me.

The pastor began the simple ceremony. He talked about the bond between man and woman, between man and God, and read passages from Scripture.

I looked at Lynne, overwhelmed by the unexpected intensity of my love for this woman. The pastor then read from the Song of Solomon: "Love is invincible facing danger and death. Passion laughs at the terrors of hell. The fire of love stops at nothing, it sweeps everything before it. Floodwaters can't drown love, torrents of rain can't put it out. Love can't be bought and can't be sold. It's not to be found in the marketplace...."

To my surprise, I was moved by the beauty of the ceremony and marveled at how happy I was now, happy to be bound to this woman for the rest of my life. The passages read by the pastor had been so unexpectedly appropriate to what I was feeling, so right for us.

If the secrets of my past didn't end up tearing us apart...

33

DARCY

I stared at the envelope containing the finished photographs, perplexed. It wasn't possible. I'd heard of this sort of thing before, but I'd always thought they were frauds.

"This is beyond weird," I told Charlie. "Ever seen those aura photographs from the psychic fairs?"

"Yeah." Charlie lit a cigarette. "What about them?"

"These are the photos I did at Duchess' wedding last night." I held up the envelope.

Charlie took a long drag. "You work fast."

"They're going back to Egypt today. I promised her I'd drop them at their hotel." I opened the envelope and passed a photo to him. "Take a look at this."

Charlie looked at the large photograph for a moment. It was Connor alone, standing by a window in the church, bathed in light. Behind him was what appeared to be a ghost figure, a woman in white who was definitely not his new wife. "Interesting effect," Charlie noted.

"I don't know where that light was coming from, Charlie," I said. "It was taken after sunset."

Charlie shrugged. "You really need to get digital cameras, pal."

"Look at this. Behind him. What do you make of this?"

"Film flaw," Charlie decided.

"That's what I thought. At first." I handed him another photograph. Connor and Lynne, standing at the altar. This time, the ghostly image stood beside them. "The lighting, maybe?" Charlie suggested.

"I don't think so. These images don't appear to be random, and if you examine them with a magnifier, they look like human beings," I told him, showing him the rest of the photos.

"Except that they're transparent," Charlie said. "That's crazy, Darcy. Tell Ally this shit and she'll ship you off to the Rubber Ramada so fast you won't know what hit you."

―――

"It won't work," Charlie protested.

"Sure it will," I insisted. "Just tell her you want to do a story for the magazine—you want to see how they work, get some background, maybe some details about the latest find—"

"And pictures," Charlie concluded.

"They made a major find there. It's newsworthy," I maintained. "You owe me this, pal."

Charlie rocked back in his chair. "We've been through so much together, I've lost track of who owes who," he said. "You might owe me, actually."

"Charlie—"

"Ally isn't going to go for this, you know."

"I'll handle Ally," I assured him.

Charlie laughed. "Right. Like you always do, I'm sure."

―――

"Out of the question," Ally insisted when I phoned her. "I need both you and Charlie elsewhere. It's just not a big enough story."

I wasn't giving up. "It could be a big story, Ally—a good story," I pushed her. "They found an old scroll, a couple of thousand years old, supposedly something important. Could be right up there with the Dead Sea Scrolls."

"Supposedly important? Is it or isn't it?" she asked impatiently. "Do you even understand the work they're doing?"

"I was married to the lady, Ally. Of course I know what she does for a living," I insisted.

"Look Darcy, I'm not about to let you use this magazine to further your latest amorous cause. You're divorced. Get over it."

"You think I want to do this because I'm jealous?"

"If it walks like a duck and talks like a duck, you can bet you're about to step in a pile of duck crap," Ally maintained.

"It's got nothing to do with jealousy, Ally. That ship sailed a long time ago."

"And sank," she reminded me.

"Yeah, like the Titanic." I hesitated. "Look, I'm going to tell you something that's going to sound a little crazy."

"No more so than some of the other crap you've told me over the years, I'm sure."

"She asked me to take some wedding photos," I started. "The pictures are, well, bizarre." I tried to explain the photographs to her.

"Well, Darcy, it was bound to happen. You've finally lost those last threads of sanity you've been clinging to for the past ten years," she responded. "You really do need that vacation, don't you?"

"About the article—" I started.

"Check the Weather Channel. When it's fifty below in hell, you can proceed with the story," she told me.

"She loved the idea," I told Charlie.

Charlie gave me a dubious look. "You sure she approved this?" he asked again. He didn't trust me, not when there was a woman involved.

"May lightning strike if I'm lying."

Charlie took ten long steps away from me. "Just a precaution," he said, glancing skyward.

"All you have to worry about is delivering her a story she'll love."

"Something she'll love so much she won't have us shot for ignoring her orders?" Charlie asked, lighting a cigarette.

I took the cigarette and pitched it before Charlie could light up. "Those things are gonna kill you, pal," I warned him again.

Charlie took another from the pack and lit it. "Nope. You're going to be the death of me," he predicted.

To say the Duchess and her new husband were not happy to see us would be like saying World War II was a peace disturbance. It was the first time I'd seen O'Halloran since the divorce, and I thought he was going to beat the crap out of me...but they reluctantly agreed to cooperate on the story.

I spent the morning on my own, taking photographs around the excavation site, candid shots of the team at work. I'd never spent any time on an archaeological site before, not even when Lynne and I were married.

I pulled my handkerchief from my pocket and wiped my brow. I'd never spent enough time with Lynne when she was my wife to have even visited one of her digs. Just one more reminder of my failures as a husband, I thought.

I had one shot left on the roll. I smiled to myself. In spite of Charlie's and Alberta's repeated insistence that I switch to the new digital cameras, I still preferred my old cameras and real film.

"You're a dinosaur, Darcy," Ally had told me more than once.

"*Come out of the Jurassic Era and join the rest of us in the twenty-first century.*"

I always ignored her, knowing even as I did that she wasn't going to go away. Unlike the other women in my life, Alberta Ashland was there to stay.

I raised my camera and focused on my real target: Connor, who was standing several yards away, talking to Tim. I adjusted my lens for the shot and took it. As I reloaded, I saw Connor glance in my direction and took aim for another shot. Connor stopped what he was doing and headed toward me.

"What the hell do you think you're doing?" he demanded as he advanced on me, anger in his eyes.

"Lynne gave me permission to take some photos—"

He ripped the Nikon from my hands. "I didn't agree to be photographed!" he snapped, yanking the back of the camera open. "I'll thank you to respect my privacy in the future."

"Hey!" I tried to stop him, but Connor pulled out the film, exposing it.

He slammed the camera to the ground, then turned and stalked away.

I stared after him for a moment, then reached for my battered camera. *Interesting,* I thought. *Does he know what comes up on film when he's photographed?*

34

CONNOR

"I think it's the bubonic plague."

Lynne was on her knees in the bathroom, hugging the toilet after vomiting for the third time in an hour.

"There haven't been any cases of bubonic plague in years," I assured her, wiping her face with a damp cloth, "and you have no fever."

"You cooked last night," she remembered.

"What's that to do with this?" I wanted to know.

"If I'd cooked, this wouldn't be a surprise," she said as I helped her back to the bed.

"My poor darling," I said, kissing her forehead.

"Sure you want to kiss me?" she asked. "I could be contagious."

"I doubt that, but I'm willing to risk it." I brushed her hair back off her face. "When did it start?"

"This morning," she answered. "I've been a little queasy for the past week, but no vomiting until now."

"You've been unusually tired," I remembered. "I've noticed you're a bit tender when I touch you."

She nodded. "A little, yeah."

I paused for a moment, then went to the drawer in the nightstand. I took out her appointment calendar and flipped through the pages. "What are you looking for?" she asked.

I showed her a page in the calendar. "Is this your last?" he asked.

"Yes." She looked up at me. "September? This is November."

I smiled. "Darlin', I think you're pregnant."

"No." She didn't dare hope.

"I told you I'd have you knocked up in no time," I said, feeling rather pleased with myself. "You had your last period in September. The doctor gave me a clean bill of health in October—we had quite a celebration that night, in case you've forgotten."

"As if I could," she said with a weak laugh.

"I believe you're now approximately seven weeks pregnant," I said confidently.

"I can't believe it could have happened so easily."

"Remember with whom you've been sharing a bed," I said with unabashed pride.

"Is it possible?" she wondered aloud.

"There's one way to find out." I went into the bathroom and returned with three home pregnancy test kits.

"If I can keep my head out of the toilet long enough to do this," she said, pulling herself upright again.

I opened one of the packages and read the instructions. "We'll do all three."

She raised an eyebrow. "Best two out of three?"

I shrugged. "One could be defective."

"Okay, let's do it," she agreed.

Ten minutes later, my suspicions were confirmed by all three kits.

Lynne was pregnant.

35

DARCY

"So tell me, Duchess—where did we go wrong?" I asked as I reloaded my camera. Lynne and I were walking across the site, Lynne providing explanations of everything I was photographing.

"Where *didn't* we go wrong?" she asked in response. "You weren't in love with me. I wasn't in love with you. It took me a while to figure that out, but when the reality kicked in, I knew we didn't have a chance."

"I loved you," I insisted. It was true. I loved her as much as I was able to love. "I just didn't know how to be a husband."

She looked unconvinced. "Darcy, you didn't know how to love," she maintained.

"That may have been true at one time, but—"

She turned to face me. "Let me guess. You've had some sort of epiphany and you came here for absolution. Am I right?"

"Partly," I admitted. "I had a brush with death, Duchess. I was supposed to be on one of those hijacked planes on 9/11. The only reason I wasn't was because the person making my travel arrangements goofed. I'm alive today because of a mistake."

She managed a smile. "Still as agnostic as ever, I see."

"If I was such a bastard, why did you marry me?" I asked then.

"My self-esteem had taken a beating. I'd been used by a man I believed loved me. I was young and foolish and I was rebelling against my father," she answered frankly. "I needed to feel loved. I met you, and you were damn good at the art of the pursuit. You pushed all the right buttons. But we didn't love each other, not really. We had no respect for each other's needs or feelings. We didn't communicate."

"You women and your communication issues," I grumbled, pushing my cap back on my head.

"There's more to a relationship—and definitely more to a marriage—than just sex," she reminded me. "Or there should be, anyway."

"We're not the same two people we were then," I said. "We're older, wiser. We've both changed."

"I've changed," she agreed. "I don't plan to repeat the mistakes of the past."

I was silent for a moment. "Is your new husband the love of your life and all that BS?" I asked.

"Connor and I have a real partnership. We respect each other's feelings and opinions. We want the same things." She pulled off her baseball cap. Strands of her hair escaped from the elastic band that held it in a loose ponytail. "He makes me feel like I'm the most important thing in his world."

I laughed. Actually, it was more a snort than a laugh. "He doesn't have to work for a living," I pointed out.

She shook her head. "You still don't get it, do you?"

That was true. I didn't. "Enlighten me," I said, frustrated.

"My husband doesn't have to be with me every moment of every day to show me he loves me," she said. "He isn't. But when we are together, I know I'm his priority, and he's mine. Darcy, I'm glad we didn't make a go of it. If we'd stayed together, I would never have met Connor. I wouldn't have what I have now." She hesitated for a moment. "We're pregnant."

I was dumbstruck. "Congratulations...I think," I said. "Duchess, how well do you know him? Really?" There were so many questions I wanted to ask, but didn't know how to ask without sounding insane.

She looked at me. "What kind of question is that?"

"An honest one. You say you didn't really know me when you married me," I pointed out. "Do you know him?"

She was defensive. "I know all I need to know."

I raised my camera for a shot of the cave where the papyri had been found. "You must be happy. He's giving you the one thing you always wanted."

"The one thing you didn't want," she said, watching me intently.

I lowered my camera and turned to face her again. "I already had two kids who hated me. They still do. I didn't see any reason to go for the Bad Daddy Trifecta." I adjusted my lens.

"Whose fault is that?" she asked.

"Mine," I acknowledged. "I was a lousy father. Which is why I knew it would be a mistake to have any more kids."

"What I wanted didn't matter," she concluded.

"Do you think it would be fair to have a child if one of the parents didn't really want it?" I asked.

"No."

"A kid deserves a better father than me." I took another shot. "Think hubby number two is daddy material?"

"He'll be a wonderful father."

"I hope you're right about him." But I didn't believe it for a minute.

"He's hard to figure out, isn't he?"

The blonde woman standing behind me had been coming on to me since I arrived at the site. "Who?" I asked, my attention on Connor, who was working on his motorcycle in front of the trailer. He was shirtless, lying on his back on an old blanket.

"The Black Knight, of course."

I laughed. "Black Knight? I take it you're not a fan."

"You take it wrong," Pam Hill said. "I'm a big fan, actually. I'd give my soul to get him into bed."

"You've tried, then." I turned my attention back to Connor.

"Definitely. And failed," she confessed. "From the day he got here, he's been all about Lynne. He's never wanted anybody but her, and truth be told, she never wanted anybody but him."

"How long have they been together?" I had the distinct feeling she wouldn't have any problem discussing private matters, and I wasn't above taking advantage of that.

"She went to London on business at this time last year and he came back with her. He moved right in with her, and they've been together ever since."

"They lived together?" I asked, surprised. She wouldn't even have sex with me until we were married.

"Surprised the rest of us, too," Pam said. "Lynne comes off as kind of a prude—but then, I guess I don't have to tell you that."

I didn't answer. I continued to watch Connor. Pam may have been willing to talk, but I was keeping what little I knew to myself. "What do you know about him?" I asked. "Where he's from, what he did before he came here, you know?"

Pam thought about it. "Not much," she said. "That's how he came to be called the Black Knight. He's our mysterious savior."

"Savior?"

She nodded. "We'd lost our funding. Tim had prepared us for what he thought to be the inevitable," she recalled. "We were about to pack it in. We all expected to be out of here by Christmas—then along comes the mysterious Connor Mackenzie with a guarantee of funding for the next five years. He dresses like a bum, but I hear his family owns half of Britain. The affluent half."

"He's paying the bills?"

"Yep," Pam said. "From the day he came, everything changed."

"How so?"

"He doesn't socialize. We'd see him at the site a couple of days a week, but never socially, and he monopolized Lynne from the day he arrived." She paused. "We used to all get together and go into Taba at least once a week for dinner or something. She stopped joining us. When she was done for the day, she'd go off to the trailer and none of us saw her again until the next morning. It didn't take a lot of imagination to figure out why. And now they're married and having a baby."

"Yeah," I said.

"He doesn't seem like father material to me, but he sure didn't waste any time knocking her up," Pam observed.

"Lynne's always wanted kids," I said, still watching Connor.

"Hey, why are we wasting time talking about them?" she asked, her tone suddenly upbeat. "I've got a place near Taba...."

36

CONNOR

I had doubts.
    I wanted to give Lynne the one thing she had always wanted. I wanted to have children with her. But I now found myself wondering if I was ready to be a father, if I was ready to share my wife with anyone, even my own child.

I'd been a loner for most of my life, unwilling to love for fear of being hurt, of losing that person as I'd lost my mother. Now that I had Lynne, I wanted to keep her to myself, at least for a while. I hadn't expected her to get pregnant so quickly, and now that she was, I didn't know how I really felt about it.

I lay beside her, watching her sleep, feeling emotions so powerful I couldn't put it into words if I had to. And something else, something that made no sense—fear, a deep, bone-chilling fear.

"*Take your child's mother and go to Christ's church.*"

I closed my eyes tightly, as if by doing so I could shut out the voices. *Leave me alone.*

"*Take her now. Go to Christ's church, and you will find a man there who will provide sanctuary.*"

This is crazy. What church? Where?

"*Take her to Christ's church. The dragon waits to devour the child as it emerges from the womb.*"

Dragon? What kind of nonsense is this?

"*The dragon knows she is with child. He lies in wait. You must take her to the sanctuary now, before it's too late.*"

I got out of bed and dressed as I hurried down the hallway to the door. I went outside and started walking without a clear destination in mind. I needed to get away, to think. I needed to take the voices into the desert so they—I—would not disturb my wife.

I didn't realize at the time that I was being watched…

37

DARCY

While waiting for our flight to be called, I took the photographs from my portfolio and studied them. I still couldn't believe what I was seeing. I'd followed Mackenzie into the desert, used high-speed film to photograph him in the darkness, and the effect had been even more startling than the photographs I'd taken in Israel. The Lord of the Geeks stood there in the desert, facing away from the camera, staring into the night...and there, at his side, two ghostly figures, sentinels, it seemed, guarding him.

"You're becoming obsessed," Charlie warned me. "What were you doing out there so late, anyway? Were you by any chance looking for trouble?"

"I was looking for answers," I said.

"Right." Charlie attempted to turn his attention back to his newspaper, but I wouldn't let it go. I was absolutely convinced I was onto something.

"It's no film flaw, no double exposure," I said, tracing the images with my fingertips. "It's not a defect. There's something going on with this guy that I can't explain."

"I can explain it," Charlie said, checking his watch. "You've finally lost it."

"Look at this, Charlie." I pushed the photo at him. "Look at this and tell me you don't see something strange here."

Charlie pushed it back at me. "Yeah, I see something, pal," I acknowledged. "Anybody who looks at it is going to see something there. The eye plays tricks on us when this shit happens. It's like looking at clouds and seeing animals or whatever. We see what we want to see. You want to see ghosts, you see ghosts."

"Have you ever known me to be irrational?" I asked.

Charlie thought about it. "No," he said slowly.

"Have I ever been a believer in spooks?"

Charlie shook his head.

"Then why do you suppose I'm seeing this shit now?" I challenged.

"Jealousy?"

"Come on, Charlie—Duchess and I went our separate ways a long time ago," I said, slipping the photos back into my portfolio when our flight was called. "If I'd wanted to get back with her, I would have gone after her when she left me."

We got in line to board. "So what is this all about, if not to get your ex back?" Charlie asked.

"I'm worried about her safety," I confessed.

Charlie's laugh came out like a snort. "Worried about her?"

"Something weird is going on with the Lord of the Geeks," I said in a low voice. "Nothing about him adds up. Pam told me—"

Charlie cut me off. "I didn't think you and Pam did much talking that night."

I ignored the comment. "She told me this guy is a member of one of the richest families in Britain—he's bankrolling their dig for the next five years," I went on. "Why would a man with that kind of money want to go off and live in the middle of nowhere like this?"

"Love, maybe?"

"I'm telling you, Charlie, something's not right here," I said, digging into my carryon for my passport and boarding pass.

Charlie handed his pass to the airline agent, who checked it and returned it to him. He looked over his shoulder at me. "Yeah," he said. "The something that's not right is you."

We boarded the plane and stashed our bags in the overhead. Charlie struggled with a seat not made for someone of his bulk. "I hate flying," he grumbled. He fluffed his travel pillow. "You want to know what I think?"

"Shoot."

"Don't tempt me." Charlie tucked the pillow behind his head. "I think you're looking to create problems where there aren't any. Give it up, pal."

"AH, THE PRODIGAL RETURNS," Ally greeted me as I entered her office. Alberta Ashland was an attractive woman in her early forties, conservatively dressed, a façade that concealed her fiery personality. She was one of the most brilliant editors in the business, due to her willingness to take risks. She was also one of the few people on the face of the earth who could actually put up with me. While other women came and went in my life, Ally was the only female constant. That was most likely due to the fact that she was too smart to ever get romantically involved with me.

"Clichés are beneath you, Ally." I plopped down in one of the chairs across from her and propped my feet up on the desk.

"Get your feet off the desk or you'll *be* a cliché," she warned. "Dead as a doornail."

I grinned. "You've got to wonder about some of those clichés—dead as a doornail, for instance. A doornail is an inanimate object, so it can't be dead. Happy as a clam—who knows if a clam is happy or not?"

Alberta laughed. "What's got you in this mood? Did Hefner give you the keys to the Playboy mansion?"

"No, unfortunately. And I'm not in a mood."

"Right. I hear you're trying to dig up dirt on the ex-wife's new husband."

"Nothing gets past you, does it, Ally?" I asked.

"You really do hate to lose, don't you?" she asked.

"What is it with you and Charlie, anyway?" I asked. "I didn't lose her to him. I lost her while he was still using training wheels."

Alberta shook her head. "You know, Darcy, there's a saying that only the good die young," she started. "If that's true, you're going to live forever. God doesn't want you and the devil won't have you for fear of a power struggle."

I ignored her sarcasm. "There's something really strange about that one, Ally," I maintained.

She looked at me accusingly. "And you're still looking for the skeletons in the old closet."

I couldn't hide my surprise.

"My spies are everywhere. You should know that by now." She seated herself behind her desk. On the wall behind her were her many journalistic awards. On the shelves, revealing her sense of humor was an R2-D2 action figure and humorous sayings, all in silver frames.

"Nothing about him adds up." I sat up straight. "And I haven't dug up anything on him. I've been trying. Big difference. I even Googled him and came up with zip. It's like he didn't even exist before he turned up in Egypt last year. I can't find birth records, academic records, anything. Duchess won't talk, and no one else on their team seems to know much about him, beyond the fact that he comes from money and his family is funding the excavation for the next five years." I took off my glasses and rubbed my tired eyes.

"What, exactly, made you suspicious of him?" Alberta asked. "The wedding ring?"

"This." I removed the photographs I'd taken from the portfolio I'd brought with me and passed them across the desk to her. "What do you make of that?"

She examined them thoughtfully, then handed them back to me. "In a word, Photoshop."

"I didn't fake these, Ally," I said. "When I developed them, at first I thought there was a flaw in the film. I've considered every possibility."

Alberta gave me a skeptical look. "And this is why you're suspicious of him?"

"He didn't want wedding photographs, Ally," I said. "He was supposedly marrying a woman he adored, but he didn't want photos."

"Do you have photos of all of your weddings?" she challenged.

"No, but—"

"If you did, you'd need a storage locker just for wedding albums." Alberta laughed. "Darcy, you're just looking for trouble—which you found when you convinced Charlie to go to Egypt after I vetoed the idea. This, I assume, is why you pulled that stunt."

"He smashed my camera after I took some shots of him at the dig site."

"So he guards his privacy. Again, not a federal offense," she pointed out.

I paused. "What did Ben tell you when you forced his confession? Did he ever find anything?"

She shook her head. "Nothing. He's clean. Was probably a boy scout."

I snorted. "I'm betting he was never a boy."

"Darcy—"

I shook my head. "I think the guy's a long way from clean, Ally," I insisted. "I'm certain he's hiding something."

"You'd like to think he is, anyway."

"Doesn't it strike you as odd that there's nothing on record about him?" I wanted to know. "I know you think I'm being paranoid, but—"

"I think you probably are, yes. I don't know about Connor

Mackenzie, but you should come with a warning from the Surgeon General—*Warning: May Cause Insanity*," she said. "I've come to the conclusion that you have far too much time on your hands..."

———

I SHOULD HAVE SAID no to another assignment, I thought as I let myself into my apartment. I should have turned her down flat.

I wasn't up for it.

I parked my duffel bag on the floor next to the front door. I hadn't been home in almost two months, but everything was in order. The place was immaculate; my mail was in the basket on the desk and the newspapers and magazines were stacked neatly on the floor. The smartest move I ever made was hiring that cleaning lady—she was a gem. All the advantages of a wife—well, almost all the advantages—with none of the headaches.

I went into the kitchen and found three cans of chili and a package of microwave popcorn in one cabinet and a six-pack of beer in the refrigerator. There wasn't much point in grocery shopping, since I'd be leaving again in a few days. I decided to get take-out from the Chinese place on the corner.

I still couldn't figure out how Ally had managed to talk me into taking the new assignment. I was supposed to be on vacation—and I needed the break. She thought I needed a shrink. I tried to reason with her—but Ally could be a royal pain. Sometimes, it was easier to just give in to her.

I rummaged through a desk drawer, looking for the take-out menus I kept there. Cooking had never been my thing. I could microwave—that was the extent of my skill in the kitchen. I called in my order and accepted my culinary shortcomings as just one more for the list of my many flaws.

I picked up a framed photograph on the desk and stared at it for a long time. My kids. The photo had been taken at least ten years ago. Sam would be twenty-nine or thirty now—I couldn't even remember how old my own son was. Christina would be about twenty-seven. I couldn't recall the last time I'd seen either of them. For all I knew, I could have been a grandfather.

A grandfather? Me? It was laughable. I hadn't been much of a father. I'd been in Moscow when Sam was born—I didn't even see my son until he was two months old. My first wife and I had already separated by the time Christina was born. I hadn't seen much of either of them while they were growing up. When they wanted me, needed me, I'd never been there for them. When they begged me to come home, to give them just a little of my time, I'd always been too busy. Now, they didn't want or need me at all. By the time they were teenagers, the only thing either of them felt for me was resentment. That resentment had been honed over the years. My son sent me a CD one Christmas—that Harry Chapin song from back in the seventies, *Cat's in the Cradle*. There was a definite message there.

It hadn't bothered me much in the past. My unwillingness to have more kids had been the biggest problem between Lynne and me when we were married. She wanted kids. I didn't. I tried to tell her I'd learned from experience that I wasn't cut out for fatherhood. Unlike most men, I'd never felt the need to have children to guarantee my own immortality—my work would do that. As far as I was concerned, I was a father because my wife had been careless.

That was how I'd felt then, anyway.

As I continued to stare at the photograph, I found myself thinking about Sam and Christina, wondering where they were, what they were doing—and wondering if they would ever be able to forgive me. I wouldn't blame them if they couldn't. I'd never been there for them. I'd never acted like a father. I acted like a stranger.

Wasn't it Thomas Wolfe who said "You can never go home again"—or something like that? It was a little late to try to make amends, much as I would have liked to. About twenty-five years too late.

The ringing doorbell interrupted my pity party. It was the delivery boy from the Chinese place. I pulled my wallet from my pocket and paid the kid, then went into the kitchen to get a fork. I didn't have the patience for chopsticks.

I put on a DVD—I had just about every movie Schwarzenegger had ever made, and when I wasn't in the mood for Arnold, there was always Bruce Willis—and parked myself in front of the TV, eating straight out of the cartons. What I wouldn't give for about six months of this, I thought.

A year ago, my doctor told me it was all going to catch up with me sooner or later. I once smoked four packs a day, before I married Lynne. I drank far too much. My blood pressure was too high and my last blood test showed there was enough crap in my veins to block the Holland Tunnel. I was courting a coronary. None of my ex-wives would believe that one. None of them believed I had a heart to damage. They'd all been in agreement on that. Three out of three ex-wives can't be wrong—or can they? I wondered.

Funny, I hadn't noticed it before—before seeing Lynne with Mackenzie—but it did seem to be catching up with me. I was not only feeling my age, I felt about ten years older.

I decided to see what Fate had in store for me. I broke one of the fortune cookies in half and pulled the narrow strip of paper from it, expecting to find the usually vague, often silly "fortune" on it.

YOU ARE ABOUT TO EMBARK ON AN IMPORTANT JOURNEY.

Enough already, I thought, tossing it aside. I broke open the second cookie.

YOUR DESTINY IS AT HAND.

38

CONNOR

"You're so tense," Lynne noticed as she massaged my back and shoulders. "Stress?"

I brushed it off. "More strange dreams, that's all," I said.

"Stranger than usual?" she kissed my bare shoulder. That almost made me forget all the rubbish that was cluttering my mind. I wish it could have.

I kissed her forehead. "Now I'm being told to take you to church."

She drew back, surprised. "Take me to church? Which one?"

"I haven't a clue. I told you it was strange."

My satellite phone rang then. "If it's Edward, don't answer it," Lynne told me. "Every time you talk to him, you end up in a foul mood."

"I have to talk to him this time, darlin'," I said, pulling away from her.

She reached for the phone on the nightstand and passed it to me reluctantly. "I'll go make some coffee," she said. "Don't let him get to you."

I waited until she left the room, then took the call. "Edward," I said. "Is it done?"

"No."

"No? Why not?"

"You have to come back here," Edward insisted. "We have people to answer to."

"Correction—you have people to answer to," I told him. "I have no obligation to anyone but myself and my wife."

"Wife? You married her?"

"Yes. As a wedding gift, you can forget you ever knew me. Won't cost you a dime."

"You have no idea what that would cost me—and you," Edward snapped. "You can't do this—"

"Try and stop me!"

"They'll never let you go."

"They don't own me, Edward."

"What about Sarah?" he asked then. "Are you going to turn your back on her, too?"

"Of course not!"

"Reconsider this, Andrew—"

"Connor."

"Reconsider. Before it's too late."

Then the line went dead.

I stared at the phone for a long moment, confused by the conversation that had just taken place. I wanted to call him back, to find out what he'd meant, but I couldn't. I wasn't about to concern Lynne with any of this bullshit. Not yet.

Not until I knew what kind of rubbish Edward was trying to pull this time.

———

Lynne was in Cairo with Tim. They would be away all day. I rang up Edward. The perfect time to have it out with him, I decided.

"Start talking, Edward," I demanded.

He hesitated, then reconsidered. "They've demanded your immediate return to London—with your wife."

"What has Lynne to do with any of this?"

"You should never have married her." There was a desperation in his voice that made no sense. "If she gets pregnant—"

"She's already pregnant," I said. "What business is it of theirs?"

"They've been waiting for you to procreate."

"What the hell are you talking about?" By that point, my patience was nonexistent.

"I was trying to keep your wife from meeting the same fate as your mother," Edward said, panic rising in his voice.

"What about my mother?" I asked, anger rising within me.

Edward told me everything.

39

LYNNE

I saw Connor's motorcycle parked in front of the trailer when Tim and I returned from Cairo. "He must not have gone to the lab today," I said.

"Maybe he's having pregnancy symptoms," Tim said with a grin. "In case you've forgotten, every time Isabella was pregnant, I had the morning sickness, weight gain, fatigue, the whole fun package," he recalled. "She had an easy time in childbirth. I had all the labor pains."

I did remember, and it made me laugh. "Connor's had a few cravings."

"Anything really bizarre?" Tim asked as he parked.

"Not for food."

Tim waved me off. "Don't want to know," he laughed. "I think you'd better call it a day, babe. Put your feet up, eat ice cream and jalapenos, watch a corny movie."

I wrinkled my nose. "That sounds hideous."

"I hope it's triplets."

"If it is, one of them is yours."

He shook his head. "No more babies for me. When Isis was born, my mother asked Isabella what we were going to name her. Isabella said, 'Enough.'"

"See you in the morning," I said as I got out of the Land Rover.

I went inside. "Connor?" I called out to him. "I'm back. Finally."

No answer.

I took off my baseball cap, removed the elastic band from my hair, and ran my fingers through it. "Connor?" I called to him again.

Still no answer.

Then I heard a muffled sound coming from behind the closed bedroom door. I found Connor there, packing our suitcases in a fury.

"Connor—what's going on?" I asked, trying to stop him.

"My mother," he said angrily, yanking shirts from their hangers. "My mother's death wasn't an accident. She was *murdered*." He threw the shirts down onto the bed.

"Murdered?" I asked. "Who told you this?"

"My dear stepfather," Connor snapped. "They killed her. The bastards killed her."

I was confused. "I don't understand."

"We have to leave here. Now. Tonight," Connor insisted.

"And go where?"

"Somewhere. Anywhere. Where they can't find us." He took one of the handguns we kept for protection from the nightstand and checked the clip.

I stopped him, grabbing his shoulders. "They—who?" I asked. "Connor, you're not making any sense!"

He sank down onto the bed, cradling his head in his hands. "There's so much I haven't told you," he said wearily, "things I should have told you before we were married."

I was apprehensive. "I'm not going to want to hear this, am I?" I asked.

He gestured to me to sit next to him, struggling to compose himself. I shook my head. "I think I'll stand for now."

He sucked in a deep breath and looked up at me. "My name isn't really Connor Mackenzie," he confessed.

My mouth opened, but no sound came out.

"My real name—my given name—is Andrew Stewart. I'm a geneticist," he went on. "I was involved in some experiments that were not exactly legal. I was—am—wanted by the authorities. That's why I've been using an alias."

"Human cloning," I guessed.

He nodded. "But that's only a small part of it. The night we met, I was already planning to leave London. You needed funding, I needed a place to hide," he said. "It was a win-win situation."

"And now they've found you?"

He shook his head. "No. They have no idea where I am."

Now I was even more confused. "Then why—"

"I'm a freak of nature."

I looked at him, not sure how to respond. He was rambling. None of this made any sense. It was all just a bizarre nightmare. Any minute now I was sure I was going to wake and everything would be all right.

"I have three university degrees. Got the first when I was eleven. My IQ has been impossible to measure," he said without pride. "It's alleged to be somewhere between 250-275."

"Einstein's was 163," I recalled. "Newton's was something like 180."

He nodded. "I was quite advanced—walked and talked by six months, I'm told. I learned to read before I was two," he said. "My stepfather sold his soul to the devil for success years ago. I was part of the deal."

"How?"

"My mother was young, she needed money," he began. "Edward's company was heavily involved in experiments involving genetic engineering. He made her an offer that would have paid for her university education. She was to be a human incubator—impregnated by in vitro fertilization with a genetically-enhanced embryo. She would bear the child—me—and hand me over after I was born. But in the course of her pregnancy, she realized she couldn't do it. There was a connection—I was her child, no matter how I was conceived. She ran away, went back to her family in Scotland. But she couldn't tell them how she got pregnant, so her zealot of a father called her a whore and kicked her out.

"She had nowhere to go. She took a job in a pub and worked until I was born. Then Edward found her. He told her his associates were planning to take legal action to get me back. He made her an offer that would put an end to any legal actions—she would have to marry him and return to London with him."

"Marry him?" I asked.

"He'd wanted her from the start," Connor said. "He knew she was scared and would do anything to keep her child. He took advantage of the situation to get her into bed."

"So she was trapped," I concluded.

He nodded. "They wanted me, and they would have done anything to get me back. I was to be the template for a master race they wished to create," he said. "Through genetic research, they planned to develop human embryos that would become physically and intellectually flawless men and women."

"They wanted to clone you?"

He shook his head. "Cloning never suited their purposes. All of the children born through cloning would look exactly alike. All the same sex. Besides, I was flawed—I'm epileptic."

I waited for him to continue.

"She couldn't live with the devil's bargain she'd made," he continued. "She had gotten pregnant with Sarah. She had no voice in how I was being raised. She felt helpless and humiliated. After Sarah was born, Mum began to plan our escape. The problem was that Edward and his associates knew what she was planning. One day when she was out, an accident was arranged...a vehicle accident. She was killed, leaving Edward the sole legal guardian of Sarah and me."

"Is Sarah—" I couldn't say the words.

"Genetically enhanced?" he asked. "No. My sister was an unplanned pregnancy. I remember Edward being furious when he found out Mum was pregnant. He wanted her slim and beautiful, his perfect concubine."

"You became a geneticist yourself," I began. "Why, after all their research had cost you?"

"I wanted to find a way to eradicate genetically inherited illnesses. Their lead scientist mentored me, encouraged me and eventually drew me into their plans. Ego took over. I foolishly believed my work would one day benefit humanity. They, on the other hand, had no interest in anything other than power and profit."

He hesitated. "Now they want our baby."

I stared at him. I was speechless.

"They—we—have been implanting genetically altered embryos into women who went to fertility clinics seeking help in conceiving," he said. "At first, I'd chosen you to be one of the surrogates."

"At first?"

"I fell in love with you. If you were going to have a baby, it would have to be mine," he said. "I took you out of the running, so to speak. When they discovered you were pregnant, they set their sights on our child."

"Why?"

"My offspring," he said. "They're anxious to see if my child has inherited my so-called gifts."

I shook my head. I felt numb. "This is insane."

"We have to leave," he insisted. "Go somewhere where they can't find us."

"I can't leave. I won't leave." I was angry. "You've lied to me. I don't even know who you are, and you expect me to just take off with you?"

"This is not open for discussion!" he snapped. "These bastards murdered my mother. They won't have any qualms about killing again to get what they want. I will not allow them to take you and our child as well. I'm leaving, and you're going with me."

40

CONNOR

I had to buy some time. Keep Edward at bay until I could come up with a plan.

"*Take her and go. Take her to Christ's church and you will find safe sanctuary. God will show you the way.*"

"God!" That made me laugh. "Where was God when my mother was being murdered?"

"*She is with Him now. He has always been with both of you. He has been looking out for you.*"

"Good job," I said sarcastically.

"*Go. The angels will guide you.*"

I stared up at the clear, star-filled sky and knew for the first time what it was like to want another human being dead.

41

LYNNE

I couldn't sleep. I lay in bed, trying to process this new reality, and wondered where Connor had gone.

He hadn't come to bed, hadn't slept, hadn't spoken since his mind-blowing confession. I wasn't at all sure I wanted to go with him in the morning, but I knew he wasn't going to give me a choice. I didn't doubt for a moment that he would carry me out of Egypt bodily if I refused. He was convinced they—whoever *they* were—would kill me to take our baby.

I'd never seen him like this before. I felt as though I didn't really know him. I found myself remembering when Darcy asked me how well I knew the man I'd married. I wondered if he knew something I didn't.

The man I married...are we even married? Is it legal?

You're married in the eyes of God.

I tried to make sense of it all, but all I could think about was that I didn't know my own husband.

42

CONNOR

The answer came to me during the night. I phoned Edward the next morning.

"You can tell them I'll give them what they want."

"That's a wise decision, son." Edward sounded relieved.

"Two weeks, Edward. We need two weeks to take care of our business here."

"I don't think that will be a problem."

"See that it's not."

"We're going to Rome," I told Lynne. "We'll be safe there for the next few weeks. We'll take only what is absolutely necessary."

She shook her head. "I can't do this," she said.

"We have no choice," I argued. "These people are killers. I'll not allow them to take our baby from us the way Sarah and I were taken from our mum. I'll not let them take you from me, no matter what I have to do."

I took our passports from the drawer and tucked them into my coat pocket. "I won't leave you here. The only way I can keep you safe is by keeping you with me."

"What about Tim and the others?"

"They'll be safe as long as we're not here, as long as they know nothing of our plans." I insisted.

"What are we going to tell them?" she asked.

"Only that we're going on holiday," I said. "We're going to Rome for two weeks because after the baby comes, we won't be able to do that sort of thing."

"And what will we actually be doing there?" Lynne asked.

"We're going there to die."

43

LYNNE

As the plane began its descent to Leonardo da Vinci International Airport, I peered through the window at the city below, wondering if I would ever see my family again. Wondering if I would ever see Tim or Isabella again. My hand rested on my abdomen. *They want our baby*, I reminded myself. *There's no choice. He's right about that. We have to protect our baby.*

Beside me, Connor was silent. He'd been working on his laptop since we left Cairo and was now shutting it down. I wondered what he was doing, what he was looking for, but I didn't ask. A part of me didn't want to know.

"We're going there to die." He intended to fake our deaths so we could escape. We would have to take new names, new identities. For how long? I wondered. For good? Will we be fugitives for the rest of our lives?

"I've booked us at the Hotel Eden," Connor said then.

I didn't respond. He was a stranger to me now, someone I didn't know at all.

He put his hand over mine. "It's going to be all right," he said softly.

I couldn't look at him. "Is it?" I asked.

He moved his hand to my abdomen. "I won't allow anyone to take this wee one from us, I promise you. I'll kill anyone who tries."

I faced him for the first time. The look in his eyes told me he meant it.

"I can sleep there, if you prefer," Connor said, gesturing toward the couch.

I hugged myself tightly as if trying to shut him out. I hesitated, almost said yes, then shook my head. "You don't have to do that." Whatever doubts I had, I was sure of one thing: he would kill to keep us safe.

He studied me for a moment as if he knew what I was thinking. "Think you'll ever be able to forgive me?" he wanted to know.

I inhaled deeply. "I don't know how to process this," I answered truthfully, looking down at the floor. "Two days ago, I was married to the man I love, carrying a baby I never thought I'd have, and I could not have been happier," I said. "Now, I don't even know my own husband and my baby's the target of a bunch of loonies."

He looked sad. "You're the only one who *does* know me," he insisted. "After I lost my mum, I dedicated myself to shutting everyone out so I'd never be hurt like that again. You're the only one I've let in."

"Do I call you Connor or Andrew?" I asked.

"It doesn't matter, really. You married a man, not a name," he said. "As far as I'm concerned, the man Andrew had become died the day I realized I loved you."

I still couldn't look at him. "That easy, huh?"

"It was never easy," he disagreed.

"How did I figure into your plan?" I asked. "How was I chosen to be one of your guinea pigs?"

"Being in the wrong place at the wrong time," he admitted. He turned away, unable to face me as he confessed. "When you mentioned you wanted children, opportunity presented itself. You were ideal for our needs. You were single, you'd exhausted every possible avenue of conception, you're healthy, intelligent—"

"Desperate," I finished.

He hesitated. "Yeah," he said finally.

"You offered to arrange an in vitro for me," I recalled. "If I had said yes to that, would you have supplied the sperm?"

"That wasn't the original plan, no," he said. "I've always been careful to make sure I didn't procreate."

This surprised me. "Why?"

"I didn't want children," he admitted. "I didn't want obligations, legal or emotional."

"So why did you volunteer to impregnate me? Did you just offer to get me into bed? Did you plan to prevent pregnancy and continue pretending to make the effort until you tired of me?"

"I might have, had I not fallen in love with you," he said. "My defenses are damn good, but you got past them."

I wished I knew how to respond. For the first time since I fell in love with him, I wasn't sure of anything.

44

CONNOR

I thought she was asleep at first, she was so still. I got into bed with her and embraced her from behind. I kissed her shoulder. "I'm glad you're still awake." I kissed her neck, stroked her arm.

She withdrew. It was only a slight movement, but it spoke volumes. I felt as though she'd slapped me. I pulled myself upright. "How long are we going to go on like this?" I asked, frustrated.

She turned over to face me. "How can you even think about sex, with all that's happening to us?" she wanted to know.

"I need my wife," I said.

"You have me."

"Do I?" I asked, unconvinced. "Do you still love me?"

She hesitated. "Yes, I do," she said. "My judgment when it comes to men is as crappy as it's ever been."

I could tell by the look on her face that she'd regretted the words as soon as she'd spoken them. I shook my head. "Your feelings for me haven't changed, but your opinion of my character has. Is that it?" I asked.

She wouldn't look at me. "I'm still trying to figure out what's real and what isn't."

I noticed she had stopped calling me by name. "My love for you is real," I tried to reassure her. Then I placed my hand on her abdomen. "This is real."

"Is there anything else you haven't told me?" she wanted to know.

"No," I answered, "but I suspect there's a great deal my loving stepfather hasn't told me."

I got out of bed, restless, and went to the window, staring into the darkness. "I always found his associates a bit strange, but Edward dismissed it as the eccentricity of the obscenely wealthy. I was too self-absorbed to question it all too carefully. They were pouring billions into my research. That's all I cared about then."

Lynne sat up. "You were going to use me as an incubator." She couldn't get past it. "What would I have given birth to?"

"A baby—a beautiful, healthy, exceptional child." I paused. "But no more so than our baby will be."

"You said there were other genetically engineered children," she remembered. "Did they know what they were getting into?"

"No. We didn't have many volunteers," I said. "We altered embryos created in vitro at fertility clinics."

"So the couples who went to these clinics ended up with babies that were not really their own?"

"Not exactly. We did use the biological parents' ovum and sperm—with some genetic enhancements," I said. "They got beautiful, healthy, highly intelligent children. There were no losers, or so I believed at the time."

"If something—anything—had been done to our baby, I'd want to know about it," Lynne said. "Is that why you were on the run?"

"No one knew about that at the time I left the U.S.," I said. "I was wanted for the genetic tampering of a racehorse. Edward owned a mare who was about to be bred. She was to be artificially inseminated. I tweaked things a bit and Icarus' Agenda was foaled. Nothing on four legs could beat him."

"The press called him the Bionic Horse," Lynne remembered. "How were you found out?"

"There was an accident at the track," I said. "A jockey was killed. One of the horses had to be put down. There was an inquiry, and in the course of the investigation, it all came out. I was in America at the time. Edward arranged for my new identity and got me out before they could arrest me."

"What became of the children born of your experiments?" Lynne wanted to know.

"I wish I knew."

"Did something go wrong?"

"The growth hormones caused the children to mature too rapidly," I said. "We realized the parents would begin to see that something was wrong. I discovered after the fact that Edward's associates had arranged to have the children collected."

"Collected?"

"Their quaint way of saying the children were abducted."

"Abducted?"

I nodded.

"Where are they now?"

"I haven't a clue."

"How fortuitous that you happened to already be in Rome," I said, extending my hand. "Connor Mackenzie."

Julian Marshall stared at me for a moment before shaking my hand. "Have we met before?" he asked.

I shook my head. "I don't believe so, no, but you came highly recommended."

"By whom?" Marshall asked cautiously.

"Interpol."

"Ah, yes. They're great admirers of my work, I hear." Marshall paused. "How did you know where to contact me?"

I smiled. "No magic to it, old chap. I saw you in the hotel lobby when my wife and I arrived two days ago."

We met for lunch in the restaurant at the Eden. I made a point of not having Lynne there. After our waiter had taken the order, Marshall said, "I was a bit surprised you wanted to meet here, Mr. Mackenzie. Such a public place."

"Exactly why I chose it," I told him. "Sometimes the best place to hide is out in the open."

"It's your call." Marshall paused. "What is it you wish me to obtain for you?"

"Interpol's files indicate you're a man who can obtain certain illegal documents," I started. "I wish to obtain falsified records for myself and my wife—passports, drivers' licenses, that sort of thing. At least half a dozen sets, using different names on each set. I will provide the photographs."

Marshall nodded. "That won't be difficult at all."

"Cost is not a problem."

"I'll need a bit of time."

"How much?"

"A week."

"See that it takes no longer."

45

LYNNE

I found a church not far from the hotel and went there in the evening while Connor was out. You can't throw a rock in Rome without hitting a church. I entered the sanctuary and took a seat in one of the pews.

Christmas was ten days away and I had no idea where we would be on that day. I wondered if we would still be alive on Christmas morning. I touched my abdomen. *It's going to be all right,* I thought, defiant. *It has to be. It took you a long time to find your way here. I'm not going to let that long trip be for nothing. No one is going to take you away from us.*

I closed my eyes and started to pray. When I opened them again, there was an elderly woman seated next to me. The woman smiled and patted my hand. "It will be all right, signora," she said softly.

"It shows, huh?" I asked.

"In Christ's church you will find sanctuary," the woman said. "You will be safe here."

I nodded. "I know."

"Your husband, do you love him?"

I hesitated, then nodded. "Yes." How did she know....

"Then you must forgive him."

I was startled by the woman's statement. "How do you know—?" Impossible. *She can't possibly know what we've been dealing with....*

"You must forgive him. You must be the wife he needs, and he will be the husband you need," the woman continued. "Go with him. Do not be afraid to love him."

Do not be afraid to love him. The words echoed in my mind. *Do not be afraid to love him.*

The woman looked at me, a look of kindness, of knowing my secrets somehow. It made me increasingly nervous. "Go with him. Have faith. God will see you through the storm."

I stood up. "I don't know how you know me, but...."

"Trust your Father. Go to Christ's church."

I got to my feet and rushed out of the church. I couldn't get out of there fast enough. The woman had not threatened me. She'd offered only encouragement. Still, the fact that she seemed to know so much—too much—instilled a sudden feeling of paranoia in me. Walking back to the hotel in a falling snow, I was convinced everyone I saw on the street was following me.

This isn't me, I thought. *I've never been like this before. Dear God, help us.*

"Do not be afraid to love him, Lynne."

"I do love him," I said aloud. "Loving him has me running for my life, for my baby's life. What else has he kept from me?"

"You are his wife. You will go with him."

"Where else could I go?"

"Do not be afraid to love him...."

46

CONNOR

The town of Subiaco is seventy kilometers east of Rome, situated high on a hill overlooking the Aniene Valley. It is home to the San Benedetto Monastery—whose abbey is built, literally, into the cliffs.

The sun was setting over that monastery when I found what I was looking for.

I'd been out all day, scouting potential locations for the accident. It had to be an isolated spot, a place where there was little likelihood of being interrupted by passing motorists. The terrain had to be rugged, and there would have to be a ravine, something deep enough to guarantee total destruction of the vehicle when I ran it off the road. This had to be an accident no one could possibly survive. If I calculated carefully, the gas tank would explode on impact.

I made a mental note: Buy petrol. Water coolers, at least three.

Now, on a deserted road above the cliffs, I parked the rental car and got out. I stood there for a long time, looking about. I saw nothing. No signs of life. Finally satisfied, I walked down a hundred yards, where the narrow road took a sharp turn. There was a guardrail, but it was old and rusted. I grabbed it with both hands and shook it hard, putting as much pressure on it as I could.

The vehicle will gain momentum rolling down the hill, I mentally estimated. *The weight of the vehicle, the speed...this will work.*

I walked back to the rental car, turning the collar of my coat up to block the cold winter wind. Once I was in the car, I took out my phone and called Lynne. "I'll be back there in about an hour," I told her. "Did you get everything?"

"It's all packed and ready to go."

"And you did pay cash?"

"For everything," she said.

"Did you get the needles and syringes?"

"Yes."

I drew in a deep breath and exhaled, thinking. "We should be out of here by the end of the week, then."

I was reluctant to leave her alone, as I had today. She was still angry, still mistrustful. She acknowledged that she still loved me, but I suspected she'd given more than a passing consideration to leaving me. I couldn't let her do that.

I wouldn't.

"When we leave here, we're not taking any of this with us," I told Lynne. "Luggage, clothing, everything will be left behind. We're not checking out. We'll still be guests of this hotel when we die."

She shook her head. "I don't think I can do this," she said, sinking into a chair.

"We have to," I insisted. "I hate having to take you away from everything you know—your family, your work—but we have no choice. These people are killers, Lynne."

She sat there, looking down at her feet, still shaking her head.

"When you think you can't go through with it all, ask yourself what matters most to you," I said sharply.

"My baby," she answered without hesitation.

"Our baby," I corrected her. Then I remembered. "I was so stupid. Edward warned me."

She looked up at me, surprised by the statement. "What do you mean?"

I scratched the back of my neck. "I suggested impregnating you myself back when we were still considering you as a participant in our program," I said. "He reacted in a way I couldn't understand. He told me it would be—his exact word—disastrous."

"But he didn't tell you why. Had you known all of this, would you have stayed away from me?" she asked.

d you known all of this, would you have stayed away from me?" she asked "I'd like to think I would have," I started, "but I was gobsmacked by the reality I'd fallen in love. I don't know. I don't know that I could have stayed away from you." I hesitated. "Would you have turned me away if you'd known?"

"I don't know, either," she admitted.

I nodded. "That's good. It's a start."

"Where do we go from here?" she asked, seeming to have finally resigned herself to what lay ahead for us.

"First, we stage the accident. Once we've convinced the world at large we're dead, we leave here. We use passports with new identities, and we head east. If anything goes wrong and they discover we're still alive, Edward will expect us to be traveling first class," I went on. "With that in mind, we'll travel like a couple of middle-class tourists. Coach seats, compact rental cars, cheap hotels—"

"I'm used to that," she reminded me.

"We'll need luggage—something inexpensive, maybe from a secondhand store," I went on.

She nodded. "No problem."

"You'll have to change your appearance."

"Me?" she asked. "What about you? They don't know me, but you...."

"I grew this after I left London," I said, referring to my hair and beard. "No one there has seen me since. A rinse to make it darker, perhaps."

"You might want to wear dark glasses, too," she said. "Your eyes are...distinctive."

I tried to smile. "That almost sounds like a compliment."

"So," she began thoughtfully, "I should get my hair cut and dyed?"

"No. Buy wigs," I suggested. "Several, different styles and colors. Pay cash for everything."

Lynne nodded.

I went to the closet brought out the syringes, needles and glass tubes. "What's that for?" Lynne asked.

"Blood."

"For what?"

"I'm going to splatter it on everything I discard at the crash site. Crime scene investigators will be looking for DNA evidence, and I don't intend to disappoint them." I sat in a chair next to her and applied a rubber tourniquet to my left arm, then attached one of the needles to the syringe. Using my teeth, I tore open a small packet containing an alcohol swab and wiped a patch of skin near the bend of my elbow. I drew blood from myself, filling several tubes, then disposed of the needle.

"Give me your arm," I told her.

And I started the process again...

"WHAT ARE YOU DOING?" Lynne asked. She'd awakened to find herself alone in bed. She came looking for me and found me at my computer, working frantically.

"Moving money. My trust fund in London, to be precise," I explained. "Since I won't be going back and don't want Edward to be able to track our movements, I'm moving the money from bank to bank to keep them from following me online. It will end up in a bank, under one of our aliases, in Hong Kong, which is where we're going when we leave here."

And I turned my attention back to the computer...

"I've got everything you wanted," Julian Marshall told me.

"Excellent. Meet me tonight for the transfer." I gave him directions to Subiaco. "I'll be arriving by seven-thirty."

"I'll see you there," Marshall promised.

After I ended the call, I turned to Lynne. "Make reservations for us under the names Ian and Marissa Campbell on the last available flight to Hong Kong. Have them hold our tickets at the counter. Be ready to leave when I get back—and don't open that door for anyone, no matter what."

"Where are you going?" she asked, concerned.

"To cause an accident," he said. "If I'm not back by midnight, leave without me."

I mentally reminded myself not to go past the posted speed limit. The last thing I wanted to do now was to call attention to myself.

It was dark and windy when I arrived at my destination. Marshall was already there, waiting in a nondescript black van. I got out of my rental car. "Punctual, I see," I said as Marshall climbed out of the van.

Marshall looked around. "How do you intend to pull this off?" he asked.

"I'll release the brake and roll it down that hill. I checked this place out a few days ago—there's a three-hundred-foot drop off that curve. I have three kegs in the trunk full of petrol. When it hits the bottom of the ravine, it will all explode, and that should cause it to burn to the point at which there will be almost nothing left."

I released the brake and he and I pushed the car along the road until it gained enough momentum to roll down the hill on its own. As I had anticipated, it crashed through the rotting wood fence along the curve and plunged to the bottom. There was a loud explosion, followed by flames shooting up from the ravine.

"It worked," Marshall said, watching the fireball engulf the surrounding trees. "There won't be much left to identify."

"Exactly." I picked up a heavy duffel I'd removed from the car and walked over to the edge of the road. I removed my wallet, Lynne's messenger bag and our cell phones, all stained with the blood I'd drawn. I tossed everything into the ravine.

Marshall came up beside me. "Impressive. You're going to a great deal of trouble to hide from someone," he observed.

"Yeah." I took a thick brown envelope from inside my coat. I gave it to Marshall, who checked the contents, then tucked it into his breast pocket.

"Good doing business with you," he said, turning to walk away.

I took my gun from my coat pocket and fired a single shot to the back of his head. Marshall fell to the ground face down. "Sorry, old man, but I couldn't let you live," I said, kneeling to make sure the other man was indeed dead. "I couldn't take that chance. You know too much."

———

I TOOK MARSHALL'S VAN. As I drove away, I saw his body in the rear-view mirror. Beyond that, black smoke billowed up from the ravine. Mentally, I considered all the possible conclusions the authorities might reach when they came upon the scene. *How long before it's discovered?*

I wanted it to be found quickly. I pulled my phone from my pocket and called Lynne. "It's done," I told her. "Are you ready to leave?"

"Just waiting for you."

"If anything happens, if I'm not back by midnight, I want you to go on without me," I said then.

"No."

"Yes," I said firmly, careful to stay well below the posted speed limit. "If I'm not there by midnight, it will mean something's gone wrong, that I've been found out. I want to know you'll be safe. What time is our flight?"

"Two a.m."

I looked at my watch. "It's going to be close," I said. "You did arrange for a car?"

"It's already here. Parked where you told me to leave it. Everything's in the trunk."

"I'll be there as soon as I can. I love you."

"I love you, too."

WE BARELY MADE it to da Vinci Airport in time to get through security and make our flight. Lynne fell asleep almost immediately after takeoff. She rested her head on my shoulder and slept peacefully. I kissed her forehead and caressed her hand. *I'll make this up to you. We will be free of them. Somehow. Some way.*

"Sir?"

The flight attendant was addressing me. "I'm sorry—what?" I asked.

"Would you like a pillow?"

"Yes, thank you."

"And your wife?"

"I don't want to disturb her, but yes, bring two—and a blanket," I said. "It's a bit cool."

"I'll be right back."

When she returned, I tucked one pillow behind my head and put the other on my lap. If she woke, I'd make her more comfortable. I pulled the lightweight blanket up over her shoulders and tucked it around her.

I was exhausted and desperately wanted to sleep, but didn't dare. I couldn't, not until I was sure we were safe.

I thought of my mother and what they had done to her. They'd taken a small boy from his mother. They'd murdered her. *You took my mum, but you won't take my wife. You won't take my child.*

You won't do to my child what you did to me.

47

LYNNE

I lay awake in the darkness, trying to make sense of everything that was happening to us. Connor was conceived by in vitro. But a superhuman? No. Perfect? No. None of it added up. Something was missing from the equation.

But what?

Then it hit me.

The prophet shall come forth from the island of the angels....

Ex insula Angelorum. England.

He must find hope before he can give hope to others...

Connor doesn't believe...

Dear God, is it possible?

I STARED at the laptop monitor, looking up as Connor emerged from the bathroom, yawning. After a week of sleepless nights, he'd finally managed to sleep for almost ten hours, but he still looked as though he could barely keep his eyes open.

"What are you doing up so early?" he asked. "You should be resting."

"I'm pregnant, Connor, not terminal." I continued to stare at the monitor.

"You're trying to do too much," he insisted.

"I'm looking for answers."

"Answers to why my stepfather aligned himself with a cartel of lunatics?" he asked. "It's a one-word answer. Greed."

"I don't think even he knows the whole story," I said slowly, scrolling down the page I was reading.

He looked at me, confused.

"The papyrus is the key," I said.

"What's that to do with any of this?" he asked.

I looked up at him. "I believe you're the prophet."

He laughed mirthlessly. "If you want to hear God laugh, tell him that."

"Have you ever seen angels, Connor?" I asked.

He managed a weak smile. "I was diagnosed with temporal lobe epilepsy when I was six years old," he said. "I had more than my share of weird, out-of-the-ordinary experiences. I not only saw them, I heard them argue with each other, fighting over me. When I was very young, I did have my own guardian angel."

"Guardian angel?" I asked.

"She said God had sent her to watch over me," he recalled. "My mother always told me God sent guardian angels to look after us. After she died, this woman appeared to me, a woman who actually looked very much like my mum. She had beautiful, long red hair, green eyes and a lovely, comforting voice. She told me God had a wonderful future planned for me. She gave me hope. Then one day someone at my school saw me talking to her—but they couldn't see her. They told Dr. Fairfield, the director of the school, and soon I was on drugs for my illness."

"She didn't visit you anymore?" I asked.

"She did. I ignored her."

"The voices drove my mother mad," Connor recalled. "It got so bad that she couldn't deal with it. She tried to kill herself. Mum used to let me get in the bath with her when Edward was away on business. One night, I went in to see if she'd let me get in with her. I saw the blood first. There was so much blood, she was so pale. I didn't know what had happened, but it scared me. The blood was in the water, on the floor."

"She slit her wrists?" I asked.

He nodded. His voice trembled when he spoke. "I was so frightened. I grabbed her bloodied wrist and begged her to wake up, to talk to me. I started to cry. I don't know how, exactly, it happened, but the wound began to heal. It healed completely, not even a scar."

"You healed her," I said.

"I don't know," he said, shaking his head. "She believed I did."

"As young as you were, to have that much power—no wonder these people want to control you." I took his hands in mine. "Connor —you are the prophet!"

"Absurd. I'm just a man, nothing more," he insisted.

"So were the apostles," I told him, "but Jesus imparted to them the power to heal, to perform miracles."

"I'm not even a believer."

"Neither was Saul of Tarses before Jesus called him to service and he became the Apostle Paul," I said. "Paul persecuted Christians. He killed many of them prior to his conversion."

"This is insane," Connor insisted.

"Humor me," I urged. "You were born in Scotland. The British Isles. The island of the angels."

He turned to the window, arms folded across his chest. Finally, he nodded. "So were millions of other men," he said.

"The papyrus says the prophet will come from the island of the angels," I said.

"Come on," he said, taking a deep breath. "You can't seriously believe that story."

"I do," I insisted. "I believe you've been having visions all these years, Connor. I believe your mother also had visions. A prophet would have visions."

"So would a bloody drunk," he pointed out.

"Dante and his people have gone to a lot of trouble to control you." I started making notes on the computer.

Connor was silent for a moment. "That's not because I'm some kind of mystic."

"Prophet," I corrected.

"No difference," he said with an offhanded shrug. "They want my DNA. They think they can create a master race."

"They killed your mother, Connor. They have us running for our lives," I said. "Whatever their motives, we need to know what they know and how far they're willing to go now to get you and our baby."

"Obviously, murder isn't out of the question," he said sullenly. "But that doesn't make me a prophet. Darlin', I'm no more a prophet than you are."

"Moses had pretty much the same response," I told him. "And the same doubts."

He didn't respond.

"The text said the prophet would be apart from God," I went on.

He turned to face me again. "That I'll give you," he said. "No one could be more apart from God than I am."

"The prophet must be made whole again in the eyes of God," I read from the computer's monitor. "Whole again...according to the ancient mystics, the soul comes to earth in two parts, and they spend their time here searching for their other half so they can become whole again."

He didn't say anything, waiting for an explanation.

"The prophet had to be made whole again in the eyes of God. Under the eyes of God. God's holy city. Jerusalem."

He frowned. "We were married in Jerusalem."

I nodded.

He raked a hand through his hair. "Unbelievable," he said. "How am I supposed to accept this?"

"Faith helps."

"The one thing I don't have, love."

I watched him with concern. Finally, I asked, "Remember the bird?"

"Bird?"

"In Egypt, the bird I found. You healed it."

"It just looked that way."

"Connor, have you ever healed anyone else?"

He couldn't hide his surprise. "Healed anyone?"

"Just what I said. Have you ever healed anyone?"

"No. Yes." He pulled up a chair and sat backward on it, leaning on its back to face her, his arms resting on the frame. "I healed you."

"Me?"

"The bruise on your shoulder," he recalled. "That night, it was quite large and dark. Purple. It should have taken a week or more to disappear. The next morning, when you got out of bed, I noticed that it was gone. There was not a trace of it."

I nodded. "You kissed it."

He still looked skeptical. "If I can raise the dead, why did I almost die myself when the bloody snake bit me?" he wanted to know.

"It doesn't work that way," I told him. "No spiritual gift is ever ours to control. The power is God's, working through us."

"So the Almighty will allow me to raise the dead, but he considered allowing the serpent to kill me." Connor scratched his head in puzzlement. "I can't be of too much value to him."

"Or he was using what happened to you for another purpose," I suggested.

MORE THAN TEN years since it was returned to China from British rule, Hong Kong is an energetic mix of contrasts: a major financial center surrounded by an unspoiled wilderness; completely Westernized, yet traditionally Chinese to its core. Its population of almost seven million occupies approximately ten percent of its geography, which made it an ideal place in which to disappear.

"How did you celebrate Christmas as a child?" I asked Connor. We were having lunch in a restaurant near our hotel and would be doing the same for dinner. There would be no Christmas tree, no celebration like the ones I'd had as a child.

"Before Edward or after?" Connor asked, his contempt for his stepfather clear in his voice. He'd been drinking heavily since we arrived, trying to drown his frustrations.

"Mum made it special," he recalled. "After she died, Edward had the staff make a huge banquet for forty people or more. There would be a mountain of gifts under an elaborately decorated tree. It was beautiful. And pointless."

I rubbed his shoulder. "I'm sorry," I said softly. "It must have been tough for you after she was gone."

"I didn't want to have Christmas. When I left Edward's semblance of a home and went to America, I didn't observe Christmas at all. Why celebrate a day for something I didn't believe in?"

I couldn't imagine what it must have been like for him. I wondered what Christmas was going to be like for our child. Would we always be on the run?

"I would imagine it was an important day for your family," Connor said then.

"Yeah, it was—is," I said, smiling at the memories that sprang to mind. "We always had pets, and never just one. Dad said we lived on Noah's Ark. Every Christmas, Mom would put up a large Nativity in the front yard. We had two identical cats, father and son. Fat Cat and Fat Cat Junior. Junior liked to sleep in the manger. Mom had a light installed in it so it could be seen at night, so it was warm in there. Junior liked that warm spot on the cold winter nights, so he'd displace Baby Jesus a couple of times a day."

Connor tried to smile. "That's what I'd like for our children," he said. "A real family, a real home, not some mausoleum masquerading as a home."

"We can have that," I said. "You can make it happen, Connor. Open the door and accept your calling. Accept the truth."

"This whole prophecy business—I can't process it, darlin'," he admitted. Connor looked uncomfortable discussing it in a public place, in spite of the fact that we practically had the restaurant to ourselves. There was only one other customer, and he was picking up take-out at the counter, having a lively conversation with a restaurant employee.

"I believe you're the prophet," I said. "I believe you've been given an enormous responsibility."

"But why?" he wanted to know. "Why me? It makes no sense."

"Only God knows why, Connor," I said softly, covering his hand with mine.

"If God is so all-powerful, why does he even need me? Why does he need anyone to be his prophet? Why doesn't he just do whatever he wants to do himself?"

I didn't have a logical answer for him. "It doesn't work that way," was all I could tell him.

"Convenient."

"Faith is believing what we can't see, what we can't prove," I tried to explain.

"The papyrus said the prophet would emerge from the Angel Isle to lead mankind, to give hope to a world that has none," he said. "How could I give hope when I have none myself?"

I didn't answer immediately. "That's it," I said finally as the realization came.

"What?"

"That's why they killed your mother," I reasoned. "You've already demonstrated certain spiritual gifts, but only by accepting God, by seeking salvation, can you achieve your full potential. Satan will stop at nothing to prevent that from happening."

He managed a short laugh. "You're saying the devil's out to get us?"

"He's out to get everyone," I said seriously. "Your mother's death, the threats against us—it's all for one purpose. It's to make certain you never turn to God, never realize your destiny."

He sat there in silence for a while, trying to process what I was telling him. "Still doesn't make sense," he said quietly. "Why didn't they just kill me when I was a wee lad if they knew all of this about me?"

"Maybe there's some reason they can't," I suggested. "If they can't destroy you, then they'll destroy everyone and everything you love in order to keep you separated from God."

"I'm an atheist. How could I be any more separated?"

HE WAS DRINKING AGAIN. He'd started drinking heavily when we arrived in Hong Kong, sometimes to the point of passing out.

I watched Connor with growing concern. I stopped even trying to convince him of his calling. I knew he didn't want to hear it. He was struggling with it. After a lifetime of being studied and tested and exploited, presumably for his incredible intelligence, now he was being faced with a reality that went against the beliefs of his lifetime. It was a mental overload, and I wondered how much more he could take.

Would it be any easier for him if he were a believer? I wondered. *It hasn't been any easier for me.*

He doesn't want the role that's been thrust upon him. How do I help him to deal with it, to accept his destiny? How do I help him learn to trust, to have faith?

Tell me what to say to him, God. Tell me how to make him see.

I took the glass from his hand. "I really wish you wouldn't," I told him.

He took it back. "It's New Year's Eve, after all."

"That's just an excuse."

"It dulls the pain."

"Connor, please."

Reluctantly, he put it down. "I can't deal with this. It's...it's...I can't even find the words," he told me. "It's insane. If I'm the prophet, why do they want our baby?"

"I don't know," I admitted, shaking my head. "I don't know. If we had the rest of the text, maybe we could figure it out, but this is all we have to work with."

He sank onto the corner of the bed. "I can't believe any of this."

I sat next to him. "Whatever we believe or don't believe, what's put us in danger is what they believe." I touched his cheek. "I can't do this alone, Connor. I need you functioning at one hundred percent." Suddenly, I let out a small gasp.

He looked at me, startled. "Is something wrong?"

I shook my head. "No, no. Something is right for once." I took his hand and placed it on my abdomen.

"What?" he asked.

"Be patient."

I could tell when he felt it by the expression on his face—a tiny, almost imperceptible stirring inside my body. "He's moving," he said, amazed.

"He? Could be she," I said.

"Not this time," he said, shaking his head. "I'd love a wee girl, of course, but this baby is a boy."

I NOTICED the man following us as we walked to the restaurant. He was hard to miss. He was the biggest, ugliest creature I'd seen since I watched pro wrestling with Tim when we were in college.

"I'm bloody sick of eating in restaurants already," Connor was saying. "I miss being able to have a quiet dinner at home. I wouldn't even mind doing the dishes."

"Connor, I think we're being followed," I said in a low voice.

He glanced over his shoulder. "The big guy?"

I nodded. "I saw him yesterday, too," I said. "He's hard to miss. There's at least three hundred pounds of refined ugly there. He might as well be wearing a neon sign."

Connor steered me into the restaurant. "Let's see if he waits for us," he said.

We ordered dinner, but I found it difficult to eat. Every time I looked out the window, I saw him, waiting, watching. "I feel like a dying hyena with a vulture lying in wait," I told Connor.

"We can't let him get us alone," he said.

"We can't stay here all night."

He took a bite. "We stay in public places. Edward's obsessive about privacy. He won't allow his hired goon to make his move in public. The cartel doesn't want the attention."

He was still watching the restaurant when we finally left. He started to follow us. I had an idea. "Let's get on that bus," I suggested.

Connor nodded.

Safety in numbers, I thought as we moved to the back of the crowded red-and-yellow double-decker bus. He wouldn't attack us in front of twenty witnesses—would he?

He did. Towering above everyone else, he pushed his way through the passengers standing in the aisles and positioned himself beside me. In the next moment, I felt something sharp against my back. A knife. He leaned past me and spoke to Connor in a low voice: "Don't try anything stupid."

I scanned the faces of the other passengers, trying to figure out which of them, if any, might be able and willing to help us. Did any of them speak English? Would they choose not to get involved? There were two large men whose clothing suggested they might be construction workers standing in the aisle maybe five feet from us. Three others looked fairly athletic—they might be able to take him if they all worked together. If they chose to get involved.

I didn't know where the tears came from, only that they surged forth in spite of my best efforts to suppress them. When the words came, I couldn't believe they were coming from me. "Why do you keep doing this?" I wailed, unable to control myself. "Why can't you leave us alone? It's been three years. Two restraining orders. Why can't you just accept that it's over? I don't love you anymore. Do you really think taking me off this bus at knifepoint is going to make me stay with you?" I was sobbing, unable to stop. "Please, just leave us alone."

The two large men turned. "Hey," one of them said to the other, "he's got a knife."

"Leave her alone!" the other shouted.

In seconds, they were making a move, the three other men following closely behind. The other passengers shifted to allow them to pass, in the process shoving Connor and me away from the monster and toward the rear exit. As soon as the bus came to a stop and the opportunity presented itself, Connor pulled me off the bus. The other passengers followed, with the two largest men forcing the monster into the street, restraining him as a young woman called for police assistance from her cell phone.

Connor tugged my arm. "We have to get out of here."

I looked back once as we crossed the street. The men were restraining him. The police had arrived. For a moment, I thought I saw the monster look directly at me. I silently prayed the police would keep him locked up.

Connor led me into a nearby restaurant, moving toward the rear. We ran through the kitchen, startling the chef. He turned, cleaver in hand, and yelled something in angry Chinese.

"Just passing through," Connor assured him. "No need for that, mate!"

We stumbled through the rear exit into an alley cluttered with battered garbage cans. A young man was taking out his frustration on an old motorcycle. "I have an idea," Connor said.

I stared at him. "You can't be serious. It's a piece of crap. Probably doesn't even run."

"We can't go back to the hotel. Can't take that chance," Connor said. "We have to get away, as far as we can, before my stepfather posts his goon's bail."

He approached the young man and spoke to him in fluent Mandarin Chinese. The transaction was brief, and even though I didn't speak the language, I knew my husband had just bought that clunker. The young man walked away with a satisfied smile, and Connor helped me onto the bike.

"Are you sure this wreck will run?" I asked as Connor made a fourth attempt to start it.

Finally, the engine started to roar. "It'll get us where we're going," he promised.

"And where is that?"

"I'll let you know when we get there."

"That's what I was afraid you'd say."

48

CONNOR

We had been on the road for hours, stopping only when it was absolutely necessary. I worried that keeping my pregnant wife on the bike for such a prolonged period might pose a risk, but staying in Hong Kong was even riskier.

I saw the approaching storm on the horizon and knew we'd have to take refuge somewhere soon, but where? I was still searching when it started to rain. I pressed on for an hour in the rain until it became a downpour that made it impossible for us to go any further.

I pulled the motorcycle into an alley behind a row of small shops, one of them a laundry.

"What have you got in mind?" Lynne asked.

"A place to spend the night."

She looked alarmed. "Here?"

"There's no room at the inn," I said.

I jerked my wet jacket up over my head and went up to the laundry's rear door. I checked carefully to make sure there was no active alarm system, then started looking for something with which to pry open the door. When I found nothing, I chose a large chunk of concrete lying next to an overflowing dumpster and smashed the glass panel in the window. I reached through the broken glass, tearing my sleeve and cutting my forearm in the process, and opened the door.

I gestured to Lynne, who stepped past me and went inside. I entered behind her and closed the door.

"I wish you'd picked the restaurant," she said. "I'm starving."

"That wasn't possible," I said. I checked out all of the windows and front entrance. "This place was the one least likely to have any kind of security."

She took off her jacket. Underneath, her wet clothes clung to her. "How could you be so sure?" she wondered aloud.

"I wasn't," I admitted, "but the odds were in our favor here. They'd remove the contents of the cash drawer at night, and who would want to steal laundry?"

"Right now, I would," she said. "My clothes are soaked."

"Mine, too." I looked around. "We're going to be here a while. We could throw our things into a dryer."

She raised her eyebrows. "And what would we wear while they're drying?" she wanted to know.

I laughed for the first time since we escaped the giant on the bus. "There's only the two of us here, and we are married, after all," I reminded her. "Why would we have to wear anything?"

"Right. If we should happen to get caught, I'd prefer not to be caught naked," she said.

"Very well," I said. "We can find something in these carts, I'm sure."

I searched through one cart while she looked through another. I finally found things that would fit but looked ridiculous. Lynne ended up with a baggy housedress with a loud floral pattern, while I donned a pair of painter's pants that had to be belted in order to keep them from falling down.

"Well," Lynne said, putting on the dress, "I must look pretty unappealing now."

"I think you look hot," I said with a grin. It was the truth. She'd appeal to me wearing a burlap sack.

She rolled her eyes. "It's official. There is absolutely nothing on the face of the earth that doesn't get you aroused."

I piled some blankets on the floor in one corner. "Better get some sleep," I told her. "We may not have a chance again for a while."

"What about you?" she asked.

"One of us has to stand watch," I reminded her.

"We take turns, then."

I shook my head. "You sleep. I'll be fine."

She pulled a comb from her bag. "I think I may have to shave it off," she said as she struggled to drag the wide-tooth comb through her wet, tangled hair.

"Here, let me try," I said, taking the comb from her. I worked it through slowly, gently, starting at the ends, until I'd removed all the tangles.

"You missed your calling," she teased me. "You could have been a darn good hairdresser. Or at the very least a great shampoo person."

"Always good to have a backup plan," I said, rolling up a small blanket for her to use as a pillow. She lay down, falling asleep almost immediately. I sat beside her, leaning back against the wall, my right hand in my pocket, gripping my handgun.

I fought sleep, drifting off, then abruptly waking myself. I had to stay awake. We couldn't be caught off guard. One slip-up could prove fatal.

I watched Lynne sleep. She was four months pregnant now. She was beginning to show. Soon, it would be impossible to conceal the pregnancy. It would be impossible to hide her. She would be unable to keep living on the run. We had to find a safe house. Somewhere she could rest and, if necessary, give birth.

I knew the risks involved in a pregnancy, especially a first pregnancy, for a woman past forty. *She needs to be getting regular prenatal monitoring. She needs to give birth in a hospital. But that might not be possible.*

I asked myself if I would still have married her, had I known the truth about Edward and his associates. I wanted to believe I would not have put her at risk, but I wasn't sure how I would have reacted. I'd been such a selfish bastard then...

"*Stop trying to be who you think you should be and allow yourself to be who you really are.*"

"Practice what you preach, Merlin."

Merlin. She was the only one who had ever given me a pet name. As silly as it was, I loved it. I loved the playfulness we'd shared before our world was shattered. I closed my eyes and saw her standing at the kitchen sink with soapsuds on her nose...the morning after the papyri was discovered, when she'd had too much champagne in celebration...the morning after we'd made love for the first time...

"I love you."

"You don't look like a man in love. You look terrified."

"I am terrified."

I twisted the gold wedding band on my finger. Even in the dim light, I could see the tiny infinity symbol engraved on it. I recalled the day we were married...standing before the preacher in that little church in Jerusalem, listening to him read from the Song of Solomon...

"*Love is invincible facing danger and death...passion laughs at the terrors of hell...the fire of love stops at nothing...*"

I recalled the day she brought me home from the hospital after my encounter with the desert horned viper. I'd been angry and frustrated by my temporary impotence—and she'd been angry with me for it.

"Is that all you think you have to offer? Is that all you believe you are to me? Listen to me—even if we could never have sex again, you are the only man I could ever want."

I drew in a deep breath. I had to put an end to this insanity. I had to protect her and the baby.

All my life, I'd been disappointed by everyone I'd known, men and women. They'd all wanted something from me, whether it was my money, my connections, my genius, or even my body. Lynne was different. She loved me for the one thing only she could see.

My soul.

I stared at the monitor, perplexed. *How have they been able to predict our every move? It's as if they know every alias we've used—*

Marshall.

I knew he was a risk. Dammit, he sold us out before he even delivered.

He was working for Edward. Why didn't I see that? He was probably the one who falsified the ID I was given to get me out of the US.

What am I missing? Why are they so determined to find us?

I gave it some thought. Lynne believed I was the prophet mentioned in the papyrus we'd found in Egypt. I couldn't wrap my brain around that. *You were born for a special purpose, Andrew.* It was my mother's voice. *You were given to me by an angel.*

Then why was that angel not there to save you, Mother?

They want you, Edward had said. *They believe you're the key to creating a master race.*

His IQ is off the charts. The headmaster at my school.

You are the future of the human race, young man, Sadowski had said.

This is impossible....

49

CAITLIN

"I was just looking at the NOTICES from Interpol," Jack said as he entered my office. "Julian Marshall's dead."

I looked up from my computer. "Natural causes or disgruntled client?" I asked.

"The latter." He pulled up a chair. "Bullet in the back of the head, fired at close range—but he must've gotten in a shot, too. His body was found at the site of a vehicle crash—SUV went through the guardrail into a ravine."

I was barely paying attention. Julian Marshall was old news. He'd been on Interpol's radar for years, notorious for providing new identities for criminals trying to stay beneath law enforcement radar. He was a master at falsifying records.

But he was not our problem. Not anymore.

"One of the two in the vehicle was American," Jack was saying. "An American—an archaeologist, Dr. Lynne Raven."

Recognizing the name, I stopped what I was doing. "Are they sure?" I asked.

"Positive ID hasn't been made yet, but there were personal effects at the site," he said. "The man with her was her husband."

"Husband?" I stopped what I was doing, closed the file and opened a new one on Marshall.

"Yeah. Just recently married, according to the report."

"Wait a minute...." I punched some more keys, then looked up again. "Apparently, Italian police found his laptop in his hotel room. They say he was meeting with somebody there, more than once. According to his engagement calendar, he was supposed to meet this man the night before his body was found."

"Anyone we know?" Jack asked.

"Someone named Connor Mackenzie," I said. "He had on his person an envelope containing a large sum of cash." I reached for my phone...

50

DARCY

I was on a flight approaching Jordan when my cell phone rang. The number on the display took me by surprise. I pushed the button and put the phone to my ear. "Cat—I always knew the day would come when you'd wake up and come back to me," I greeted her.

"Shut up, Darcy." She was in no mood for my warped sense of humor. "This isn't a social call."

"The FBI wants me? If you'll tell me what I'm guilty of, I'll know how to plead."

"You're a world-class SOB, but unfortunately, that's presently not a capital offense," she said.

"I knew you still loved me," I chuckled.

"I need some information on your ex-wife," she said impatiently.

"Which one?"

"Number three. The archaeologist."

I laughed at that. "Why would the Feds be interested in Lynne?" I asked. "She's as squeaky-clean as it gets."

"Are you aware that she remarried?"

"Yeah. I was their official wedding photographer. He's an odd one. He didn't like the idea of me being there, let alone photographing the ceremony."

"And that qualifies him as strange?" Caitlin asked skeptically.

"No, but you didn't let me finish," I said, waving off the flight attendant who was trying to tell me I'd have to end my call until the plane landed.

"He's secretive. I photographed him at their wedding, but he erupted when I tried to get shots of him working on the excavation site. When he saw me taking his picture, he took my camera, tore the film out of it, then smashed it."

Caitlin laughed. "You still use film?"

"Yeah, what about it?"

"You said you photographed him—did you salvage any of those photos of him?" she wanted to know.

"Yeah."

"E-mail them to me." It was an order, not a request.

"Sure, but why?"

"What did she tell you about him?"

"Not much. Why?"

"E-mail me those photos, Darcy," Caitlin told me again. "I have to go."

"Wait a minute!" I halted her. Now the flight attendant was threatening to confiscate my phone. "Aren't you going to tell me what this is all about?"

"You know I can't discuss my cases." She hung up.

51

CAITLIN

"Wake up, Jack!" I gave a sharp kick, sending my sleeping partner crashing to the floor. He often napped in the office, making me wonder what he did all night when he should have been sleeping. He opened his eyes and gave me a dazed look. "I think I have the missing piece to the puzzle," I told him.

"What puzzle?" he asked, still not quite awake.

"The Sadowski puzzle, numbnuts," I responded impatiently. "I believe we finally have a link between Rhys-Williams, Marshall and Sadowski."

"Great," he said, rubbing his hip as he made his way across the room to the table where his computer was set up. "What am I looking for?"

"Three men. Three different men. The man on the right is the elusive Dr. Stewart, Sadowski's right-hand man. The one on the left is the man who calls himself Connor Mackenzie, the one who supposedly died in Subiaco."

"And the one in the center?"

"Edward Rhys-Williams' stepson, Andrew Stewart. Dr. A. J. Stewart."

52

DARCY

I tried to call Lynne's satellite phone three times but it went to voicemail each time. Finally, I located a number for her partner, Tim O'Halloran. I called and waited through several rings before a male voice finally answered. "Tim O'Halloran."

"This is Darcy, Tim. Is Lynne there?" I asked.

There was a long pause. "You don't know," Tim said slowly.

"Don't know what?" I asked impatiently. Where was Lynne?

"Lynne and Connor—they were killed in an accident a few weeks ago."

I was stunned. "Killed?" I couldn't have heard correctly.

"They were in Italy. Their car went off a cliff." Tim sounded distracted. "Look, there's nothing else I can tell you. We're shutting down the excavation here."

The line went dead. I stared at the phone in my hand for a moment, then put it aside. I leaned forward, elbows on the desk in front of me, head in my hands. I knew it. I knew something wasn't right. No one would listen to me....

"I was just about to call you," Alberta told me when I reached her in New York. "I have some news about your ex-wife."

"I already heard. She and the Lord of the Geeks are dead." I shook my head. "What the hell did Mackenzie get her into?" I wondered aloud.

"How can you be so sure this was her husband's fault?" Alberta asked.

"Come on, Ally! Lynne is—was—such a straight arrow, she wouldn't even litter," I said, irritated. "She gets involved with him and—wham! She's dead, and the FBI is investigating her and her husband. Doesn't take a rocket scientist to connect those dots! What does anybody really know about him or his family?"

"Maybe it's time someone found out," Alberta said quietly.

"I want this story, Ally," I said. "This time, it's personal."

"You're a photographer, not a journalist," she reminded me.

"Then put Charlie on the story and assign me to do the photos," I persisted.

"For once, Darcy, you and I are on the same page."

"Caitlin, don't hang up, please," I said quickly, as soon as she answered her phone.

"Did I hear correctly?" she asked. "Did you actually say please?"

"I need answers," I said, not bothering to even try to conceal the desperation I was feeling.

"I told you before, I can't discuss my cases," she responded, knowing what he was referring to.

"You came to me for information. You owe me an answer," I argued.

"I owe you?" she asked incredulously. "I owe you?"

"Look, I know I treated you like shit," I admitted. "I know I was a real pig—"

"Pig?"

"SOB?"

"For lack of a better word."

"You grill me about my ex-wife but give me no explanation. Then I find out she and her new husband are dead—"

"We don't believe the Mackenzies are dead," Caitlin said quietly.

I was stunned. "Not dead?"

"For reasons we have yet to determine, your ex-wife and her new husband may have faked their deaths," Caitlin revealed.

"Why?" I asked.

"We don't know—yet. There was a man shot at the accident site, a known criminal wanted by us and by Interpol. Notorious for helping criminals establish aliases." She paused. "We're still trying to piece it all together. We have very few answers at this time."

"I knew the guy was weird, but nobody would listen when I was trying to warn them," I told her. "I remember how he regaled the group at the dig by telling us how to clone Jesus."

"*What?*"

I could almost hear the light going on in her head. "Yeah. One of the people working on the archaeological site said he once told them that it would be possible to extract DNA from the Shroud of Turin and use it to Xerox the Almighty. Crazy, huh?"

She cut me off abruptly. "Darcy, I have to go. Let me know if you think of anything else."

"And you'll do the same?" I asked.

"I can't."

"Yes, you can," I insisted. "Quid pro quo."

"Darcy—"

"I'm tired of being treated like a mushroom, Cat," I said.

"Mushroom?"

"Yeah. Kept in the dark and fed a lot of shit."

"All right," she reluctantly agreed. "Quid pro quo."

"Okay, I know, I owe you an apology," Charlie conceded. "I thought you were just shitting me."

"I wish I had been," I said.

Charlie looked at me, surprised by my grim manner. "This has hit you hard, huh?" he asked.

My jaw tightened. "I knew, Charlie," I said. "I knew right off there was something not right about that guy. Everybody thought I was either nuts or jealous. I knew, dammit."

Charlie patted my shoulder. "It sounded crazy, pal," he acknowledged. "You couldn't have been surprised nobody bought your spook theory."

I looked at him. "If anyone had, they might still be alive."

"Yeah, right." Charlie negotiated a sharp turn on the road leading to the crash site. "As I recall, Mackenzie had some pretty bizarre ideas on religion and cloning and the like. Maybe he was actually involved with some global cult. You know—bring about the Second Coming in a lab. Or maybe even the antichrist."

I leaned back in the passenger seat. "Sometimes I think he *is* the antichrist," I said.

53

CONNOR

I lay in the darkness, staring up at the ceiling, trying to shut out the voices that had roused me from sleep. I didn't know what time Lynne had finally fallen asleep. I wanted to tell her it was going to be all right, but the truth was that I was no longer certain of anything except that I would do whatever was necessary to protect my wife and child.

"*Take her to Christ's church. There you will find sanctuary.*"

Leave me alone. I have enough crap to deal with.

"*Take your child's mother to Christ's church. There she will be safe. She will give birth there in the wilderness, attended by angels.*"

Right.

"*You will all be safe there, under God's protection.*"

Stop talking in riddles, dammit!

"*Take her to Christ's church....*"

54

DARCY

"How many times has Ally fired you now?" Charlie asked as we climbed into a taxi at Heathrow Airport. He gave the driver the address of our hotel.

"I've lost track," I admitted. "She fires me, I act like I don't give a rat's ass, then she cools off and offers me my job back, always making me understand that I have to be reprimanded."

"You two act like you're married," Charlie observed.

"Ally's lasted with me longer than any of my wives," I said. "She understands me better than any of them ever did."

"That explains why you two have never been involved," Charlie said with a chuckle.

"Ally and me?" I laughed at the thought. "We'd end up killing each other."

"You always been drawn to hotheaded women?" Charlie asked.

"I used to be," I admitted. "When I was younger, I was attracted to the excitement and unpredictability of a difficult woman. Now that I'm past my 'use by' date, I don't have the fortitude for the fights."

"You and the doc—did you two fight often?" Charlie asked.

I thought about it. "In the beginning, yeah," I recalled. "She was ticked that I was away so much. We fought about having kids. She wanted 'em, I didn't. She'd get all fired up and I'd leave. I dealt with our problems by avoiding them, until finally she got tired of it and walked out."

"I'm surprised she stayed as long as she did."

I was silent for a moment. "She was pregnant, you know."

Charlie looked surprised. "No, I didn't know."

I nodded. "When we were in Egypt, she told me."

Charlie said nothing, waiting for me to go on.

"There she was, married to a man who was willing to give her that one thing she always wanted, and just when she was about to get it..." I couldn't finish.

"You want to know why," Charlie guessed.

"Yeah," I said. "I want to know why. And then I want to know who, and I want them to pay."

―――

"I'll make some calls, see who's willing to talk," Charlie told me when we checked into the hotel. "The Phoenix Foundation. Division of Icarus International. High-profile conglomerate, low-profile founder," he said. "Edward Rhys-Williams hasn't given an interview in over thirty years. None of their executives ever gives interviews, in fact. Trying to get information out of them is like trying to get information from the CIA. In fact, getting into the CIA would probably be easier."

"Makes them sound like they have something to hide, doesn't it?" I suggested.

Charlie shrugged. "Howard Hughes was obsessively private," he pointed out.

"I rest my case."

Charlie stopped at his room and slipped his card key into the lock. "I'll see if I can get an audience with Stepdaddy."

"If he turns you down, we'll just ambush him outside the stronghold," I decided.

———

"THERE ARE no records of anyone named Connor Mackenzie ever having attended Cambridge," I told Charlie over breakfast in the hotel restaurant.

"I made some calls, but I was unable to find anything," Charlie said, adding sugar to his coffee. Noting the way I was looking at him, he defended himself. "What? I need the energy boost."

"No wonder you're diabetic."

"You should talk," Charlie said, reaching for more sugar. "If I die, I die happy."

"And get buried in a piano crate," I said.

Charlie nodded and sipped his coffee. "Any idea where Mackenzie was born in Scotland?"

"I recall Duchess saying something about it in passing," I said, trying to summon up the memory. "Inverness, Inveraray, something like that."

"I guess that means we have to turn over every rock in Scotland," Charlie said.

"Try Loch Ness."

"I called Icarus. We've been turned down by everybody who's anybody there," Charlie told me.

"What a surprise," I said sarcastically. "Did you try the janitor?"

"Couldn't even get a peek at the trash."

"We could always hijack the trash. Might be worth a little dumpster diving." I said.

"You don't have any other information on Mackenzie?" he asked. "Anything at all?"

"Just what's been in the news since that bogus accident," I said. "And my photographs."

"You're sure? If you can think of anything, even some little thing mentioned in passing, because right now we've got nothing," Charlie said.

I STAKED out the Icarus Tower while Charlie continued his search for information back at the hotel. I watched everyone who entered and left the building, armed with one of the rare photographs I'd been able to find of Edward Rhys-Williams. I looked at my watch. I'd been there almost seven hours, with not even a sighting of the man. *Does he live in the freakin' building?* I wondered.

Then, a limousine pulled up to the curb and parked. I snapped to attention as the driver got out and spoke briefly to one of the security guards at the entrance. Moments later, Edward Rhys-Williams appeared, accompanied by a woman who looked familiar.

"Mr. Rhys-Williams!" I called out. "I need to speak with you!"

I never got the chance. My path was blocked by two security guards, who held me at bay until my target was in the limo and it had pulled away from the curb. I tried shouting to get the man's attention, but to no avail. As I turned back to the building, I noticed the woman was still there.

"Sarah Stewart?" I asked, now recognizing her.

She nodded. "You're American," she said. "Your accent."

"Oh, yeah."

"I should be flattered that you've recognized me," she said, smiling.

"I haven't been here long, but long enough to catch the local TV news," I said, shaking her hand. "You scored a coup there."

She looked puzzled. "I don't understand."

"Rhys-Williams. I hear he never does interviews, but there you were with him," I said. "How'd you do it?"

"Nepotism," she answered. "He's my father."

I couldn't hide my surprise.

"My surname's a bit unwieldy," she said. "I decided early on to use my mother's maiden name professionally."

"A smart move," I said. "I'm sorry, I didn't introduce myself. Phillip Darcy, Viewpoint."

"You're also a journalist, then."

"Photojournalist, actually." I patted my camera case. "Are you free for dinner?"

She seemed to be about to accept my invitation, then abruptly changed her mind. I looked over my shoulder. One of the security guards was watching us, shaking his head. "I'm sorry, no," she said. "I really do have to run. It was good talking to you."

I watched her walk away. *Stewart*, I thought. *She's his half-sister. Different fathers, same mother....*

I TRIED to call Charlie on my way back to the hotel, but there was no answer, either in the room or on his cell. Knowing Charlie, he probably went out for donuts and left his cell at the hotel, I thought. The man had a death wish. He'd been diabetic since his teens, and still he didn't take the whole thing seriously enough.

When I returned to the hotel, I saw a housekeeper working on our floor. She was knocking on Charlie's door. "Housekeeping," she announced as she took out her passkey.

I had just unlocked my own door when I heard the woman scream. I ran back to Charlie's room and found her standing over Charlie, who was lying on the floor. I went to Charlie, dropping to my knees. "Call for an ambulance!" I shouted.

The housekeeper, struggling to regain her composure, nodded and went to the phone. I patted Charlie's face. "I told you those damn donuts were gonna catch up with you, buddy," I said. "Come on, Charlie, wake up!"

Charlie's face felt cool. He didn't appear to be breathing. Instinctively, I pressed two fingers to the carotid artery. There was no pulse.

Charlie was dead.

"Insulin shock," the doctor told me. "He apparently overdosed."

I shook my head. "He was diabetic most of his life," I said. "He knew what he was doing with the needle. He wouldn't have made a mistake like that."

"Perhaps it was not a mistake," the doctor suggested.

"Are you saying—no, that man was not suicidal," I insisted. "He was a little reckless with his diet, sure, but he didn't really want to die."

"I'm sorry," the doctor said.

"Me, too," I said.

I had to call Ally. Charlie's wife had to be told, and Ally would be the one to break it to her. I found a quiet place and made the call to her cell.

"Darcy, why are you not calling the office number?" she asked. "It is, after all, regular business hours. You didn't get arrested again, did you?"

"It's Charlie, Ally," I said. "He's dead."

There was a momentary silence on the other end. "I'm not sure I heard you correctly."

"Charlie's dead." I told her everything I knew. "I don't think this was an accident, Ally."

"Why do you say that?"

"For one thing, Charlie never made that kind of mistake with his meds," I said. "I've been on so many assignments with him...he played Russian roulette with his diet, but he never made a mistake with the insulin. He had the crazy idea he could get away with eating crap as long as he got the insulin right. And he'd already injected himself, before I even left the hotel."

"What are you suggesting, Darcy?"

"I'm suggesting Charlie was murdered," I said, anger rising

within me. "I'm guessing that whatever Connor Mackenzie is hiding, Charlie was just one more piece of collateral damage."

"I want you on the next flight out of London," she told me. "Let the police deal with this."

"No way," I said stubbornly.

"You're not a writer, Darcy."

"I'm going to write this story," I insisted. "I'm going to find out what's so important that someone is willing to kill for it. Fire me if you want, but I'm staying."

55

CONNOR

"Take the child's mother and go to Christ's church. There she will be safe. There she will give birth to your son."

I slept fitfully, the voices relentless, refusing to leave me alone. I tossed and turned so that I woke Lynne.

"What's wrong?" she asked.

"It's nothing. Bloody nightmares," I tried to brush it off.

"Again?"

"Go back to sleep, darlin'," I told her. "It's all right now."

"The same nightmare?" she asked, curling up against me.

"Yeah. I'm still being told to take you to church," I said, embracing her.

"Where, exactly, are you being told to take me?" she asked.

"Just Christ's church. Not a specific church, just church."

Lynne was silent for a long moment.

"What if it's not a church but a location?" she asked finally. "Christchurch—New Zealand."

I thought about it. "Why Christchurch?" I questioned.

"I have no idea, but I think we should go," she said.

I sat up. "Go to New Zealand because I heard it in a dream?" I asked.

"No. Go because we've both been told to go," she said.

"You've had the dream?"

"No. Just before we left Rome, I went to a church. You were out that night. There was an old woman there. We talked. She told me to go to Christ's church—Christchurch. Connor, this is the only explanation that makes any sense," she said. "What have we got to lose?"

"Our lives," I answered.

56

DARCY

"I'm onto something," I told Ally. "Mackenzie's half-sister is Sarah Stewart, a TV news anchor here. They had the same mother, different fathers. She told me she uses her mother's maiden name professionally. I located her birth record. Mother's name was Anne Stewart Rhys-Williams."

"And?"

"Stewart, Ally. Not Mackenzie," I pointed out. "Mackenzie's not his real name. It's Andrew Stewart. Once I had the mother's maiden name, I got his birth record from Scotland. Mother, Anne Stewart. Father listed as unknown."

"And do you also know why he's using an alias?"

"Yeah. Do you recall a scandal involving a genetically-engineered racehorse a couple of years back?"

There was a brief silence on the other end. "The Sadowski case."

"Joseph Sadowski's protégé was a scientist named A. J. Stewart," I said. "Andrew James Stewart, to be precise."

I ARRIVED at the Highgate Institute late in the day and bullied my way into the office of the director, Dr. Edgar Fairfield, a portly man in his late sixties with a warm, earthy demeanor that I suspected was just a front.

"What can I do for you, Mr.—" Fairfield asked as I seated myself across the large mahogany desk.

"Darcy. Philip Darcy. From *Viewpoint* magazine."

The other man nodded slowly. "American," he said with distaste. "I should have known." Then, after a pause: "And what is it that was so important that you couldn't go through the appropriate channels?"

"I couldn't go through channels because you wouldn't take my calls," I said. I'd tried everything but a decree from Parliament.

The man stiffened. "I'm a very busy man, Mr. Darcy. Again, how can I be of assistance?"

I wasted no time in getting to the point. "I'm looking for information on one of your former students. Andrew Stewart."

"I am not at liberty to discuss any of our students, past or present," Fairfield stated firmly, letting me know there would be no exceptions to the rule.

I wasn't giving up. "A genius, wasn't he?" I asked. "Isn't that why he was here?"

"Was? You're speaking in past tense. Has something happened to him?" Fairfield wanted to know.

Bingo. The door had been opened. Just a crack, but enough to get my foot inside, to keep it from slamming in my face. I said, "He was killed in an automobile accident last month in Italy." Don't let on you know they're not dead until you know where he stands.

"I am sorry to hear that. What is it you wish to know about him, Mr. Darcy?" Fairfield asked hesitantly. "There are things I can't divulge—"

"How long was he here?"

"Six years. He went to Cambridge at age nine."

I nodded. "Impressive."

Fairfield smiled a genuine smile for the first time. "He was without a doubt the most gifted young man alive," he said proudly, as if Andrew Stewart's genius were somehow his own accomplishment. "There is no limit to his potential. Einstein himself once said human beings use only a fraction of the brainpower they possess. He claimed anyone who did would become pure energy. This young man comes closer to such a realization than anyone I have ever examined."

"Did he have any—problems—while he was here?" I wanted to know.

Fairfield immediately turned defensive. "I'm not sure I understand what you mean by problems," he responded cautiously.

"Problems. Troubles. You know," I prodded. "Was he difficult?"

Fairfield leaned back in his chair and seemed to ponder the question. "With genius comes certain difficulties," he reasoned. "Yes, of course he had his share of difficulties."

"Such as?"

"I can't discuss that with you, Mr. Darcy."

"Mental problems," I pushed the envelope.

"I can't discuss that with you." Fairfield repeated firmly.

"Was he ever treated for psychosis?"

"I said—"

"I know what you said, Doctor," I said, rising to my feet. I placed my hands on the desk and leaned forward. "Could he be dangerous?"

"I can't tell you that!"

"You had better!" I shot back at him. "People are dying, and I believe it's because of this man. My ex-wife—my pregnant ex-wife—was one of the casualties. My best friend and colleague was another. Let me go on the record by saying I'm not going to rest until I know why."

Fairfield's entire body sagged, and he nodded slowly. "I haven't seen the young man in many years, Mr. Darcy. I thought he was cured."

I eyed him suspiciously. "Cured?"

Fairfield looked up at me. "He lost his mother when he was very young. He didn't cope well," he recalled. "He had problems. We did what we could for him, but he was so angry and bitter. We never saw him again."

"Maybe you'd better tell me more about his problems," I suggested carefully.

Fairfield nodded again. "He had hallucinations."

I said nothing, waiting for him to continue.

"He said an angel was with him, protecting him from us."

AN ANGEL. A FREAKIN' angel, of all things.

This just keeps getting more and more bizarre, I thought as I entered my hotel room.

Mackenzie was apparently regarded as some kind of miracle child, a genius with a real "gift from God." He was also deeply disturbed. He once believed he'd had an angel who had protected him.

Angels...the figures in the photographs look like ghosts... spirits...angels?

Connor Mackenzie, the self-professed atheist, had a guardian angel. Two months ago, I would have scoffed at all of it, convinced it was either a tall tale or the ravings of a lunatic. But now....

I took out the photographs I'd taken and studied them again, Connor Mackenzie, God's experiment gone horribly wrong. People are dropping like flies just for being associated with him. And he has someone—something—protecting him.

Okay, if You're really out there, I can handle a challenge, I thought. But if You're listening, could I at least get a decent road map?

57

CONNOR

New Zealand is one of the most beautiful, unspoiled places on earth, for the most part removed from the so-called "rat race" plaguing the rest of the world. It's a land of mountains, glaciers, fjords and rivers, of grassy fields, lakes and evergreen forests. Three quarters of the population inhabits the North Island, but it is the more remote South Island to which Lynne and I went in search of a safe place in which to take refuge while we awaited the birth of our baby.

Christchurch, founded in 1850 as a colony of the Church of England, was named for Oxford University's college, where the city's founder received his education. It's a blend of the old and the new, evidenced in its blend of contemporary architecture and the earlier Gothic structures. The compact downtown area, built around the willow-lined Avon River, is complete with bridges, boatsheds and ducks.

We checked into a small hotel and set out to figure out how to find the sanctuary we'd been promised in the visions. "Where do we begin?" I asked as we wandered into a small café for breakfast.

"The vision said we were to come to Christchurch and we would be directed to a safe house, didn't it?" she asked.

I nodded.

"I think we should look for a place to rent. Make our intentions known," Lynne said. "In the New Testament, the apostles were instructed to go into Jerusalem and look for a man with a donkey. In other words, they had to take certain actions to set things into motion."

"I wasn't given any other instructions," I said, still skeptical of the whole thing.

"That's why we play it by ear for now."

We took a table and ordered. "I hope wherever this promised safe house is, it has a suitable kitchen so we can cook." I paused. "So I can cook. I think we should keep you out of the kitchen. I want you to get as much rest as possible."

"I'll be fine, once we can stay in one place," she assured me.

When the server brought our meal, I asked, "Do you know of any homes in the area for rent?"

The girl thought about it. "Not nearby, no," she said, "But I'll ask Sam—my boss. If there's anything to be had, he'll know. Sam knows everybody."

"Thank you, we'd appreciate that," I said. "My wife and I are new to your country."

She smiled. "Welcome."

Lynne ate as though she were starving. "This baby's got an unbelievable appetite," she told me.

I was amused. "Are you sure it's the baby who's so hungry?" I asked.

"Of course." She took a bite. "It has to be."

"Excuse me." A man approached their table. I was immediately defensive, but Lynne put her hand over mine and shook her head. "I couldn't help overhearing you talking to Mindy," the man was saying. "You're looking for a house?"

"Yes, we are," Lynne said.

The man looked to be in his seventies, a smiling, rotund fellow with a broad smile. "Calvin Hawkes," he introduced himself. "I may be able to help you."

"Please, sit down, Mr. Hawkes," Lynne invited him.

He nodded and pulled up a chair. "I've got a place, owned it for over thirty years now. My wife and I lived there until she passed away last year," he said. "Much as we loved the place, I just couldn't stand to live there without her."

"I can understand that," I said, giving my wife's hand a little squeeze.

"It's a big house," Hawkes went on. "I should tell you, though, it's in a bit of a remote area. Don't know if that's something you'd want."

"It sounds perfect for us," I said.

"It's been closed up for almost a year," Hawkes said. "We have caretakers. There's a little cottage on the property. They live there. They haven't had much to do with Mary and me gone, but I kept them on because they were so loyal to us."

"That could be a big help," Lynne said.

"My wife is pregnant," I told Hawkes. "She needs to rest as much as possible."

"Then Gabriel and Rafaela will be a good fit for you," Hawkes said. "Rafaela's a midwife."

Lynne and I exchanged looks. It seemed to us that we had already been directed to our safe house.

———

THE HOUSE WAS ALL we could have hoped for. It was secluded, the closest neighbor at least five miles away. It sat on a hill, surrounded by tall trees. It was a large, rustic house, all flagstone and wood beams, with two working fireplaces. The windows were large, offering a spectacular view of the valley below. The caretakers, a pleasant older couple, were preparing the house when we arrived.

"We've stocked the pantry and refrigerator," Gabriel told me. "Rafaela has laundered all the linens and made the bed in the master suite for you and your wife. If there's anything you require that's not here, just let us know."

"Thanks, mate," I said. "I think all my wife needs right now is a hot meal and a good night's sleep."

"The linen closet is stocked with towels and bed linens," Rafaela said. "And I've prepared dinner. It's in the warmer. I thought you might be too tired to cook after the long drive."

"Thank you," Lynne said. "We appreciate that."

"If that will be all, then, we'll be going."

"What do you make of them?" I asked Lynne after they returned to their cottage.

"They seem very nice," she said. "Why?"

"I suppose I'm a bit paranoid, given all we've been through," I said. "I can't quite trust anyone."

"Mr. Hawkes said they've been here a long time," she said. "It's not as if they just got here ahead of us."

"We don't even really know him," I reminded her.

Before we got into bed that night, I put my handgun on the nightstand. I was taking no chances.

58

LYNNE

When I woke the next morning, I was ravenously hungry. Connor was still asleep. Not wanting to disturb him, I said a silent prayer of thanks that I was not vomiting and went downstairs in search of food.

First, I checked out the large, restaurant-style refrigerator. It was filled with fresh milk, orange juice, fruits and vegetables, lean meats, fish and poultry. There was freshly baked bread in a warmer. The cupboards contained assorted herbal teas, oatmeal and whole-grain cereals.

"Lynne!" Connor called to me from upstairs.

"Down here—in the kitchen," I called back to him.

I could hear him running down the stairs. He gave a heavy sigh of relief when he saw me. "I woke and you weren't there," he said, embracing me from behind.

"I got hungry."

"No vomiting this morning?"

"Not yet, thank God."

"You should have woken me," he scolded me. "I would have come down and fixed a tray for you."

I gave him a disapproving look. "What are you going to do, keep me on a pile of pillows and spoon-feed me until this baby is born?" I wanted to know.

"I might."

"I'm perfectly capable of doing almost everything I did before I was pregnant," I assured him. "Women have been having babies for centuries, you know."

"Maybe—but you're the only one having my baby."

I opened the refrigerator again. "Was this your idea?" I asked.

"I told Hawkes to let the caretakers know I wanted you to have only fresh, healthy food," he admitted.

"And here I am, craving chocolate."

"Chocolate?" He cocked an eyebrow. "Now, I might be persuaded to give you a bit of chocolate."

"Persuaded?"

He took a chocolate bar from a drawer. I licked my lips. "Come to Mama!"

"Not so fast!" he halted me. "What will you give me for it?"

"Give you for it?" I started to laugh. "I'm going to have to bribe you for a candy bar?"

I made a grab for it, but he raised his hand high over his head, putting the chocolate bar just beyond my reach. As I stretched to reach it, his mouth came down on mine. He kissed me, lowering his arm just enough for me to snatch the candy from him. Then he lifted me up so that I was sitting on the counter. I kissed him deeply, then turned my attention to my reward.

He plucked an apple from a basket next to me on the counter, but I took it from him. "Better not eat that. I'm pretty sure in Paradise, apples are off-limits."

59

DARCY

I had no trouble locating Mackenzie's birthplace...but after thirty years, locating people who remembered him and his mother was another story. Finally, I found a former neighbor, an elderly woman named Maddie MacDougal.

"I used to sit with the wee one when Anne was out," the woman remembered. "He was so smart, that one. But so sad."

"Sad?" I asked.

"Anne was a troubled lass," she said, shaking her head. "She tried to take her own life more than once. The wee boy, he loved her so much, but he could not depend on her."

"She was mentally ill?"

She nodded. "Heard voices, that one. Quite unstable."

"But she married well."

"That she did," the woman said, smiling for the first time. "Anne was very beautiful, and that was what Mr. Rhys-Williams wanted. A beautiful young woman for his bed. He pursued her, until she said yes. He married her and took her and the boy to London to live. We never saw them again, but we heard she got pregnant, had another child. Heard the poor lassie died while her baby was still nursing. Most of us thought she finally did herself in."

"Why would she do that, with so much to live for?" I questioned.

"She was sick, that's why." Maddie MacDougal paused. "It was an odd thing about the boy. He had a way of knowing things."

"Knowing things?" I asked.

Maddie nodded. "I had cancer. The doctors held out no hope. I'd not told anyone of it, but the wee boy knew. He climbed up on my lap one day, gave me a big hug and told me he was sorry I was ill, that he didn't want me to die."

"Obviously, you didn't," I said, feeling like an idiot for saying it.

"No, and that's the strange part," Maddie said. "I had cancer. There was no doubt. But after that day, I went back to my doctor, and I had not a trace of it. It was gone. It was a miracle."

"A miracle?"

Maddie nodded. "The wee boy, he was a healer. He had the gift."

A LARGE PART of England and Wales was hit by an earthquake measuring 4.8 on the Richter scale. Buildings shook for up to thirty seconds in parts of Wales, London, Wiltshire, North Yorkshire and West Midlands. Aftershocks were felt later that morning from what was believed to be the United Kingdom's largest quake in ten years. Seismologists from the British Geological Survey said the quake was not connected to temblors occurring in other parts of the world.

Flights in and out of Heathrow Airport were cancelled. Tired and frustrated, I arrived early to get a flight to New York, only to find it was one of many cancelled. I called Ally. *Might as well get the execution over with.*

"Darcy—where are you?" she demanded impatiently. "I've been trying to reach you."

"My cell was dead," I said.

"Is your computer dead as well? Have you even checked your e-mail?"

"Truthfully? No."

"Would you care to explain?"

She was mad, but I knew she would be. I tried to think fast, to come up with a way to soothe the savage beast. "I'm still in London. I'm stuck here," I went on. "The damned earthquake brought everything to a halt. No planes are taking off—at least not yet."

"If you're lucky, the earth will open up and swallow your sorry ass," she snapped. "If not, I'll do the job myself."

"And what, may I ask, is responsible for this delightful mood you're in?" I had to know what I was up against.

"I pulled you from this assignment," she reminded me. "Charlie's dead and you're going to get yourself killed."

"So you do care about me," I chided her.

"Don't press your luck, Darcy."

If I believed in reincarnation, I'd say Ally was a Mafia hit man in another life. "I'll get out of here as soon as I can," I assured her.

"I'll believe it when I see it."

The line went dead. I stared at my cell phone for a moment, fairly certain the call hadn't been interrupted by an act of God.

ON THE FLIGHT back to New York, I found I couldn't stop thinking about what I'd discovered in Britain. He believed an angel was protecting him...

"I had cancer, Mr. Darcy. I was told there was no hope. He hugged me...it was a miracle...."

"He was the most extraordinary genius I have ever encountered...."

They look like ghosts...spirits...angels....

"His mum believed he had been chosen for a divine mission...."

"He believed Christ could be cloned...."

"He genetically manipulated an average racehorse and nothing on four legs could beat him...."

"We're pregnant, Darcy...."

Lynne was pregnant. She was having Mackenzie's baby. The question is, what kind of baby would it be? I wondered.

60

CONNOR

I was worried about Lynne.

In less than five months, she would give birth, and I was no closer to finding a way to deal with Edward and his associates than I had been the day we left Egypt. I had no idea what I was really up against. How could I fight an adversary I couldn't identify?

I walked alone on the hillside near the house. Lynne was inside, resting. She tired more easily now. She would often sleep for an hour or two in the middle of the day. I wondered if I would be able to take her to a hospital when the time came to deliver the baby, or if we would have to deliver the baby here, without the benefit of medical facilities, should they be needed.

Every time I looked at her, every time I felt the baby move, I was overcome by guilt. I couldn't feel joy without being reminded of what I'd done to those other children and their parents. There were kids out there somewhere who might never get to go home again, who might never have a normal life because of me.

Frustrated, I picked up a large rock and threw it.

I was accustomed to being in control of every situation. In my lab,

I'd always been in charge. I knew all the facts. I knew how to proceed. Everyone under me deferred to my judgment.

But now....

"*It's difficult for you, being out of control, is it not?*"

I shook my head. "Not you. Not now."

"*You already know the truth. You know what must be done. You refuse to face it.*"

"Truth?" My laugh was hollow. "You expect me to believe some crazy story about Satanists who think I'm the key to the Apocalypse?"

"*Do you not see they've gone to a great deal of trouble to control you? Even as a child, you were a threat to them. They were willing to kill your mother to prevent you from fulfilling your destiny. They are willing to kill your wife with the same objective in mind.*"

"Why do they want my child?" I asked.

"*They know he will be his father's son. Only by facing the truth can you protect him.*"

"Even if I believed this crap, what difference would it make?" I wanted to know. "How would I be able to deal with them?"

"*Alone, it will be impossible. You must surrender yourself to your Father. He will work his will through you.*"

"My father?"

"*Your Creator.*"

"Right. I'm going to place the fate of my family in the hands of an entity in which I don't believe. I'm many things, but suicidal is not on the short list."

Autumn had arrived in the southern hemisphere, and Lynne was now almost six months pregnant.

To me, she was a marvel. Her hair was long and loose, the way I liked it. Her eyes were bright, her cheeks flushed in the crisp, cool air. She wore baggy shirts and sweaters over maternity pants, and she looked ten years younger. Her body seemed to be blossoming with her advancing pregnancy.

I never thought of pregnant women as being attractive. I'd heard others gush about how beautiful a woman was when she was expecting a child, but I'd always found pregnant women to be somewhat grotesque, with their skinny arms and legs and bulging bellies. But my wife was not like the other pregnant women I'd seen. Her whole body seemed to have ripened, like the women depicted in the masterpieces in Edward's art collection.

My doubts about becoming a father so soon after we married dissolved as I watched her body change and anticipated the arrival of my son. *My son,* I thought. I knew the baby was a boy. It wasn't the wishful thinking of a man who wanted a son to carry on his name. That didn't matter to me at all. I simply knew, the minute the baby began to make his presence known, that this child was a boy.

And once again, I found myself thinking of the children whose lives I had ruined, and the guilt threatened to consume me.

"You're developing some muscle here," Lynne said, stroking my bicep. "All that wood chopping is turning you into a real lumberjack."

We were curled up on the couch in front of the fire I'd built in the massive stone fireplace. A storm had descended upon the valley, and power had been out for the past two hours. We could see flashes of lightning through the windows.

"Is it, now?" I asked, amused.

"Next thing I know, you'll be wearing plaid flannel."

I kissed her. "You know, these muscles didn't come from chopping wood," he told her.

She gave me a puzzled look. "They didn't?"

"No," I said solemnly. "They came from carrying you upstairs every night. You're not exactly a light load these days."

She punched me. "In case you've forgotten, you're responsible for this extra poundage."

"I told you, didn't I?"

"Told me?"

"I told you if you stopped saying no to me, I'd have you pregnant in no time."

"You know, we need to start thinking about names for this little guy," Lynne said, patting her belly affectionately. "After all, if you're right and I am about to pop—"

"A boy's name," I said confidently.

"You're absolutely certain?" she asked, still doubtful.

"You're the one who thinks I'm some kind of mystic," I reminded her.

"Prophet," she corrected.

I shrugged. "What's the difference?"

Lynne shook her head. "For a brainiac, you can be dumb as dirt sometimes," she chided me. "If, by some slim, remote chance this baby is a girl, I was thinking we should name her after your mother."

I was surprised. "Are you sure?"

"I think we could not make a better choice."

She shifted on the couch as I drew her legs across my lap. Now that she was nearing full term, by the end of the day her legs and feet were swollen and painful. Every evening after dinner, I massaged them and gave her a backrub.

"We could name a boy after you," she suggested.

I shook my head. "Every child should have his own name," I maintained. "They should never be named for anyone who's still living."

"All right," she said with a nod. "I've also been thinking of Biblical names—Adam, Jacob, Joshua, Noah, David, Micah, Levi. What do you think?"

"He's a Scot," I said. "He should have a Scot's name."

"He's half American," Lynne reminded me.

"And he's probably going to be born here in New Zealand," I said. "Perhaps we should call him Kiwi?"

She smacked me playfully. "Kiwi?"

"You have a better idea?" I continued to rub her feet.

"I was going to ask you that question, but if Kiwi is the best you can do—"

"Sean," I suggested.

"Sean Mackenzie." She thought about it for a moment. "It has a good sound, but we already have a Sean in the family. My eldest sister's son. Might get confusing."

"Colin, then." I massaged her calves, moving slowly up her legs.

"I love it—but too often Colin is mispronounced 'Colon'," she said.

"That's not a mispronunciation," I told her.

"That's what concerns me."

"What about Daniel?"

She nodded. "Daniel Mackenzie. I like it."

I leaned down to kiss her belly. "Well, wee lad, at least you'll have a name when you make your appearance."

Her mood suddenly changed. "Think they'll let us live once they have him?" she wondered aloud.

I stopped what I was doing and regarded her with equal seriousness. "They're not going to touch him, and we're going to be fine," I promised. "I'll find a way to deal with them."

"You already know how to deal with them, Connor."

I shook my head. "From what you're telling me, that requires a faith I don't have," I said. "A belief I don't have."

"To believe, you have to open your heart. You've already done that."

"I opened my heart to you—not that I had much choice. My heart wanted you from the start."

"Your heart?" She smiled again. "I thought that was another part of you."

"It was both," I insisted. "The problem was that my heart and I had been strangers for so long, I didn't recognize it when it spoke."

The sound of someone entering the house startled both of us. I went for my handgun, pointing it at the movement in the shadows. "Hands up, where I can see them!" I shouted.

The man stepped forward. It was Gabriel, and he was unfazed by the sight of the gun. "You have nothing to be afraid of," he assured us.

I lowered the gun. "Don't startle me like that, old chap," I said, my body sagging with relief.

"I apologize," he said. "Rafaela and I are going to retire for the night and I came to see if there's anything you might need."

I looked at Lynne, who shook her head. I turned back to Gabriel. "No, thank you. We're quite all right."

"Good night, then." He turned and left the house.

I turned back to Lynne. "Sometimes I think he's a bloody ghost," I complained. "He moves so quietly, I never know he's around until he's right here with me."

Lynne rubbed my shoulder. "Maybe he's a ninja," she suggested.

I managed a smile. "Maybe we should put bells on him."

"Orion."

We were walking near the lake, enjoying an unusually pleasant evening. Lynne was now eight months pregnant, and looked as if she might give birth at any moment.

"That's easy," Lynne said. "Everyone knows Orion."

"And I suppose you know all the difficult ones," I responded with mock indignation.

"As a matter of fact, I do," she said, naming several of them. "The Southern Cross, Phoenix, Lepus, Columba, Hydra, Libra."

I smiled. "Ah, a stargazer," I concluded.

"If I weren't an archaeologist, I'd probably be an astronomer," she confessed. "I got my first telescope when I was eight. When I was ten,

I won a science fair competition with a project on space. When I was twelve, I told my parents I wanted to be an astronaut."

"So instead of digging up the remnants of long-dead societies, you could be on the space shuttle," I said.

"Maybe." She paused. "What about you? What would you be if you weren't a geneticist?"

I didn't hesitate. "A porn star."

She rolled her eyes. "Seriously."

"I am serious," I deadpanned. "Don't you think I have the right stuff?"

"I'm not going to answer that," she laughed.

"Actually," I said, "I'd want to be a pianist."

"A musician?" She couldn't hide her surprise. "Concert pianist?"

I shook my head. "Rock star." I started to sing to make my point.

Lynne laughed as I followed her around, singing. "You have a beautiful voice," she told me. "You know, you're going to have to handle the lullaby department when Kiwi arrives. I had to lip-sync in church."

"My mother played the piano," I said. "She learned as a child, and she taught me early on. We had so much fun playing together before she died—before she was killed. Edward had a grand piano at the house in London, but after my mum was gone, it was decided music was a waste of my alleged brilliance, that it was time to put aside the frivolous."

"But you were just a little boy!"

My jaw tensed. "I don't think Edward ever saw me as a child."

"I can't imagine what your life was like."

"I can tell you, beyond a shadow of a doubt, that it wasn't something to be envied."

"Something you can teach Kiwi here," she said.

I put my hand on her belly. "I want our children to savor every moment of their childhood."

I would kill for you, wee one. I already have...

61

DARCY

It was all over the newspapers. Agents of the FBI and Scotland Yard showed up at the corporate offices of Icarus International and at the Belgravia residence of Edward Rhys-Williams early one morning, armed with search warrants. They seized files, computers, and bank and phone records. Edward Rhys-Williams was arrested a week later, charged with fraud and tax evasion. I had yet to convince Ally to put me back on the story, so I was doing this on my own. I was going back to London, determined to find the truth.

I hated the security procedures at JFK Airport, but I knew they were necessary. I removed my shoes and emptied my pockets into the pan the screener offered and allowed myself to be scanned and patted down. I cheated death once, I reminded myself. No point in tempting the Grim Reaper again.

I was on my way back to London, to find the missing pieces to the puzzle that was Connor Mackenzie. Icarus might be a fortress, but the king's in the slammer now. No knights to surround him. No one to keep me away from him.

Ally was furious when I told her where I was going.

"This story's going to be big, Ally," I predicted.

"I don't doubt it," she said. "I've already lost one man because of it."

I grinned. "You're the one who said God didn't want me and the devil wouldn't have me," I reminded her.

I had to see this one through. I owed it to Charlie, and I owed it to Lynne.

———

"I WASN'T sure you'd agree to see me," I said as I seated myself across from Edward Rhys-Williams. A glass partition separated us, and we spoke by telephone.

"Your message said you wished to speak with me about Andrew," Rhys-Williams said. He looked around, as if he thought we were being watched. Of course we were, but he looked frightened by the thought.

"Your stepson is married to my ex-wife," I told him.

He nodded.

I didn't hesitate. "I know the truth," I said.

He looked at me, a blank stare. "What truth is it you think you know?"

"I know he has special—abilities," I told him. "I know he's a genius. I also know he's a healer."

"His mother was mentally ill, Mr. Darcy. She had many strange notions about her son," he said. "Some people actually believed her. You're not the first."

"How do you explain this?" I removed the photographs from the envelope I'd brought along and held them up to the glass.

He turned away.

"Angels," I said. "Your stepson seems to have a pipeline to the Almighty."

"Don't be absurd."

"If it's just bullshit, why is someone killing people left and right to find him?" I challenged.

He was silent for a moment. "This was a setup," he said finally. "I'm no longer useful to them, so they've cut me loose."

"They—who?" I asked.

"I was about to lose everything," he started. "Thirty-five years ago, I was facing bankruptcy. A young man showed up at my door with some big promises. I had nothing to lose, so I took the bait."

"Bait?"

"They wanted to recruit me, so to speak," he remembered. "They were part of some cult. They had some unbelievable ideas. I didn't take it all seriously at the time. I suppose I should have."

"Maybe you'd better explain," I said.

He nodded. "They believed some bizarre prophecy about a prophet who would come to give hope to the world. I don't know all of it, but they believed Andrew to be that prophet, and they wanted to prevent the prophecy from being realized."

"What did they need you for?"

"They had to gain legal custody of him. He was only four years old at the time," he explained. "They gave me success, and in return, all I had to do was marry Andrew's mother so I would become his father legally."

"What happened to his mother?"

"We were married less than two years," he said. "Anne gave birth to my daughter, Sarah. Then she was murdered. I became Andrew's sole guardian. It was in name only."

I wasn't sure I understood.

"They dictated everything—where he would attend school, what he was and was not allowed to do," he said. "They controlled his life until he was of legal age. It had a profoundly negative impact on him."

"If they wanted to prevent fulfillment of the prophecy, why didn't they just kill him?" I asked. "They apparently don't have a problem with taking lives."

"I don't know," he said. "I think they believed they were mocking

God by taking His chosen one, I'm not certain. They went to great expense to try to draw him into their plans."

"Plans?"

"To create a superhuman race," he said. "It all sounds absurd, I know, which is why I didn't take it seriously. They were trying to duplicate what made Andrew special. Then he became a geneticist himself, and they were only too happy to take him into the fold."

"The US authorities have been looking for him," I said.

He nodded. "I know. They arranged for falsified documents to get him out of the US."

"So he became Connor Mackenzie," I concluded.

He nodded again. "He met your ex-wife and wanted to stay with her, and when she became pregnant, they targeted the child."

"Targeted the child?" I asked.

"The prophecy makes a claim regarding subsequent generations," he said. "The child is believed to be even more powerful than his father."

"Do you know what you're saying?" I asked.

"You have the photographs. You've seen for yourself," he said.

"I need names," I said, taking out a small notebook....

62

CAITLIN

"Caitlin, it's Darcy," the caller identified himself.

"Not again—" I started.

"Hold your fire. Are you still on the Mackenzie case?" he asked.

I hesitated. "His name's not Mackenzie," I said finally.

"I know. He's Dr. Andrew Stewart, genius gene manipulator and stepson of Mr. Megabucks," he said with unmasked sarcasm. "Worked side-by-side with Dr. Frankenstein himself, I hear."

I was surprised by how much he already knew about the case. "All right, you have my attention," I said, perching on one corner of my desk. "What else do you know?"

"He's a healer. There's a woman in Scotland who claims he cured her cancer."

"Right. Any more ridiculous claims?" I asked, my patience wearing thin.

"He had a guardian angel."

"What?" I almost laughed.

"When he was five years old, he claimed to have a guardian angel," Darcy said.

"Where did you hear this?" I asked. To Jack, who came in as we were talking, I mouthed "Darcy."

"I strong-armed the head of the private school the Lord of the Geeks attended," Darcy told me. "If you'd stop playing by the book, you might not have to hear this crap from me."

"Anything else?"

"He's epileptic. The kind that sees and hears things."

"Excuse me?"

"He hallucinates. Some people think he's having religious experiences, which is why he and my ex-wife had to fake their deaths."

"And you know all of this—how?" I asked carefully.

"I just had a little chat with his incarcerated daddy."

"And you believe all of this garbage?" I asked.

"I believe something screwy is going on," Darcy said. "I believe a lot of people, including a very good friend of mine, died because of it."

63

DARCY

I boarded the flight back to New York and found my seat. As the plane taxied down the runway and lifted off, I closed my eyes and took a deep breath. *I've done all I can, pal,* I thought. *Charlie, I'll do anything I can for your family. This is my fault. If I hadn't dragged you into this, you'd be here now, griping and whining. I'd give anything if you were. I'd even let you have that damn donut.*

Lynne's disappearance, Charlie's death, the incredible claims made about Connor Mackenzie...I had been forced to take a good, hard look at myself, and I didn't like what I saw. That self-examination that had begun on the roof of my apartment building on the morning of September 11th, 2001 had come to a head when I found Charlie dead in that hotel room.

Duchess was right. I don't know how to love.

My kids had grown up with a self-absorbed, absentee father. No wonder they felt like orphans. No wonder they wanted nothing to do with me.

My wives had never been more than sex partners for me. Cat and I should have worked. We were a match in every way, more than any other woman I've known, I realized. Trouble was, there were three of us in that relationship, too: Cat, me, and my ambition. She couldn't compete.

What was it Duchess said? She could have named my career as a co-respondent in the divorce petition.

I hadn't seen my son in five years, my daughter in four. Sam was an executive at a Madison Avenue advertising agency. Christina was a dancer in a Broadway musical. Did I have grandchildren? I didn't know.

I took out my satellite phone as soon as it was allowed and placed a call. "Sam? It's your father. Don't hang up, please...."

64

CAITLIN

Harry Lambert's call took me by surprise. "Edward Rhys-Williams is dead."

"Dead?" I asked. "How?"

"They claim it was suicide," Lambert told me. "Supposedly, he hanged himself in his cell."

"Supposedly?"

"I talked to a couple of people on the inside," Lambert said. "They say he was found hanging, all right—with his hands tied behind his back."

65

LYNNE

I woke during the night with a vague ache in my lower back. I tossed and turned, unable to find a comfortable position. Finally, I got out of bed and walked around, rubbing my back, trying to remember what I'd eaten in the previous twenty-four hours that could have made me feel so queasy.

Connor turned over and felt my pillow, then raised his head. "What's wrong?" he asked.

"Just a backache," I told him. "I'm okay. Go back to sleep."

"Come back to bed and I'll give you a backrub," he said, patting the mattress.

Desperate for relief, I stretched out beside him, facing away. He massaged my lower back with gentle pressure. I relaxed. "That feels good," I said.

"Does it still hurt?" he asked.

"No. I don't know what you did, but it's gone now."

He bared my shoulder, then kissed the exposed flesh. "I've had it with celibacy," he said.

"Now there's a surprise."

"Think about it," he said, drawing me closer. "When we first met, we lived together under the same roof for six months before you'd let me into your bed. Then I was sidelined by that bloody snake. After you learned the truth about me, you banned me for a month. And now—how long has it been? Almost two months?"

"It'll be another six weeks after the baby comes," I reminded him, turning over to give him a sympathetic kiss.

He groaned loudly.

"Ow! The pain's back," I said.

"Mine too." He put his hand on my swollen belly. "The lad's been quiet, hasn't he?"

"No movement since yesterday," I said. "That's normal just before birth."

He didn't respond. His hand still rested on my abdomen. Pains at regular intervals. The baby was still. The due date was tomorrow. I wanted, needed to go to a hospital now, but it was out of the question.

I was certain I would give birth before the night was over.

66

CONNOR

"Rafaela—I need your help!" I shouted. "My wife is in labor!"

Rafaela ran up the stairs. Lynne was in bed, I was at her side. I had prepared carefully for the birth. The mattress was covered with a vinyl protector and an extra layer of sheets. At the foot of the bed were clean towels, a washbasin and scissors for cutting the umbilical cord. On the nightstand was a large bowl of ice chips, which I was hand feeding to her.

I wiped her face, whispering to her. "It's going to be all right," I told her.

"When did the pains begin?" Rafaela asked.

"About one-thirty, I think," I said. "Her contractions are at five-minute intervals."

"I thought it was just cramps at first," Lynne said as she braced herself for another contraction.

"That's how it normally starts," Rafaela assured her. "Let's see how things are progressing."

She pulled up a stool at the foot of the brass bed and examined Lynne. "She's almost ready. Let's move her down here. She can push her feet against the railing if need be." She looked at the thick socks on Lynne's feet. "You'll have to take those off. When she pushes, they could cause her feet to slip and injure her."

"Just trying to make her comfortable," I said.

Rafaela nodded. "She can have them after this baby has been delivered."

I gently pulled the socks off her feet and put them aside. "If they get cold, I'll massage them for you."

"My water broke," Lynne gasped as they moved her closer to the foot of the bed.

I looked questioningly at Rafaela, who nodded. "It's all right, my love," I told her. "It will be lovely to have a waterbed."

"You're disgusting," Lynne gasped as I fed her more ice chips.

"You didn't find me disgusting the night this wee one was conceived."

She let out an agonized cry. I turned to Rafaela. "Is there nothing we can do to ease her pain?" I asked, empathizing with her pain.

Rafaela shook her head. "You might give her something to bite down on when the pain comes."

"I can think of something—" Lynne was gripped by another contraction. "They're getting stronger."

I checked my watch. "They're two minutes apart."

Rafaela examined Lynne again. "I can see the baby's head. Push, Lynne."

Lynne pressed both feet to the brass rail and let out a scream. I held onto her. "It's almost over, love. Push again."

"I can't!" Lynne wailed.

"Just a few more pushes, Lynne, and you'll be a mother," Rafaela encouraged her.

"Come on!" I urged.

Lynne sat up, her feet pressed hard to the rail, and reached between her legs, gripping the rail with both hands. She arched her back and pushed with as much force as she could summon up. She was gasping, unable to speak. I held her tightly, urging her on. "Once more and he'll be out."

She pushed hard. "That's it," Rafaela said. "It's a boy."

Lynne fell back, panting. The baby started to cry. I kissed her. "You did it, love," I said. "You did it."

"You get to carry the next one," she told him. "Give me my baby."

Rafaela placed the baby, still covered in blood and amniotic fluid, on Lynne's chest, then handed me the scissors. "Cut the umbilical cord," she told me.

I tied the cord in two places, then cut between them. I looked at my wife. She was exhausted but had the most beautiful smile on her face. "Look at him, love. He's perfect. Ten fingers, eleven toes—"

"Eleven?"

"Oh, so that's not a toe, is it?" I laughed. "I think I should take him to be cleaned up."

"How soon shall I nurse him?" Lynne asked.

"Not until tomorrow. He won't be hungry until then," Rafaela said.

"I need a bath."

"Not yet," Rafaela said firmly.

"I'll wash you up as soon as I get this lad ready to lie with his mum," I promised, taking the baby off to the bathroom. I was relieved. Had anything gone wrong, I don't know how we would have dealt with it...

I COULDN'T SLEEP. Trying not to disturb Lynne, I got out of bed and settled into the old rocking chair next to the bassinet. I watched my infant son sleep, overcome by the powerful emotions I felt for the baby.

As if sensing his father's presence, Kiwi opened his eyes and looked up at me. I reached into the bassinet, and the baby immediately seized my finger. I laughed. "Already you have advanced visual and motor skills," I said proudly. "You might not want to be showing off in front of your mum, though. She might get the wrong idea."

The baby tried to suck on my finger. "Ah, I know what you want," I said, lifting him into my arms. "Tell you what. You promise not to wake your mum, and I'll take you to her."

The baby whimpered. "Ssh," I hushed him, putting a finger to his lips. "Your poor mum's exhausted. She doesn't have to be awake for this."

I cradled Kiwi in one arm and dragged the chair over to the bed where Lynne slept. I sat down and with my free hand uncovered her breast. I positioned Kiwi there and he immediately began to nurse. I watched until he was finished, then lifted him to my shoulder, patting him gently until he burped.

"It's a good thing your mum doesn't sleep on her back, isn't it?" I asked as I carried my wee son back to the bassinet. "That could have been a bit difficult to navigate."

I sang to him until he finally went back to sleep, then got back into bed with Lynne. She turned over and snuggled against me. I held her, unable to sleep, lost in thought.

I STOOD outside in the cold night air, oblivious to the chill. I wished I had one of my motorbikes with me. I needed to be alone, to think. I didn't know how to tell Lynne what I was going to do, what I had to do. It would take all the willpower I could summon up to leave her and the baby, but it had to be done. It was my obligation, my responsibility.

I zipped my coat and pulled up the hood. It was starting to snow. I'd have to make sure there was plenty of firewood before I left.

"It will be difficult to leave them, I'm sure."

Startled, I turned. Gabriel stood behind me, watching with concern.

I couldn't hide my surprise. "How did you know—"

"You've been considering it for weeks now," Gabriel said,

checking the firewood. "You know what you're planning is dangerous."

I nodded. "There's no other way."

"You know the truth," Gabriel said, staring up at the star-filled sky. "Why do you continue to resist?"

"Truth?"

"Who you are, why you were sent."

"I see you've heard the rumors," I said, absently pushing a rock with the toe of my shoe. I realized Gabriel must have been eavesdropping, but I no longer worried about it. They had proven themselves to me, and if they were a bit strange, I accepted that. I knew I would have to depend on the couple to look after Lynne and Kiwi until I returned. If I return.

"You can't accept it?"

"I was brought up to believe only in what I could see, prove."

"You were brought up, at least in your early years, by a mother who taught you to believe, to love, to embrace the calling for which you were created," Gabriel contradicted him.

"My mother was a scared, sick woman," I said with deep sadness.

"No, she was not ill at all," Gabriel said. "And her only fear was for you. She simply saw what others could not. People fear what they don't understand. Your mother understood because her heart was open. She could see a miracle because she expected to see one."

"And look what it cost her."

"Ask yourself this: is this the world in which you would like your son to grow up?"

I frowned. "No. I don't want him to be caught in some maniac's crosshairs simply because he's my son."

"Then you already know what must be done."

67

LYNNE

"No. You can't. It's suicide," I protested when Connor told me of his decision over breakfast.

"I either go back to London, or we all remain here in exile indefinitely," Connor said.

"Then we stay here," I said stubbornly. "I need you. Your son needs his father."

"What do you think they would do to me if they did catch me?" he asked, reaching for his coffee. "They won't kill me. I'm too valuable to them, remember?"

"If I'm right, Connor, you're now a threat to them," I insisted, having suddenly lost my appetite. I pushed my plate away. "Once you rejected their plans, you became a liability instead of an asset."

He rolled his eyes. "I'm no prophet," he said with certainty.

"How do you explain the way you healed your mother? And me? And the bird?" I challenged him.

"I don't know, but there has to be a logical explanation."

"And the visions?"

He took a bite. "I'm epileptic. Goes with the territory."

Kiwi slept peacefully in his carrier, oblivious to the tension around him. "He's the reason I have to do this," Connor maintained. "I'll not have him grow up a fugitive."

"I don't think we can avoid that."

"If I go to the proper authorities now, if I deliver the evidence to them, those bastards can be stopped. Kiwi would be safe and all those children could be found and returned to their parents."

"You told me yourself they have people everywhere," I argued. "How do you know you wouldn't be walking into a trap?"

"I don't," he admitted, "but I have to do something."

"Even if you go to a legitimate law enforcement officer, you're a wanted man, Connor," I reminded him. "You'll be arrested. What good will that do anyone?"

"It will make them investigate—and hopefully shut GenTech down."

"Hopefully." I repeated the word, frustrated.

"When we first arrived in Egypt, when we first met," he began, reaching across the table to take my hands in his, "There was a young woman at the airport. When I bumped into her at the baggage carousel, I had a vision. I knew she was carrying explosives. I did nothing, and two hundred people died when the plane she boarded in Cairo exploded as it was about to land in New York. I was a selfish bastard then. You changed me, darlin'. You made me a better man. The man I am now can't sit back and do nothing. I owe this to you and to my son. I owe it to all those children and their parents whose lives I destroyed on my ego trip."

"I'm not going to let you be a sacrificial lamb for my sake!" I shouted, waking the baby. He started to cry, and I took him from the carrier. "It's all right, Kiwi," I said softly, holding him close.

"What about for his sake?" Connor asked. "My mother sacrificed herself for me. Should I do less for my child?"

68

CONNOR

"You should try to get some sleep," I said, stroking Lynne's hair.
"I can't."

We were lying in bed, holding each other in the darkness, neither of us able to think about anything except what the morning would bring. "You've got to take care of yourself," I insisted. "Kiwi needs you."

"He needs his father, too, but that's not stopping you from leaving," Lynne said, tears welling up in her eyes. "You've talked about how it felt, growing up not knowing who your father was. Is that what you want for him?"

"Of course not," I said, my heart breaking. "But if I can't come back, he'll have what I didn't—his mother, who can tell him about me, about how much his daddy loves him."

"Are memories supposed to take the place of having you there?" she wanted to know.

I sighed heavily. "We've been through this already—"

She sat up. "You've told me that your mother wasn't there for you when you needed her, that even though she'd made sacrifices to ensure your future, the money and education she'd obtained for you didn't really matter," Lynne reminded me. "You resented her for it, Connor. Do you want your son to resent you, too?"

"I know you won't let that happen. You know I'm doing what's right."

"I should be proud of you for doing this," she said, "but all I can think about is how hard it is to say goodbye. Connor, please, don't do this."

"If I don't, we spend the rest of our lives in hiding and those kids might never be found," I said. "Lynne, I'm responsible for the suffering of all of those families. It's my fault the kids were abducted. I have an obligation to them, too."

"Yes, you do. But you don't have an obligation to put your life on the line. Mail it to them," she urged me. "Put it in a mailer and send it to them."

"I considered that," I said. "I can't be certain it will be accepted as credible if I don't go. There's so much there the lay person couldn't begin to understand."

"I'm not proud of myself for saying this, but all I care about is keeping you here with us," she admitted. "I want our son to have his father. I want to have my husband with me like this every night."

"One day, when this is all over—"

"It's never going to be over!" she snapped. "They'll kill you, Connor! If you go back there, you're as good as dead."

I sat up and held her close, wishing there was something I could say or do to comfort her, to make her see that I wouldn't be able to live with myself if I didn't go.

It was snowing the morning I left. I looked at Lynne and knew she was barely holding it together. Her eyes were red from crying, her face puffy. She held Kiwi, heavily bundled, in her arms, watching silently as I put my bags into the trunk of the car. Gabriel was already in the driver's seat, starting the engine. I closed the trunk lid and went to Lynne.

She made a last-ditch attempt to stop me. "Please don't go," she said softly.

"You're the one who's always urged me to answer the call," I reminded her.

"You never believed," she said. "Why now?"

"I want to," I admitted. "I want redemption."

"I want you alive," she said.

"I want our son to be proud of his father."

"You don't have to be dead for that."

"I'm planning to come back here very much alive," I told her.

"They'll find you if you leave here."

"Not if I'm careful." I turned the blanket back to kiss my wee laddie's face, then kissed Lynne. "I love you," I said softly.

She nodded. "I love you, too."

I finally broke away from her and got into the car with Gabriel. "Are you having second thoughts?" Gabriel asked, starting the engine.

"Oh, yeah," I confessed. "Second, third, fourth."

"You know what you have to do."

"Only too well," I said as we drove away. I looked at the rear-view mirror. Lynne had broken down. Rafaela was taking the baby from her. I could tell she was crying uncontrollably, and my own tears came freely.

"So, Gabe—am I ever going to see them again?" I asked, finally regaining my composure.

"Only God knows," Gabriel answered honestly.

69

LYNNE

"Dinner is ready," Rafaela said as she entered the master bedroom.

I sat in the old rocker by the window, nursing the baby. "I'm not hungry," I said.

"You have to eat," Rafaela reprimanded me. "You're nursing. Your child needs the proper nourishment."

I nodded. I had to think of him. "Could you bring it up? Would you mind?" I asked. "Kiwi needs me."

Rafaela gave me a disapproving look. "I suspect you need him more than he needs you right now," she said. "But you may have your dinner alone, if that's what you want."

As Rafaela started to leave the room, I said, "It's not fair, you know."

"It's up to God to decide what's fair and what is not," Rafaela disagreed.

"God wanted us to be together, and now He doesn't," I said, unable to contain my bitterness. "Where's the fairness in that?"

Rafaela sat on the foot of the bed. "You've known for months now who you married," she pointed out. "You know of his calling. You know who we are and why we came."

"I thought you came to protect us." I lifted the baby to my shoulder and burped him, then kissed his forehead.

"Knowing his destiny, you had to know a time would come when he would have to leave you, that he would have to risk his life to fulfill his purpose," Rafaela said.

"And what's my purpose?" I wanted to know. "To be alone? I've lost my family, my colleagues, and now my husband."

"Yours is to love him, to teach him to love," Rafaela said patiently. "To bear his child."

I shook my head. "I can't do this. I'm not strong enough," I said, fighting tears.

"Then you must lean on the Father. You already know this," she said. "And you are definitely not alone. You know this as well. You have a beautiful son, Lynne. A living part of the man you love. Remember that, at least, and you'll find a way to keep going."

70

CONNOR

I tried to sleep during the long flight to the UK, but found it impossible. I took my phone from my pocket. There were half a dozen text messages from Lynne:

PLEASE COME HOME.

GET THE NEXT FLIGHT BACK HERE AND WE'LL BE WAITING.

PLEASE DON'T DO THIS, CONNOR.

YOUR SON NEEDS HIS DADDY.

PLEASE, CONNOR. COME BACK TO US.

. . .

I LOVE YOU. WE LOVE YOU.

I'D LOST track of how many times I considered calling her, just to hear her voice one more time. I always managed to stop myself just short of making the call, knowing it would only take one more plea from her to make me turn around and go back.

It would be so easy to get off at the layover in Athens and catch a flight back to Christchurch, to go back to everything in this world that really mattered to me. I wanted to be with my wife and son, even if it meant living in exile for the rest of our lives. I wanted to see my son grow up. I wanted the life Edward and Dante had stolen from me.

"You've always known the truth." It was my mother's voice. "I told you from the beginning, my darling, that you came to the world for a special purpose. God gave you to me, and I gave you back to Him."

"What about Lynne? What about my son? What happens to them now?"

"God will protect them."

Once again, I wished I could believe....

71

CAITLIN

I was roused from sleep by the ringing telephone. I rolled over, groaning, and snatched the receiver off its cradle. "Hullo?" I mumbled as I pressed it to my ear, upside down at first.

"Blondie, it's me."

"Jack?" I was instantly alert. "What time is it?"

"You don't want to know." He paused. "Harry Lambert's dead."

I sat up in bed. "How?"

"Would you believe suicide?"

"No." I pushed my hair away from my face. "Would you?"

"He was found at his place, supposedly having ODd on barbiturates and booze," Jack said.

"Harry didn't drink," I remembered. "He had an ulcer."

"He also had some kind of lead on the GenTech case."

"Meet me at Reagan National," I said.

"I'm already on my way."

"The official story is that Rhys-Williams also committed suicide," I told Jack when we picked up the rental vehicle at the airport in London. "However, one officer I spoke with told me, strictly off the record, that he was the one who found the body. And his hands were indeed tied behind his back."

Jack grinned. "Hmm...think foul play was involved?"

"According to Scotland Yard, Andrew Stewart was spotted at a hotel in Kensington," I said as I buckled my seatbelt. "You talk to the police about Rhys-Williams. I'll see what I can find out about Stewart."

72

CONNOR

I checked into a hotel upon my arrival. I made some calls—I wasn't going to simply surrender myself to the authorities without legal counsel. I scheduled an appointment with a solicitor who came highly recommended.

I tried to visualize every possible scenario. *Best case scenario, I get a light sentence. Worst case, Dante and his people get to me first and I'm a dead man. Worst case, those kids are never found and my own son grows up without a father.*

Like I did.

I had to see Sarah, but I'd have to be careful. She was probably being watched. I dressed in jeans and a hooded jacket, concealing my face, and went to the house in Belgravia where we'd grown up after making sure she was now living there.

She opened the door and looked at me as though she'd seen a ghost. "Andrew!" she gasped, hugging me tightly. "Father told me you were dead!"

"He knew full well I wasn't," I said, withdrawing from her embrace slowly.

"You know—"

"That he's dead? Yes, I know." I removed my jacket and followed her into the drawing room. "Probably at the hand of one of his own business partners."

"Nicholas Dante," she said.

I couldn't hide my surprise. "You know him?"

"I've met him. He makes me uncomfortable." She paused. "Tea?"

I shook my head. "Not now, Princess," I told her. Then I told her everything...the whole, bizarre story...

UNABLE TO SLEEP, I phoned Lynne when I returned to the hotel. Sarah had wanted me to stay with her, but I knew it wouldn't be safe for either of us. Dante's goons would be watching her. It was eight hours later in New Zealand, and I was sure Lynne would be up with the baby. "Edward's dead," I told her, giving her details of the arrest. "Sarah says the official story is suicide, but I don't believe it."

This did nothing to put her at ease. "Come home," Lynne pleaded. "Don't let them kill you, too."

"I can't," I said, considering it even as I said the words. "I have to do this. I'm the only one who can. I have the proof, Lynne. I can show them where the bodies are buried—literally and figuratively. I may be able to make a deal for myself. I help them, they reduce my penalty."

"If you live that long," my wife said, unconvinced.

As I EMERGED from the hotel the next morning, I was approached by an attractive blonde woman moving toward me with determination. "Dr. Andrew Stewart?" she asked.

I shook my head. "I think you've got me confused with someone else." I kept walking.

She followed. "Okay, let's try Connor Mackenzie," she called after me. "Does that name work for you?"

I stopped in my tracks and turned back to her. She held up her FBI badge and official ID. "Caitlin Hammond, US Federal Bureau of Investigation," she identified herself.

"Am I under arrest?" I asked. The wind was blowing. It was starting to rain.

"Not at this time," she answered, putting away her identification, "but I do have some questions for you."

"About?" I opened my umbrella. She followed suit.

"A lot of missing kids. Your stepfather's business interests. A man named Julian Marshall. Take your pick." The wind threatened our umbrellas, jerking them about. Hers turned inside out. I grabbed it and made the necessary adjustment to fix it for her.

"Dr. Stewart?"

"Not here," I said, scanning the faces on the street, wondering if any of them worked for Dante.

"Where would you suggest we do it, then?"

I looked around. There was a church down the street. It would be safe—or so I hoped. "There," I said.

She clearly found the suggestion baffling, but didn't object. "All right. Let's go."

We crossed against the light and went inside. The sanctuary was deserted. I breathed a sigh of relief. We weren't likely to encounter any of Dante's people here. I closed my umbrella.

"Looks like God has trouble getting his wayward children to visit," Caitlin observed as she closed her folding umbrella and looked for a place to put it. Water dripped from it onto the floor. I took both umbrellas and placed them on a coat rack.

"Here," I said, gesturing toward one of the pews. Caitlin sat down, and I slid in next to her.

"Why here?" she asked, still curious. A loud clap of thunder startled her. The rain was pouring now, pounding the church's roof.

I was oblivious to it. "We ran the risk of being watched out there," I said.

She gave me a wry smile. "Paranoid, Dr. Stewart?"

"Not at all. I know what I'm up against, that's all."

"And what would that be?"

I inhaled. "A group of powerful, connected people who want something I won't give them."

"Not to mention possible criminal prosecution."

"The least of my worries, I assure you."

"You could have come to the authorities," she suggested.

"That was my intention."

"A little late, don't you think?"

I frowned. "It's been my experience that a badge doesn't automatically ensure trustworthiness," I said. "The cartel has far too many of their own in positions of authority on their extensive payroll."

"Point taken," she conceded.

"This might surprise you, but you and I want the same thing, Agent Hammond," I said then. "You want to find all those missing kids. So do I."

"I want to find them, yes, but I also want to bring those responsible to justice," she said.

"So do I."

"You were involved." It was a statement, not a question.

"I was involved in experiments that were illegal," I told her, "but I was not involved in the abduction of those children."

"And why should I believe you?" she challenged.

"Because I've been in hiding for the past several months. Because the people who are responsible want me dead. Because you would never have found me if I had not chosen to come back," I pointed out. "Because I have the proof to bring the guilty ones down. What I don't yet have is the location of those children."

"So even if we get your associates," she began, "we may not ever find those kids—dead or alive."

I nodded. "These people have resources beyond anything you can imagine. By the time you could get inside their offices, they would have gotten wind of your plans and the proof you need would have evaporated into thin air."

"You make them sound like the Mafia," she said, mildly amused.

"They're worse," I told her. "They have unlimited connections and resources. They believe they get it directly from Old Nick himself."

"Old Nick?" she asked.

"In Britain, Old Nick is a nickname for Lucifer," I explained.

"Lucifer?" She laughed mirthlessly. "You expect me to believe—"

"It doesn't matter what you or I believe, Agent Hammond," I told her. "The fact that they believe it makes them dangerous. They're both capable and willing to do things normal human beings would be morally and psychologically incapable of doing."

She looked at me, surprised. "You're serious."

"I've known for months how dangerous they are," I confided. I told her everything I knew. "My wife believes in God, Agent Hammond. She believes that He gives us what we need when we need it and sees us through the dark times. She would say you and I crossed paths as we did so that we could find those kids."

"What about you?" Caitlin asked. "Do you believe?"

"I don't know," I said truthfully.

"Suppose I were to believe all this bullshit," she started. "What are you suggesting we do—together?"

I thought about it and made an impulsive decision. "Put a wire on me. I'll confront Nicholas Dante. I'll make him tell me."

She took a few minutes to process all of it. Then she said, "You do realize if everything you're telling me is true—and I'm still not totally convinced—you would be risking your life in doing this."

"They killed my mother," I said. "They've forced me to leave my wife and child in order to keep them safe. The advantage of a man who has nothing left to lose is that he doesn't mind dying for the sake of revenge."

73

LYNNE

I wished I knew what was happening in London.

I stood at the front door, looking out across the valley. In my mind, I could see him chopping wood...meditating on the stump...waving to me to join him.

Will I ever see him again? I wondered.

"You haven't been sleeping."

I turned. Rafaela stood in the doorway, a look of disapproval on her face. "I can't sleep when he's not there with me," I said.

"You slept without him for forty years," Rafaela reminded me.

I didn't smile. "I didn't know him then," I said. "I didn't love him."

"You knew him," Rafaela disagreed.

I looked at her, confused.

"You knew him before either of you came into this world. Your souls have been entwined from the beginning of time."

As she walked away, I sank onto the bed. There was a time I would have believed what Rafaela had just told me without question. Now, I doubted. I was no longer sure of anything.

I wanted to believe again. I wanted my faith to be restored. I wanted my son to grow up with faith, with hope. I wanted him to grow up with his father.

I bowed my head and began in a low voice: "Dear Father, I have doubts. I need my faith restored...."

74

CONNOR

I returned to my hotel room alone. I removed the two flash drives from their case, then took two envelopes from the drawer. I addressed one to Sarah, one to Caitlin Hammond. I put one flash drive in each, along with a brief letter to my sister. Then I phoned a courier service and had the envelope for Sarah picked up for delivery the next day. *In the event anything goes wrong,* I thought.

I phoned Lynne. "This is it, darlin'," I told her, explaining what the FBI agent and I had decided to do.

"You can't be serious," Lynne objected. "This is suicide, Connor."

"It's the only way I can see to locate those missing kids," I said.

"What about your own son?" she wanted to know.

I wished I could make her understand. "I love you."

"I love you. We love you," she said. I could tell she was crying. I hated what I'd done to my once strong, fearless wife. She was no longer that woman, and it was my fault.

I left the hotel and walked to my meeting with Caitlin Hammond, hoping I could trust her. I knew only too well that nothing, no one was what they appeared to be. I could only trust my own instincts and hope they wouldn't let me down.

There are no other options, I thought.

I was vigilant, aware of everyone and everything around me as I walked. If Dante knew I had returned to London—and I was almost certain he did—he would have his goons looking for me.

I scrutinized every face I encountered on the street, always wondering, *is he one of them?*

"Excuse me, sir."

I looked at the old woman approaching me. "Can I help you?" I asked.

"I do hope so," she said with a smile that revealed two missing teeth. "I seem to have dropped my keys and I can't find them."

"Where?" I asked.

"There." She pointed.

I knew I should keep going. I didn't want to be late for my meeting with the Americans. But I looked at the old woman, and I felt for her. "All right," I said, following her.

I located the missing keys quickly. "Here you are," I told her, extending my hand.

"Thank you so much." She grabbed my hand and I felt a sharp prick. And after that, darkness....

75

CAITLIN

"What are the odds of this working?" Jack asked.

I shook my head. "Somewhere between slim and none," I admitted. "But as far as I can see, this is all we've got."

"You think this cartel was behind Harry's death?"

I nodded.

"Think Stewart will show?"

"Yeah. He'll be here," I said confidently.

"Still think he's coming?" Jack asked hours later.

I was seething. I'd been so sure of his sincerity. I had trusted him and he'd bailed on me. "If he ever shows his face on US soil, I'll be waiting," I said with unmasked contempt.

76

CONNOR

I opened my eyes. My head was splitting and my mouth felt like it was stuffed with cotton. I was disoriented. I tried to talk, but the words wouldn't come. My limbs felt heavy, too heavy to move.

"I'm truly disappointed in you, Andrew."

Nicholas Dante. Edward's second in command. I couldn't see him, but I could hear his voice. He was close by. Very close.

"I'm surprised you're out and about in the light of day, Nicholas," I said. "I thought you'd be in your box, waiting for the sun to go down."

"For someone as brilliant as yourself, you didn't handle this well at all," Dante gloated.

I finally found my voice. "What did you do to me?" I asked.

"I saved your life," Dante said, coming into view, walking around me, circling me like a predator about to seize his prey. "You collapsed on the street. Don't you remember?"

"I remember a sting. A tranquilizer, I presume. It was one of your people, no doubt."

"As a matter of fact, it was."

"Where are they, Nicholas?" I demanded. "What did you do with the children?"

"Why do you care?" Dante's voice was cold. "You created the freaks. Why would you want to be exposed?"

I inhaled sharply. "How bad?"

"Excuse me?"

"The accelerated maturation. How severe is it?"

"Their chronological ages, as you know, are seven to eight," Dante said. "Their physical age is now ten to twelve. At the current rate of development, they will reach full maturity within nine months."

"They're still alive," I concluded from Dante's use of the present tense.

"For now."

"They're children, Nicholas!" I protested the unspoken threat. "You can't just dispose of them as if they were yesterday's rubbish!"

Dante's smile was malevolent. "Becoming a father has changed you, Andrew," he observed. "It's made you soft. Almost human, I think."

"My child is dead," I said. "Because of your hired goons, we couldn't get my wife the proper medical care. There were complications. She died in childbirth."

Dante leaned over me so that our faces were only inches apart. "I don't believe you. We will find them, Andrew. With or without your cooperation, we will find them."

"You have me. Is that no longer enough?" I asked, frustrated.

"No, as a matter of fact it's not."

77

CAITLIN

"This is Sarah Stewart," the woman's voice on the phone identified herself. "I'm Andrew's sister. I know my brother met with you and that you were supposed to meet again. I have something I believe he gave me for safekeeping. Something I know he would want me to turn over to you..."

"My brother sent this to me by courier just before he disappeared," Sarah Stewart said as she took the flash drive from her bag. She passed it across the desk to Jack, who immediately inserted it into the USB port on his laptop.

"Why have you come to us, Ms. Stewart—Ms. Rhys-Williams—" I asked.

"It's Stewart now," Sarah said.

"Why not take it to Scotland Yard?" I asked.

"You met with my brother, did you not?" Sarah asked.

"Yes," I said, nodding slowly. "He had security concerns."

Sarah nodded. "He told me in the event of his death, I should get this to you." She gave me the letter that had accompanied the drive.

I raised an eyebrow. "You believe he's dead?"

"I believe *something* has happened to him," she admitted. "He's dealing with a dangerous man."

"And you know this—how?"

"They killed my father." she said with certainty. "They manipulated him and used him. When he was no longer of use to them, they disposed of him. The man behind all of this is, I am fairly certain, Nicholas Dante."

Jack and I exchanged looks. "Dante," I repeated.

"Then you know of him."

"His name has come up in the course of our investigation," I admitted.

Jack opened the files on the flash drive. "Bingo."

I turned to look at him. "What is it?"

"Joseph Sadowski's missing files."

78

LYNNE

Something was very wrong.
    I could feel it. The vague sense of foreboding wasn't due to the fact that he had not called again. I knew that might not be possible. No, what I was feeling came from another place, deep within my soul.

You knew him before either of you came into this world. Your souls were entwined before time began.

Rafaela's words echoed through my thoughts now. Is it possible? I wondered.

It would have been so easy to accept those words a year ago, when my faith had not been so severely tested.

You chose him to be your messenger, I thought angrily. *Will You let it end like this? You told me not to be afraid to love him—but You didn't tell me I'd lose him so soon. Why?*

I had to know if he was all right. I went to the drawer and got the last of the prepaid phones we'd bought when we arrived in New Zealand, hoping I could get a signal in this remote area. Connor had told me they couln't be traced,. If he'd been arrested, would I have any way of knowing? If he didn't answer his phone, would anyone answer? If not, I'd know nothing, no more than I did now.

I punched in his satellite number. It rang...and rang...and rang...and rang. Then it stopped ringing, and a man's voice came on the line. Not Connor's.

"Hello, Mrs. Mackenzie. I've been waiting for your call."

I dropped the phone.

79

CONNOR

"That was your wife, Andrew." Dante tossed my satellite phone aside and leaned back in his chair. "I'm sure she misses you. As soon as we trace that call, she'll be able to join you."

"You're mistaken. My wife is dead."

"She sounded very much alive just now," Dante said.

I didn't respond. I maintained an emotionless expression, silently hoping Lynne had used one of the throwaway phones.

If not, it was only a matter of time.

80

LYNNE

They've got him.

I was frantic. I didn't know what to do, who to call. Darcy? No...Darcy had never understood. I couldn't tell him the truth. He'd never believe it.

Trust no one.

Connor wanted me to stay here, with the baby. He wanted to know we would be safe. Yes, I promised him I wouldn't leave...but now I wanted to go to London, to do whatever I could to help my husband.

The authorities? Interpol? Scotland Yard? The FBI? Connor said Edward had told him all of those agencies had been infiltrated. Trust no one.

I scanned all the news stories on the internet. *Nothing*, I thought anxiously. *If he were dead, wouldn't someone have found the body?*

No. They wanted his DNA. They would keep his body. Dear God, they would cut him up like a chunk of meat.

I wished Tim were here. I could trust him. I could call him for anything and he would have been there for me. If only I could call him.

NORMA BEISHIR & COLLIN BEISHIR

God help me. Tell me what to do...

81

CAITLIN

Sarah Stewart was determined to find her brother. She convinced Jack and me to go with her to the hotel where he'd been staying. We went to the front desk. "I'd like to speak with the manager, please," she told the front desk clerk.

He nodded. "One moment, miss."

The manager appeared almost immediately. "Aaron Rudd. May I be of assistance?" he asked.

"I'm Sarah Stewart," she introduced herself.

His eyes lit with recognition. "Of course, Ms. Stewart," he said. "I see you on the telly often."

"My brother was staying at this hotel." She showed him a photograph of Connor. "He was most likely not using his real name, as he was in some legal difficulty. Perhaps you recognize him?"

He studied the photo for a moment, then showed it to the clerk. "That's Mr. Ryan, sir," the clerk said. "He's in 407. He hasn't collected his messages in days, however."

Rudd pulled up his file on the computer, then turned back to us. "His things are still in his room. He paid by credit card and thus far he has not checked out, so..."

"Could I have the key, please?"

"I don't know..."

"My brother is *missing*, Mr. Rudd," Sarah said. "There may be something in his room to help me in finding him. Would you have him meet with a bad end to protect your foolish rules?"

"No," he stammered, "but—"

She extended her hand. "The key, Mr. Rudd."

"I can't."

"Shall I do a story on this for my network?" she threatened.

He hesitated. "I'll take you up."

"I would appreciate that."

We didn't speak in the elevator. He unlocked the door and let us in, then looked on like a silent sentinel while Sarah searched everything. Nothing.

"Thank you," she told Mr. Rudd as we walked out.

Once we were in the elevator again, she took out her mobile phone and called what I presume was a former colleague, switching to speaker mode. "Sidney—are you still the best hacker in the United Kingdom?" she asked, turning on the charm.

"I ain't in prison, am I?" asked the male voice on the other end of the line.

"Might I hire you?"

"Is it illegal?"

"Possibly, but you could help me save a man's life," she told him.

"Count me in."

She ended the call and turned to Jack and me. "If Sidney can't hack the files, nobody can."

"Babe, this is the like trying to break into the system at MI-6," Sidney told Sarah an hour later.

"You have nothing for us?" she asked, frustrated. "Time could be running out for Andrew."

"Not yet."

"Keep trying," she instructed him.

"You're going back to the US?" Sarah asked incredulously. "But my brother is still out there somewhere!"

I tried to be understanding, but the likelihood of finding Andrew Stewart alive grew less likely every day. "Your brother is most likely dead, Ms. Stewart," I told her. "It's been weeks, and there's no trace of him. This isn't even our jurisdiction. We've been ordered to return home."

"I'm not giving up," she said stubbornly. "Somehow, I will find him."

82

CONNOR

I felt like a caged animal.

I knew where I was. I was at the GenTech research facility outside London. I'd been involved in its design. I knew it was state-of-the-art, an impregnable fortress. There were seven stories, three of which were underground. Security was tight. The security fence was concealed by a high hedge, and armed guards were posted at the gates and patrolled the premises continually. There was no way I would be able to escape.

I knew I was being held prisoner on the lowest level. My twelve-by-fifteen room was much like a jail cell, windowless with drab gray concrete block walls, and only the barest minimum of furnishings. I had a bed, a table, and a tiny bathroom. The door was locked from the outside, with an opening large enough to accommodate meal trays.

"I see you've settled in."

I turned as Dante entered the cell. I lunged at my jailer, but was immediately shoved away from the door by a man I recognized: the giant Lynne and I had encountered in Hong Kong. I fell backward, hitting the bureau, then slumping to the floor.

"Why don't you go ahead and kill me, Nicholas?" I asked, scrambling to my feet. "Get it over with."

"In time, I might," Dante said calmly, "but not until I'm convinced you are of no further use to us."

I dropped onto the bed. "You don't trust me. Why would that change?"

"If we keep you—detained—long enough, we will break you," Dante reasoned. "Then we may be able to make use of your considerable assets. If not, at least your DNA will be of value to us."

I looked at him. "You're planning to clone me?"

Dante's smile was cold. "We already have."

83

LYNNE

It was September, almost spring in New Zealand. I took Kiwi for long walks, talking to him, telling him about his father. He was three months old now, and I couldn't look at him without thinking of Connor. Our son was a constant reminder of what I'd lost. I wondered what I would do if Connor never returned.

The answer was simple: I couldn't accept that possibility.

That was when I decided to keep a journal. I would videotape Kiwi's first steps, his first words. I'd write down my thoughts and memories. I'd document everything so that when Connor came back to us—and I had to believe he would—he would not have missed a moment of his son's life.

When he comes home. Not if. When.

HE'S DEFINITELY *his father's son, Connor,* I wrote. *He looks exactly like you. I look into his tiny face and I see you. It breaks my heart. If I didn't have Kiwi, I might crawl into bed and never get up.*

He's saying words already. Six months old and he's talking! His first word was "Daddy." It made me cry. He needs you. I need you. Please come home to us....

———

CONNOR, *where are you? Are you still alive somewhere?*

It was a beautiful day. The sun was shining. Not a cloud in the sky. I wondered if I'd ever get used to the difference in seasons in the southern hemisphere.

You should be here with us, I thought angrily. *You should be celebrating your son's first Christmas with him.*

Why did you have to do this?

84

CONNOR

I was not allowed to see a TV or listen to a radio. I was not given any newspapers, magazines or books, and I had no computer. I had only my own thoughts with which to occupy myself for hours on end. I knew I'd been there at least four months.

My moods fluctuated wildly. I went from anger to depression to mania to despair in the course of a day. I wanted to kill. I wanted to die. And I wanted to live, to return to my family.

But I knew there was little chance of that happening. It would take something in which I did not believe. It would take a miracle.

I raged at God. "I'm your prophet, am I? What good am I to you here?" I demanded. "If I were your prophet, you would not allow me to be imprisoned this way. How could I possibly be of use to you here?"

And the seizures began. Without my meds, I had no idea what to expect. *You have no power on your own, my child. This is a battle you cannot win alone. If you are to survive, you must accept this truth and surrender yourself to your Father....*

I WAS SITTING on the bed when Dante entered the cell, the door locking behind him. I didn't look up. I sat there, elbows resting on my thighs, my head in my hands, staring down at the floor. Ignoring him. The bloody bastard.

"Where are the children, Nicholas?" I asked after a long, deliberate silence. "Where are you keeping them?"

Dante took a seat at the table. "They're here, of course," he said.

I looked up. "Here? You're holding them here?" I asked.

"Where else would I take them?"

"They're children, Nicholas," I said.

"Not for long," Dante said. "Your growth hormone formula is out of control, Andrew. They're maturing far too quickly."

"Let them go. Send them back to their parents." I pounded my fist on the mattress, wishing I could do the same to Dante's face.

"Do you really think their parents will want them if they see them?" Dante was amused by my demand. "They'll reject them as soon as they realize their sweet little boys and girls are growing up far too fast. Is this what you wish for these children? Rejection?"

"You don't care about them," I said.

"You're right. I don't." Dante leaned toward me. "But I do care about *your* child."

"My child is dead."

"How long will you continue to lie to me?" Dante asked, seething beneath the surface.

I refused to look at him. "My wife and son are dead," I repeated.

I HEARD someone say it was Christmas.

It was just another day to me, but I remembered how important it was to Lynne. She probably had a tree. She probably hung stockings by the fireplace and had gifts for our son. I wish I could see them now. I wish I could hold them both....

JANUARY...ANOTHER month had passed. The only thing that kept me going was the thought of my wife and son, of finding a means of escape, of returning to them. I had no photographs of them—but their images in my mind were more detailed than any photograph could ever have been. Every day, I visualized myself with my family—playing with my son, making love with my wife.

Kiwi took his first steps. He was a bit unsteady at first, but a brave lad. Two or three steps, and then he fell into his daddy's arms.

Lynne watched while I sang my baby to sleep. Maybe we'll start trying to make him a brother or sister soon.

He'll start school soon. I'll take him to school and pick him up after. Maybe we'll stop for ice cream. His mum's been having cravings again.

And then reality destroyed those beautiful images....

I WISHED I WERE DEAD.

I would have taken my own life if I'd had the means to do so. I was slowly losing my grip on my own sanity. Even the voices had deserted me. I'd never felt more alone.

Not since they killed my mum, I thought.

I thought about my wife and son, and that galvanized me. *Nicholas is hell bent on finding them,* I thought. *If he does, he'll kill Lynne and take our son. My Kiwi will not grow up the way I did.*

I have to get out of here before he locates them....

85

LYNNE

I watched Kiwi take his first steps through the video recorder and wished Connor were there to share the moment with me.

Kiwi is nine months old. He took his first steps today, Connor. He's your kid, all right. He wants to run before he's mastered walking. He's impatient, doesn't want to wait for anything.

Kiwi was at my side, trying to climb into my lap. I offered him a bottle to placate him long enough for me to finish the journal entry. "No!" he responded angrily, slamming the bottle to the floor.

He's like you in every way, I wrote. *I can't even think about what he's going to be like in a few years. How am I supposed to raise this wild child alone?*

And the tears came....

86

CONNOR

I lay on the bed, fingering the St. Jude medallion Lynne had given me. *You say you're a lost cause, I say you're not...nothing's ever hopeless.*

"Interesting medallion. Religious symbol, isn't it?"

I looked up as Dante entered the cell. "Have a closer look, Nicholas," I invited with sarcasm. "Touch it. Let it burn your miserable flesh."

"You're still a smartass, aren't you?"

"Why did you let me keep this?" I asked.

"As a reminder. Every time you look at it, you think of them, don't you?"

"You bastard."

Dante pulled up a chair and sat facing me. "Make this easy on yourself. If you tell us where they are, you can have your wife with you in here," he offered. "Wouldn't that be more pleasant than being here alone?"

"I would never have allowed you to turn my son into a lab rat," I responded.

Dante looked around the cell. "It would appear you don't even have control of your own circumstances," he said, smiling. "I don't believe you can stop me."

———

I LAY IN THE DARKNESS, thinking, remembering....

I was in living Boston, working with Sadowski, when the call came from Edward. *"You have to return to London immediately,"* he told me. *"The FDA is coming after Joseph. A government site review committee will come to GenTech tomorrow morning. They will order the laboratory closed."*

"We've already destroyed the files," I told him.

"You must not be there when the committee arrives," Edward insisted. "A courier will deliver a package to you tonight. In it you will find new documentation—passport, driver's license, credit cards, everything you will need. Tomorrow morning, you will meet the Icarus jet at Logan Airport and it will bring you back to London. You can continue your work here."

"Until they follow the trail to the parent company," I predicted.

"We'll deal with that when—if—it happens."

It never happened. I knew why. Nicholas and his people had managed to prevent it.

How?

———

As SOON AS the lights went out, the ghosts arrived....

"This is a good school, Andrew. It's for gifted children like you." The voice belonged to Dr. Fairfield. "You'll be able to interact with other children like yourself."

"There are no other children like him."

The voice had not been Edward's. It was Nicholas Dante who had delivered me to the Highgate Institute...

WITH THE DARKNESS CAME PEACE. I welcomed the night, welcomed a respite from the beatings, the humiliation of the experimentation.

Today, they had drawn blood. They had taken skin samples from various parts of my body. And they'd triggered a memory....

"Joseph, I've found the solution," I said, barely able to contain my enthusiasm. "The growth hormones are working. The new clones are developing on schedule."

"It's too late." Sadowski looked crestfallen. "The FDA is onto us, Andrew. They are about to shut us down."

I remembered helping Sadowski destroy the files. We'd gone to Sadowski's home and built a fire in the fireplace, tossing document after document onto the blazing fire, eliminating the proof of all we had accomplished.

I took a deep breath. I'd taken the two flash drives with me when I was summoned back to London. The drives I'd given to Sarah and to Caitlin Hammond. The files on those drives had revealed an unbelievable truth to me weeks after Sadowski's sudden death....

THEY'D DRUGGED ME. Not for the first time.

I saw the needle marks on my arm, and I knew. What did they give me? Did they finally make me give away Lynne's whereabouts?

I tried to move, but I was in restraints. I'd been in my cell when the goon came for me. I had only a vague memory of the big man hitting me, of losing consciousness....

I had to find out what, if anything, I had told them. I had to know if they now knew where to find my wife and son. I had to know if I had put my family in danger.

Dante came into the room. He looked frustrated. A good sign? I wondered.

Dante leaned down, his face only inches from mine. "Sooner or later, Andrew, we will find them."

"Look in the cemetery, you bastard," I said in a low voice. "They're dead."

"I don't believe you." Dante pulled up a chair. "If they are indeed dead, why are there no death certificates?"

"I couldn't take her to a hospital. I told you this already," I said, staring up at the ceiling. "She went into labor early. She hadn't been able to see a doctor because your goons were hunting us. There were complications. The baby was stillborn. My wife hemorrhaged and I lost her as well. How many times will you force me to relive this?"

"As often as it takes for you to convince me," Dante answered.

"Why would you want my child?" I demanded.

Dante didn't respond.

―――

I LAY on my back on the bed, staring up at the ceiling. I knew it was night because the lights had been turned out. With no windows and no clocks within my range of vision, this was the only way I had of distinguishing day from night. I mentally tried to keep track of the days, the months that had passed, but it was not always clear to me.

Sometimes I meditated. Sometimes I practiced visualization exercises. And then there were the nights the ghosts came. Sometimes they were comforting. Other times, they were disturbing. Like tonight....

"*I want my mum!*" *I screamed.*

"*Your mum is gone, Andrew,*" *Edward had attempted to explain.* "*She drowned—*"

"*No!*" *I cried.* "*She can't be!*"

"*She was quite sick, child.*"

"*No, you're lying!*" *I hit my stepfather repeatedly, unable to control my anger.* "*My mum's not dead! She's not!*"

I remembered going to my room, curling up in a fetal position on my bed, refusing to eat, refusing to talk to anyone. I wasn't sure when I stopped crying.

When I stopped feeling....

"Where are they, Andrew?"

"They're dead!"

The giant called Caine hit me hard, a sharp blow to the head that sent me crashing to the floor. I looked up, waiting for the giant to come after me again. Dante stood in the doorway, his face contorted by rage. "I'll ask you again, Andrew. Where are they?"

"They're dead!" I shouted.

Dante nodded to the goon and left the room. The big man grabbed me by the front of my shirt, hauling me to my feet. This time, the blow connected with my jaw. I fell backward, hitting the concrete wall. The goon hit me again. I doubled over in pain. Another blow landed me face down on the floor. The big man jerked me upward again, punching me hard in the abdomen.

Finally, mercifully, the beating stopped. The goon threw my battered body onto the bed and left the cell. I heard the familiar clicking sound of the locks being activated. I lay there for a long time, motionless, trying to determine if anything was broken. My jaw felt as if it might be. I knew it would heal quickly, but for the moment, I was in a great deal of pain.

Tomorrow, I would be subjected to another round of testing.

A short time later, the lights went out. They always went out at the same time every night. I looked forward to it. That was the only time I had any real peace. I practiced visualization techniques to help me maintain my sanity throughout the degrading tests, the interrogations and the beatings. My mental control was becoming more focused with each session.

Tonight, I was going to put it to the test.

I lay supine on the bed, closed my eyes and focused on the pain in my jaw. Finally, the pain subsided. I touched my jaw. The pain was gone.

I continued to focus, this time on the house in New Zealand. I was climbing the stairs. I could see it clearly. I entered the bedroom. Lynne was asleep. I went over to the crib and wondered why Lynne hadn't moved the baby to the nursery we'd prepared before I left.

My son slept soundly, unaware of the turmoil surrounding him. I wanted to touch him, to hold him, but reluctantly decided not to wake him.

I turned to my wife. She lay on my side of the bed, hugging my pillow. I sat next to her, watching her sleep. I could tell she'd been crying. *I did this to you,* I thought, overwhelmed by guilt. *I took you away from everyone and everything you knew, made you a fugitive, and then I left you. I wonder if you'll ever be able to forgive me.*

I brushed a strand of her hair off her face and kissed her cheek. She stirred a little, turning onto her back. I kissed her again and she wrapped her arms around my neck, holding me tightly. I kissed her again, pushing the blankets away so there would be nothing between us....

———

I OPENED MY EYES. My heart thumped wildly inside my chest. I was back in my prison.

It had only been a dream, but it felt so real. I'd been there, in the house in New Zealand. I'd touched my son. I'd made love to my wife. I could still feel her in my arms. I could smell her, taste her. Tonight, my visualization exercises had exceeded my expectations. I'd left my earthly prison. I'd somehow left my physical body. I'd transcended time and space and had made love to my wife.

How?

87

LYNNE

I love you....
    I lay in bed in the darkness, unable to stop crying. It was a dream, but it felt so real. He'd come back to us. We made love. I felt his lips, his body, his breath on my skin. I felt the familiar softness of his beard.

I was screaming inside, my love for him mingling with the deep sadness I felt at my loss—and my anger at him for leaving. *Why did it have to be you? Why couldn't you have just mailed it to the authorities? Why did you have to do it yourself?*

The baby started to cry. I went to him, lifting him from his crib, cuddling him. He was so perceptive. As young as he was, he sensed my pain. He picked up on my fear, the fear that had prompted me to move his crib into my bedroom so that he would never be out of my sight. *He's all I have left,* I thought angrily.

Two short years ago—had it only been two years?—I had my work, my family, and a man I loved in spite of my best efforts. Now, my work was gone. My husband was gone. I lived in fear that this child I wanted so desperately, Connor's gift to me, would be taken from me as well.

I never left the property. Gabriel and Rafaela saw to it that all of our needs were met. I had everything I needed.

Everything except my husband.

I sat in the rocker, nursing Kiwi, wondering if we'd ever have a normal life again. Wondering if Connor was alive, if I would ever see him again outside my dreams. I needed answers. I needed closure. I imagined him being beaten. I imagined him being killed for defying the cartel. I looked down at the baby in my arms and wondered if Connor would see our son grow up.

No. He's alive, I thought. He was here, tonight. He was in this room. He made love to me.

He's alive, reaching out to me....

I STARED at the computer monitor for a long time, at the open email form. I wanted to contact my family, contact Tim and Isabella, let them all know I was alive. I wanted to pick up the phone and call them. I wanted to get on a plane and fly to the US or to Egypt...but I couldn't.

Trust no one, Connor had told me. *Stay here.*

I knew he was right. I knew if I left, Kiwi and I would be at risk. The minute we surfaced, it would be open season.

Could I e-mail Tim?

It can be traced, Connor had warned me. *They'll be watching, waiting....*

I'm a prisoner in my own home, I realized, though not for the first time. Then an idea began to form. How easy would it be to trace snail mail? I wondered. Even the postal service has a problem with that. She took paper and a pen from the drawer and started to write...

Dear Tim and Isabella,

I'm sorry for all the trouble I've caused you. I'm sorry for all you've had to suffer alone. I wish I could have told you why Connor and I had to leave so abruptly, but we believed we could protect you by remaining silent. I can't tell you now. I can't even tell you where I am.

I can introduce you to our son, Kiwi. Actually, his name is Daniel Ewan Mackenzie, but we called him Kiwi before he was born. It stuck. As you can see, he's a carbon copy of Connor. I was just the incubator. I hope one day soon, you'll get to meet him.

*Love,
Lynne*

88

CONNOR

I was on my knees beside the bed, my eyes closed tightly. I didn't know how much more I could take. The beatings were more intense and more frequent with each passing day. I wanted to die. I wanted it to be over. I endured only because I knew when they finally allowed me to die, it would mean they had found Lynne and my son.

I bore the pain and humiliation believing that in doing so, I was protecting my family.

"Now you begin to understand."

I looked up. There was a woman standing beside me—beautiful, with long, brilliant red hair and eyes that gleamed like emeralds. She looked so familiar—at first, I thought I was looking at my mother, but I quickly realized it was not Anne.

"I do know you," I said slowly.

"Yes," she said in a soft, melodious voice. "I've been with you all of your life."

I got up slowly. "You're—"

"Rafaela."

I didn't understand. "Rafaela is with my wife," I started. "She's an older woman, a bit frumpy, quite a bit shorter—"

"Like this?" She seemed to morph before my eyes, becoming the caretaker who had delivered my son, then resuming her more attractive form. I was sure I was hallucinating. Was it a seizure, or was it the drugs they'd been giving me?

"How did you get here? Are you working for them?" I was horrified.

"I work only for God," she assured me.

"God?"

"Gabriel and I were sent to protect you and your wife while you awaited the birth of your child." She sat on the edge of the bed. "Gabriel performed your marriage ceremony. We witnessed the birth of your son. As I delivered Daniel, Gabriel delivered you."

I sank down next to her. "I was delivered by an angel," I said slowly.

She nodded.

"But he wasn't my father?"

"No."

"You know who my father was," I guessed.

"No," she said. "Only God Himself can answer that question for you."

"Why do they want my son?"

"Dante has interpreted the prophecy," she said. "He knows that Daniel will one day follow you in your calling, and that it is he who will do battle with one of his own blood."

"Who will he have to fight?"

"I do not know."

"What's your role in this insanity?" I asked then.

"I have been your guardian since your birth," she explained. "It was my duty to protect you, to guide you to your destiny."

I shook my head. "Then why am I here?"

"You had to be irretrievably broken before you could finally begin to relinquish control to God and allow him to work through you,"

Rafaela said patiently. "Even now you fight what you know in your heart to be the truth."

"I see you here, now, and still I can't believe," I confessed.

"Honest communication. That's a start," she said.

"Why did my mother have to die?" I asked.

"God did not kill your mother."

"He didn't prevent it, either." The resentment surged to the surface. "Why did he not protect her?"

"You had to live without love so that you would realize how precious it is."

"Collateral damage? Is that all she was?" That made me angry.

"Had your life not taken the course it has, you would not have become whole again."

"Whole?" The prophet must become whole again in the eyes of God.

I thought of Lynne and Kiwi.

"I whispered to you the night your sister asked you to go with her to the lecture," Rafaela told me. "I encouraged you to go with her so that you and Lynne would meet, and you would go with her to Egypt."

"Did you also bring my mother and Edward together?"

"Nothing happens by accident," she said.

I nodded slowly as it all began to sink in. "Lynne was right, then?"

"That you were chosen to be the prophet? Yes, she was correct." Rafaela put her hand on mine. "Connor, there is not much time. You must surrender yourself to God and allow his power to come through you."

"If you're an angel, you know my name isn't really Connor," I said, withdrawing my hand.

"It is now," she said. "As I've told you, there are no coincidences. Andrew died the night you confessed your love to the woman who became your wife, and you became Connor Mackenzie. Do you know what that name means?"

I shook my head.

"Wise, intelligent leader," Rafaela said. "That's what you'll become."

I forced a short laugh. "The wisdom of Solomon, is that what's expected of me?"

"Something like that, yes."

"I can't be a prophet." I got up and walked to the other side of the cell, then turned to look at her again. "That would really be the blind leading the blind."

"You are what you are. You cannot change that," she said.

"I don't know *how* to be a prophet."

"Being a prophet is an act of obedience," Rafaela explained. "The prophet's role is to bring light into darkness, to speak the truth."

"Why me?"

"Only God can answer that. He's chosen you. He chose you before you were born."

"Have I been drafted, then?"

She nodded. "In a sense, I suppose you have been," she answered.

"I can't refuse?"

"You can, of course," Rafaela said as she looked around the cell, "but why would you want to?"

I shook my head, still unable to accept it. "I can't do this. I can't even process it."

Rafaela stood up. "They'll kill you. What purpose will that serve?"

"If what my wife has told me is the truth," I began, "no matter what I say to God, he'll know if I'm not being honest."

"Yes, He will."

"I'm not there yet," I confessed. "I want to be, but I'm not."

"Then tell Him that!" Rafaela urged him. "Down on your knees, confess your doubts! Allow Him to change your heart! Do it, Connor, and be free!"

I went to my knees, but I didn't know where to begin. "I'm not sure what I believe," I started. "I find it hard to believe you could be real when my mother, who loved you and trusted you unconditionally was allowed to be killed for her faith. It's hard for me to believe when my wife had to give birth as she did, putting her life and our son's at risk. It's hard for me to believe I could have some kind of special favor with you, given the life I've had...."

The longer I prayed, all the anger and bitterness I'd carried with me all my life surged to the surface, a kaleidoscope of emotion that threatened to swallow me. In my mind, I was in that cold, dark, turbulent sea of my nightmares, swimming, struggling to stay above water, fighting the undertow...

I saw the light on the boat. I could see Lynne, calling out to me. I could hear the baby crying.... Then I saw something else...a serpent, rising from the sea, headed for the boat...and I started to struggle against the current, trying to reach the boat before the serpent could attack it. I raised my arm, and found there was a sword in my hand. It was a huge, gleaming sword, and I drove it into the serpent. When I did, the serpent was swallowed up by the sea, which instantly calmed. The darkness turned to light, and I swam to the boat.

When I opened my eyes, Rafaela was smiling. "Now what?" I asked.

"Now the battle begins," she told me.

"ANDREW."

I looked up as Sarah was let into the cell. "Why have they brought you here?" I asked.

"I came here of my own free will." She sat next to me on the bed. "Are you all right?" she asked, embracing me. "Have they hurt you?"

"I'll live. For now," I told her. "How did you get access—"

"I let Nicholas think I could persuade you to cooperate."

I shook my head emphatically.

"He intends to kill you, Andrew."

I nodded. "I know."

"I'm not going to let that happen," she said then.

I couldn't hide my surprise. "You can't stop him, Sarah," I said. "He'll kill you as well."

"He allowed me to see you because he wants me to convince you to tell him where you've hidden your wife and child," she continued. "I don't know why he wants to know."

I remembered the prophecy. "I do," I said, "but it's not going to happen."

"I never intended to ask you to tell me anything," Sarah said. "I came to tell you I'm going to get you out of here. It might take me a day or two, but if you'll trust me, I'll send you home to them."

"I can't ask you to put yourself at risk for me."

She took my hands in hers. "You haven't. But I'm going to do whatever I must to gain your freedom."

I COULD HEAR the guards outside my cell.

"What the hell?"

The closed-circuit camera in the cell was apparently malfunctioning and they were frantically attempting to adjust the equipment. The audio was out, while the video was distorted by static.

"What's wrong?"

"I don't know. It was working just fine an hour ago."

Divine intervention? I was starting to believe it.

"Sarah, Dante's holding some children here. He told me they're in this section," I said, seizing the opportunity.

She nodded. "I know," she said.

"If and when I leave here, I have to take them with me," I insisted.

She was hesitant. "I don't know if I can manage that," she admitted.

"You have to. *We* have to," I said. "I owe it to these kids to get them out of here and back to their parents."

She looked uncertain. "I want to get you out before he kills you. I could send the authorities," she suggested.

I shook my head. "They'd be dead before all the warrants could be issued," I told her. "We have to take them with us."

"Andrew. Andrew."

I heard Sarah's voice as she fumbled with the security lock on the door. I got to my feet. "How did you get past the security guards?"

"There's a major security breach in another section," she told me in a low voice. "We don't have much time. Ten minutes at best."

I suppressed a laugh. "I had no idea my wee sister was so devious. The children?" I asked then.

"I've got the access codes for all of the cells."

The door finally opened. I rushed out and looked around. "Give me the codes. You go. Now."

She shook her head. "You'll need my help if you're to get out of here before they return," she said.

I hesitated, then nodded. "All right."

The two of us worked frantically to unlock all ten cells. Some of the children were reluctant to go with us. "It's all right," Sarah assured them. "We're here to take you home."

Many of the children didn't speak English, but the others dragged them along. They all followed Sarah and I down a long corridor normally used for deliveries, chattering among themselves. I knew they were frightened. I was as well. I knew what would happen if we were caught.

I had helped design this facility. I'd been the one who demanded state-of-the-art security. I set the strict requirements for the manpower that patrolled the facility. I also knew where the chemicals were stored, and there was a storage room on the route we were taking. "Keep them moving," I told Sarah. "I'll catch up."

"No," she protested. "We can't go without you."

"You won't be," I told her. "I'll be right behind you."

I went into the storeroom and found what I was looking for—a canister of benzene. If they caught us, this would slow them down a bit. Combustible, highly toxic. Deadly.

I ran down the corridor, catching up to the group. "That way, Sarah!" I called out to her.

Sarah directed the group toward the rear exit, with me silently praying we'd make it. I knew Dante well enough now to know that he would never allow any of us to leave there alive.

I could see the service exit a few hundred feet ahead. *We're going to make it,* I thought, stepping up my pace.

"Andrew—don't do anything foolish!"

Dante was behind us with at least a dozen armed men. "Stop now and I won't kill them."

I turned. "Who do you think you're kidding, Nicholas?" I demanded loudly. "You never intended to let any of us survive."

"Don't move!" one of the guards called out.

I stopped in my tracks. "Nicholas—do you know what this is?" I asked in a loud voice.

Dante's eyes fixed on the canister. "Don't be stupid, Andrew," he said.

"We're leaving," I shouted. "Make your goons stand down, or I'll open it."

"It's combustible," Dante warned.

"We're leaving," I said again. "Try to stop us, and I'll bring this place down."

"With all of you inside?" Dante wasn't convinced.

"If necessary."

One of the guards raised his gun. Sarah, seeing he was aiming at me, rushed forward. "No!" she screamed.

Startled, the guard fired, his bullet hitting Sarah. She let out a cry and fell to the floor. I threw the canister as a second shot was fired. The bullet hit it, igniting the chemicals. It started a chain reaction, all the chemicals in the storeroom exploding. Flames immediately engulfed the corridor, blocking Dante and his guards from pursuit. "Keep running!" I yelled to the children. I scooped Sarah up in my arms and carried her out of the building to safety as the complex exploded.

"Go," Sarah whispered as I placed her on the lawn, kneeling beside her. "I'm going to slow you down."

"I'm not leaving without you," I said softly. The children had stopped and were gathered around us, looking on expectantly.

"You can't help me." Blood from a chest wound soaked the front of her silk blouse. "Go, back to your wife and son."

I hesitated, remembering...my mother's wrists bloody, my tears falling on them...Lynne's shoulder, one moment covered by a dark, ugly bruise, the next without a trace of it...the bird, dead in the box, then flying away. I placed my hand on my sister's wound and closed my eyes. *Please don't deny me now. Please save her. Please....*

Sarah's eyes opened. She gave a sharp gasp. "I was dying. I could feel it," she whispered.

Thank you, Father.

"You're going to be fine, I promise you," I told her, pushing her hair back off her face. "We've got to get out of here now, so if you still feel weak, I'm going to carry you."

"I think I can stand."

I helped her up and put an arm around her, supporting her as her strength returned. We made our way to the rear security gates, opened now as the fire department arrived on the scene.

I looked back once as we made our escape. The entire complex was in flames. *You're all going back to Hell, where you belong*, I thought.

No one could have survived that....

THE CEMETERY WAS DESERTED. I walked alone among the gravestones. A blue hooded jacket concealed my face as I made my way to two graves marked by a large marble gravestone topped with a sculpture of an angel. The angel looked heavenward; arms outstretched. A dove perched on one hand.

I knelt at my mother's grave and placed a single pink rose on the earth. "You were right, Mum," I said softly. "You knew."

"I thought I'd find you here."

I looked up. Sarah stood there, smiling down at me. "How are you feeling?" I asked.

"As if I'd never been shot," she said. "So you're the real deal, are you?"

"So it would seem."

"Our mother was not insane, then."

"No." I reached up and took her hand. "Thank you for taking in the kids."

"I certainly have the room now," she said. "Are you sure you don't want the house?"

I made a face. "That mausoleum? My wife would never go for it."

"Have you talked to her yet?" Sarah asked.

"I haven't been able to reach her," I said. "Dante had my phone when she last called. That may be why she's not picking up. I'm going home as soon as I can. At least I'll surprise her."

"I'll call Nigel and have the corporate jet ready to take you whenever you're ready to go."

"I appreciate it," I told her. "It's not over, you know. You will have to leave London and join us in exile."

"Nicholas is dead. There's no more threat."

I shook my head. "Edward told me this is a global conspiracy," I recalled. "He said their people were everywhere. The cartel has interests in banks, universities, a wide range of businesses. They also had a good many politicians in their pockets. I have to bring them down. All of them."

She was silent for a moment. "What do we do, Andrew?" she finally asked.

"Andrew is dead."

She gave me a puzzled look.

"I am no longer Andrew Stewart. The prophet has been reborn, I'm told," I said. "I am now and forever Connor Mackenzie."

"That will take a bit of getting used to," she told me. "What about Icarus?"

"I've no interest in running it," I answered honestly.

"Neither do I," she said. "What shall we do about that?"

"You'll think of something, I'm sure."

"Me?"

"I'm not staying, remember?"

"So you aren't." She gave a heavy sigh. "You never stay anywhere for long, do you?"

"Wrong." I grinned. "When I get back to New Zealand, I just might stay there forever."

89

LYNNE

The news of the explosion at GenTech forced me to face a reality I'd subconsciously denied since the day he disappeared in London: Connor was dead. He was never coming back. Up until that moment, I'd hung onto that slim thread of hope that he was alive somewhere—but now I knew he could not have survived. If he were alive, he would have come back, now that Dante and his associates were dead.

His sister Sarah and the children escaped the fire that killed Dante. There had been no mention in any of the news reports of Connor.

I wonder if he knew he accomplished what he set out to do? I blinked back a tear as I viewed online footage of the missing children being reunited with their families. I wish our family could have been reunited.

I wasn't sure when I'd made the decision to leave. I'd been restless for months, living in isolation, not knowing if my husband was dead or alive, not having any human contact other than my son, Gabriel and Rafaela. Now, I could no longer bear to stay there in exile without my husband, without hope that he would return to us.

If he were alive, he would have come home by now, I thought. *No way would he stay away.*

I remembered that day I'd tried to get him on his cell phone....

"Hello, Mrs. Mackenzie. I've been waiting for your call."

I had never heard Nicholas Dante's voice before, yet I knew instinctively who was speaking. That night, I'd thrown that cell phone, the last of the prepaid phones we'd purchased, into the lake.

A part of me did want to stay here. This was my home, the home Connor and I had shared. This was the place where our son was born. In spite of the circumstances that brought us here, we'd made it a real home.

Connor wanted us to stay, I thought. *He wanted us to be safe. But it's over now.*

Kiwi needs to be around other children. His cousins. He needs a normal childhood, if he can ever have anything remotely resembling normal.

I sorted through all of the fake IDs and passports Connor had obtained for us in Rome. There were some we hadn't used. I could play it safe for now, use one of those. Just in case.

But what do I do about Kiwi? He doesn't have a passport.

I can go to the US embassy here. He's an American citizen by birth. I can get him a passport.

He doesn't have a birth certificate.

"Is there a problem?"

I looked up. Rafaela was standing in the doorway, carrying a tray. "Is it lunchtime already?" I asked.

Rafaela nodded. "You've been preoccupied," she observed. "Is there a problem?"

"My son doesn't have a birth certificate," I said. "How do I get him a passport without a birth certificate?"

"Why do you need a passport?" Rafaela placed the tray on the table.

"I have to go home," I said.

"This is your home, is it not?"

I nodded. "This will always be our home," I said. "But my husband's gone and I have family back in the States."

"Do you think it wise to leave?" Rafaela asked.

I wasn't sure. "Connor's dead. I need to start living again, at least as best I can without him," I said.

"Then perhaps the answer you seek is in his files," Rafaela suggested, nodding toward the computer on the table.

I nodded. "It's worth a shot." I logged on and found a file Connor had encrypted. The file was labeled Kiwi.

In it, I found six birth certificates. "Date of birth, June 22. Male, eight pounds, two ounces. Length, twenty-one and one-quarter inches. Name, Daniel Ewan Mackenzie. Father, Connor Ewan Mackenzie. Mother, Lynne-Marie Raven Mackenzie," I read aloud. The other birth records were identical in statistics. Only the names were different.

"How did he do this?" I wondered aloud.

"He planned for all possibilities, did he not?" Rafaela asked.

"Always, but—"

"Does God not always provide?"

"Yes, but—"

"God be with you if you must do this," Rafaela said resolutely.

I LOOKED out the window as the 747 began its descent to Lambert-St. Louis International Airport. How long had it been since I'd been home? I couldn't remember. I secured Kiwi in his seat. "It's all right, honey," I told him. "We'll be there soon."

"Daddy's coming."

"No, Daddy's not there. I wish he were," I said, kissing the top of his head.

I wondered what the future held for us. *I could return to fieldwork. Tim and Isabella had assembled a new team and returned to the Middle East. I could go back there, too. Or could I?*

I can't go back. Nothing's ever going to be the same again. I'm never going to be the same again.

90

CONNOR

As the plane taxied down the runway and lifted off, I leaned back in my seat and closed my eyes. I couldn't wait to get back to Lynne and our son. I imagined the look on her face when I arrived, and it made me smile.

I tried to phone her again, but still there was no answer. *I'll surprise her,* I told myself again.

I was anxious to get there, and grateful to Sarah for taking responsibility for the children, for making sure they got back to their parents. I thought about the children. *Will their parents accept them, once they know the truth?*

If not, Lynne and I will become their parents. For as long as they remain children.

God willing...

"Lynne!" I called out as I entered the house. "Darlin,' I'm home!"

There was no response.

I looked around, floored by the sudden realization that I was alone. There was no one there. Where could they have gone? Were they safe? I climbed the stairs to the master bedroom. The bed was made. Everything was in order. The bassinet still sat near the bed.

I opened the closet. It was empty. Their clothes were gone.

My heart sank. They were gone—and I had no idea where they had gone. I dropped into the rocking chair, the same chair in which I'd rocked my newborn son. I buried my face in my hands and cried openly. I was finally free, and they were gone.

"Tell me where they've gone!" I shouted. "Let me go to them!"

"Not yet."

I looked up. Gabriel stood in the doorway.

"Where are they?" I demanded.

"They're safe. Protected."

"Where?" I asked again.

"You can't go to them. Not yet."

"Why not?"

"You made a promise," Gabriel reminded me. "You have an obligation—or did you only make that promise to be free of the cartel's prison?"

"No, of course not." I insisted. "But I didn't know I wasn't going to be allowed to return to my family."

"You'll see them again."

"When?"

"After you achieve communion with God."

91

CAITLIN

"I just got a NOTICE from Interpol," I told Jack. "Believe it or not, Andrew Stewart is alive and well and spotted at the airport in Christchurch, New Zealand."

"Where do you think he's been all this time?"

I thought about it. "Haven't a clue." I continued to stare at the NOTICE.

"What would he be doing in New Zealand?" Jack asked.

"That must be where he stashed his wife and kid," I decided. "Now that he's resurfaced, we have to bring him in. And unfortunately, there's still the matter of the murder of Julian Marshall."

"The evidence there is circumstantial at best," Jack said.

"They still want him—and his wife—for questioning."

"If he did kill Marshall," Jack said, "he should get a medal for it."

92

DARCY

I put my new digital camera in its case and began the task of sorting through my extensive photo files from the past. That was when I found the photographs I'd taken of Lynne and Connor Mackenzie's—Andrew Stewart's—wedding.

Were they legally married? I wondered now. Wouldn't marrying her using a false identity constitute fraud?

I doubted that would matter to Lynne. I looked at the wedding photograph for a long time. Her eyes...the way she looked at her new husband...she'd never looked at me that way. She'd forgive him anything, I think. How had she put it? They were joined at the soul.

I put it aside and picked up the shots I'd gotten of Connor alone: at the little church in Jerusalem, waiting for Lynne; at the excavation site in the Sinai; out in the desert...always flanked by those two ghostly figures.

Spirits, I thought. What a nutty idea.

I knew Lynne was still alive, but I had no idea where she was now. I knew she'd want these photographs. She'd want them for her kid, so he'd at least know what his father looked like.

Her partner, Tim. He'll know how to contact her, I thought, going to my computer. I'll send them to him. He'll see that she gets them....

93

CONNOR

I rented a camel and camping gear from a Bedouin guide. I didn't understand what I was about to do, but that was, it seemed, part of the plan. I had to do this as a test of faith.

"Go to the summit and wait."

"Wait...for what?"

"Your Father will tell you in his timing."

"How long will I have to stay up there?" I asked.

"Your Father will tell you in his timing."

"When can I see my wife and son?" I asked impatiently.

"In time."

I was still struggling with this new reality. I had surrendered myself to God, but could I go through with it? Could I be the prophet I was supposedly created to be? Could I give up control of my life? All I wanted was to be a normal man with a normal life with my wife and child.

"There's no turning back now," I told myself.

I zipped up my jacket, pulled up the hood and mounted the camel. The wind was in my face as I began the climb to the summit....

I SET up camp at the top of the mountain and filled my canteens from the natural spring there. "This is the only mountain in the Sinai that has a natural spring," Lynne had told me. "The Bible says the mountain Moses climbed had such a spring."

She had wanted to climb this mountain because she believed Moses had climbed it thousands of years ago. My wife wanted that kind of communion with God. I, who had never sought such a thing, had been summoned to receive it. Why? Why me?

I took the Bible she'd given me from my backpack and sat near the fire I'd built. I tried to read, but found I couldn't concentrate. I couldn't stop thinking about Lynne and Kiwi. *Please, let me go to them, wherever they are. Let me put my mind at ease so I can focus.*

"You can't bargain with God, Connor."

I looked up. Gabriel stood near my tent, a look of disapproval on his face. "I don't understand," I admitted. "I don't understand it at all."

"No, you don't, but you will soon," Gabriel assured me.

"Lynne and Daniel—I need to know they're safe," I said.

"They are quite safe," Gabriel assured me. "Protected."

"Where are they?"

"In time, you will be reunited with them," the angel promised. "First, however, you must prove yourself to God. You must stay until He sends you back to them. You must accept the calling for which you came into this world."

"I do accept it!" I insisted. "Am I wrong to want to be with them? It's been a year and a half."

"You will not have to wait much longer," Gabriel told me.

But for me, even a day longer was too long.

94

DARCY

"I've decided to publish your spook photos," Alberta told me.

I looked at her, trying not to laugh. "My *what?*"

"The photographs you took of Andrew Stewart, Connor Mackenzie, whoever the hell he is," Alberta said. "He's news, with the break in the GenTech abduction case."

"You're all heart," I said, flopping into one of the chairs in her office.

"You never liked the man," Alberta reminded me. "Why does it suddenly matter to you?"

"I would imagine Duchess—Lynne—won't take it well," I said, making it clear my concern was for Lynne.

Alberta softened. "Have you heard from her?" she wanted to know.

I shook my head. "Not a word since she and Mackenzie faked their deaths—not since I left their dig in Egypt, actually," I said. "I don't even know where she is. I did contact her former partner, Tim O'Halloran. I sent her copies of the photographs through him. Thought she might want them for her son. As I recall, he didn't allow many to be taken of him."

Alberta was leafing through the photographs. "Looking at these, I can see why."

95

LYNNE

"I've thought about it, but I can't, Tim," I said, cradling the telephone on my shoulder. "Not yet."

"It would be hard to be here without Connor, I know," Tim said.

I was silent for a moment, thinking. "It would be impossible—for now," I admitted. "It took me so long to find him, Tim. How do I go back to business as usual without him?"

"I don't know," he said, "but I know you'll make it. You've always been tough."

"We all have our limits," I said.

"And you have that baby you always wanted," he reminded me.

I managed a little laugh. "Not such a baby anymore," I said. "He's actually a miniature version of Connor."

"Lynne, about that—I sent you a package. Forwarded it from Darcy," he said.

"Darcy?" I asked, surprised. "Why would he be sending me a package?"

"I think you're going to want this," Tim told me. "It's photographs. Of Connor."

I sank into a chair. "The only one I had of him was taken at our wedding," I said quietly.

"I know. That's why I figured you'd want these."

I had to struggle to maintain my composure. "At least Kiwi will know what his father looked like."

I HELD the large cardboard mailer in my hand, not sure I was ready to see what it contained. It was labeled PHOTOGRAPHS: HAND CANCEL. How hard was it going to be to look at them?

I sat on the couch and carefully opened it, withdrawing the contents. The first photograph was of Connor at the church before our wedding. He was standing at the window, bathed in light.

From where? I wondered. We had a candlelight ceremony. At night.

Then I noticed the transparent figure behind him. At first, I thought it was a flaw. I examined it closely. The form appeared to be human.

Double exposure?

The same figures appeared in all of the photos. Is it possible? Could they be angels?

"Mummy?"

I looked up from the photographs in my lap. Kiwi was watching me, a puzzled expression on his small face. "What's that?" he asked.

I smiled. "Come look," I said, patting the couch. He climbed up next to me, and I showed him each of the photos. "That's your daddy," I told him.

He smiled up at me, and seeing his face next to the images of his father's was painful. Kiwi really was a tiny version of Connor. I imagined my son at thirty, looking exactly like his father, and it broke my heart.

He frowned. "Don't cry, Mummy," he said, patting my arm. "Don't cry."

I wiped my eyes. "I just miss your daddy, baby," I said.

"Daddy's coming home," the child said.

I pulled him into my arms and held him close. *When does the pain stop?*

96

CONNOR

I didn't know how long I'd been on the mountain. I'd lost track of time. I watched the sun rise every morning. I read my Bible. I prayed. I fasted when it was demanded of me. I slept—and I dreamed. Still, I did not understand why I was here or what was expected of me.

I dreamed of my family, of Lynne, of Kiwi, of Sarah, of my mother. And I talked to God.

"I know I should be able to forgive Edward, but I can't. Not yet," I confessed. "The man destroyed us, Sarah and me. He used my mother and let them kill her. He would have let them kill Lynne as well. How do I forgive that?"

"If you don't forgive him, you're the one who will suffer. It will poison your soul."

"He's dead now. He got what he deserved," I said.

"Yes, he has been judged."

"I hope he's burning in hell."

"You must let go of the past. Only then can you fulfill your calling."

"I'm not sure I ever can," I said, pushing the dying embers of the fire about with a stick.

"You must. You cannot let anything stand in the way of your mission."

"Maybe you've got the wrong man, then."

And the next day, the dialogue would begin anew....

97

LYNNE

"I'm not sure I can stay here," I told Tim, "but I don't know what I want to do or where I want to live."

"Come back to work," he urged me once again.

"Maybe one day, but not now," I said with deep sadness. "I need to start over, I think."

"But you're *not* starting over," he argued. "You say you've accepted that he's really gone, but you still wait for him to come walking through your door."

"I've been offered a teaching position in Baltimore," I said then, trying to change the subject.

"You're no desk jockey, babe."

"I don't know what I am anymore."

"You don't have to work at all," he said. "Connor left you an obscenely rich woman."

"That's going into a trust for Kiwi," I insisted.

"Think you'll ever come back to us?" he asked.

"I don't know," I admitted. "I've lost the ability to think beyond today."

98

CONNOR

I had reached the breaking point.

I had no idea how long I'd been on the mountain. I knew only that food had become scarce, I was dirty and smelled of sweat and filth. My hair had grown long, as had my beard. I was a broken man who was desperate to be reunited with my family, a man trying to be what was expected of me but afraid I could never measure up. On this mountain, my wealth meant nothing. My genius meant nothing. My education meant nothing. My past meant nothing. There was only now.

Please, just tell me what you want of me so I can go home, I thought.

"Where is home, prophet?"

I looked up. "I don't know," I realized. "I no longer have a home."

"Yes, *you do.*"

"My home is wherever my wife and child are," I said. It was the only answer I could give truthfully.

"Yet *you have come and you have stayed as you were commanded to do.*"

"I believe. Is that what I need to say? Is that what I have to prove?"

"Why do you assume you have something to prove?"

"I've spent my life proving myself."

"You have accepted your calling. I will direct you and you will lead the nonbelievers from the darkness."

"I don't know what to do, what to say," I despaired.

"You will not need to know. I will direct you. I will give you the words when you speak. You have only to surrender yourself wholly."

"Kneel, Connor."

I turned. Gabriel and Rafaela stood behind me. "What?" I asked.

"Kneel," Rafaela repeated. "Humble yourself before God."

I nodded, lowering myself to a kneeling position. I bowed my head. "I am your servant," I said in a low voice.

There was no verbal response, but a disturbance in the heavens erupted at that moment—thunder, lightning, a meteorite shower that pelted the desert every few seconds. A cloud of smoke enveloped the top of the mountain. I remained kneeling, eyes closed, praying, trying not to give in to the fear that engulfed me.

"Rise," Gabriel told me.

I got to my feet slowly. I couldn't believe what I was seeing. It was the most incredible light show I'd ever seen. I raised my arms as if to try to embrace my father for the first time. "Yes!" I cried out. I turned to face Gabriel and Rafaela. "Yes, Lord!"

That was when I discovered I was alone on the mountain.

I REGAINED CONSCIOUSNESS SLOWLY. I opened my eyes to unfamiliar surroundings. *Where am I?* I wondered.

"Ah, you are awake, finally."

I looked up with eyes that wouldn't quite focus. The man who stood over me was unmistakably Bedouin, tall and swarthy. He held a bowl in his hand. I didn't know what was in the bowl, but it did smell good.

I tried to pull myself upright, but was too weak. I fell back against the pillow, frustrated.

"You must first regain your strength," the Bedouin told me. "Now that you are awake, you can eat." He sat next to the cot on which I was lying. He offered me a drink.

I suddenly realized how thirsty I was. I felt as if I'd had a mouthful of sand. "Do not drink too fast," the other man warned, but I couldn't help myself.

"Where am I?" I asked.

"Our camp is at the foot of the mountain, not far from where you came down." The Bedouin spoon-fed me. "You collapsed. We have been tending you since."

"How long have I been here?"

"Two weeks."

"Two weeks!" I tried to get up again, but the man stopped me.

"You must be patient."

"My wife and son—I have to find them," I insisted.

"Not until you are well enough to travel." He put the bowl aside and studied me for a moment. "You saw the face of Allah on that mountain."

I shook my head. "I don't know what happened up there."

"He has sent you. For all of us. And we will tend you until you can go safely." The man smiled. "We have been waiting a long time for this day."

———

I STOOD on the side of the highway, arm extended, trying to hitchhike to Cairo. Car after car passed me by. I'd been there for almost two hours, and not only had no one stopped, most had hit the accelerator as they passed me.

Finally, a truck slowed to a stop. "Where you headed?" the man behind the wheel asked. He spoke in broken English.

"Cairo," I told him.

"You're in luck. That's where I'm going."

I took one last look over my shoulder as I climbed into the truck and headed for civilization, wondering why the two angels had abandoned me....

———

I CHECKED into a hotel in Cairo—after my credit card was approved and a call to Sarah in London convinced the front desk manager it hadn't been stolen. I went to my room and soaked in a hot bath for more than an hour. I called room service and ordered a meal large enough to feed a family of four. I looked forward to sleeping in a soft bed again—though I didn't look forward to being in that bed without my wife.

I had to find Lynne and Kiwi. I couldn't conceive of the idea of sleeping alone any longer. I missed curling up with Lynne, holding her in my arms, dispelling all the loneliness I'd felt all those years before we found each other. I missed all the talks we'd had in the middle of the night. I missed her. I missed my son. I missed the love I found with them.

Kiwi would be almost two years old now, I thought as I stood in front of the bathroom mirror, trimming my beard. The last time I saw him, he wasn't even two months old.

Where are you, Lynne? Why did you leave New Zealand? Why won't they tell me where you are?

99

CAITLIN

Jack and I were going over the files for our current case when Randy Baker found us. "Thought you'd want to know—Andrew Stewart's been spotted again."

That came as a surprise. "Where?" I asked.

"Cairo."

"We thought he was dead," Jack said.

A thought occurred to me. "Do you remember that news story a few weeks ago—that freak storm in Egypt?"

Baker nodded. "The Egyptian military was on alert. Thought they were being attacked."

I nodded. "Darcy told me a pretty outrageous story about how the men behind the child abductions believed Stewart was some kind of divine messenger."

Jack rolled his eyes. "Right."

"Sarah Stewart rescued the kids from GenTech's London facility," I went on. "How did she do it? She couldn't have done it alone."

"You think Andrew Stewart was there?" Baker asked.

"More than one of the kids reportedly told their parents that there had been a man with them when they escaped. Here's the weird part. All of the kids claimed Sarah Stewart had been shot during the escape," I said. "They said the man who was with them touched her chest wound and healed it."

100

DARCY

"I still can't believe it," Alberta said as she and I walked through the gallery together, checking out the exhibit before the opening. "You, doing a one-man show."

I laughed. "You can't believe I'm good enough, or that I agreed to it?"

"I've always known you were good enough," she assured me. "I just never thought of you as the type to do a gallery exhibit. You're the man who wants to be on the front lines, in the midst of the action."

"The past few years have given me a lot to think about," I confided. "I'm not a young man anymore."

She feigned shock. "You? No—you're ageless!"

"Like Stonehenge," I scoffed. "I'm actually happy to hang around for a while. My son and his wife are expecting—I'm going to be a grandfather."

She was genuinely happy for me. "Congratulations, Gramps."

My cell vibrated in my pocket. I checked the number and raised an eyebrow. "The FBI?"

She gave me a look. "What have you done now?"

"I guess I'll have to find out. I'll just be a minute." I walked away as I put the phone to my ear. "Darcy. Talk."

"Darcy, it's Caitlin."

"Caitlin? Just can't stay away from me, huh?"

"Be serious," she said impatiently. "Have you heard from your ex?"

"Do restraining orders count?"

"I don't have time for this—"

"Come on, Cat. My exes all hate me," I said. "You, of all people, should know that. After all, you're the one who put everything I owned, including my boxer shorts, out for the Goodwill truck."

There was silence on the other end.

"All right, I get it. To answer your question, no, I have not heard from Lynne. I sent her some photos I took of the Lord of the Geeks back when I saw them in Egypt—under the circumstances, I thought she might want them for her kid. But I sent them in care of her partner, Dr. O'Halloran."

"Give me his number," Caitlin said.

"Don't have it with me. I'll have to call you back with it when I get home." I paused. "What's this all about?"

"I need to locate her."

"She's a US citizen—why would Uncle Sam be keeping tabs on one of his own?" I asked.

"Citizen or not, she's married to a man who can help us nail the cartel." Caitlin paused. "And unfortunately, they're both wanted for questioning in a murder case."

"In Italy."

"Two words, Darcy. Extradition treaty," Caitlin said impatiently.

"But isn't this all after the fact?" I asked. "He's been dead almost two years now."

"Presumed dead," Caitlin corrected me. "He's not only not dead, I've got a NOTICE from Interpol indicating he's on the move."

"I'm not surprised he's not dead. I'm the guy who always said he couldn't be taken out without a silver bullet," I reminded her. "I never did get what Duchess saw in him, but I'll tell you this: if she and the boy are here, he will come for them. I'm surprised he's waited this long."

"Get back to me with that number, Darcy." She ended the call abruptly.

I pushed my cell back into my pocket and rejoined Alberta in front of a large photograph that was the centerpiece of the exhibit: black and white, Mackenzie in the Sinai desert in the darkness of night, illuminated by a brilliant white light. There were two ghostly figures, almost transparent, flanking him.

The placard beneath the photo read *The Deliverer*.

"Ever figure out what that is?" Alberta asked, pointing to the figure on the left.

I shook my head. "They do look human, don't they?"

"I think that's why this particular photograph's garnered you so much recognition," she said, her fingertips tracing the ghostly outline. "There are some, including religious leaders, who believe you managed to photograph two angels."

"With him?" I laughed at the thought.

101

CAITLIN

I put the telephone back on its base and looked up at Jack. "He left Cairo yesterday," I said. "He's got a stopover in Paris. Flight 1103, due in at Reagan National at 10:45 this morning."

"We'd have to intercept him at Dulles," Jack said. "We may have to hand him over to Rome in the Marshall case. What's he thinking?"

"He's not," I said.

He munched a handful of chips. He offered the bag to me, but I shook my head, wrinkling my nose in disdain. "Blondie, I worry about you. Ever since you started dating that French chef, you've become a food snob," he said. "As for Mackenzie—Stewart—whoever he is this week, if it were me, I'd risk it and come for my wife and kid."

"Not surprised," I said. "I've always known *you* were nuts."

"Think about it," he urged. "Why wouldn't he come for them?"

"Why wouldn't he *send* for them?"

"His wife thinks he's dead. Not something he can break to her over the phone." He looked up at the clock on the wall. "Well," he said, "if we have to bust him, we'd better get a move on. That flight's on time, according to Dulles. It'll be arriving soon."

"I don't believe this," I said.

We were stuck in bumper-to-bumper traffic on the bridge over the Potomac. It was at a standstill. "I wonder what the problem is?"

"I'll go find out," Jack volunteered. He got out of the car and picked his way through the sea of vehicles. I took out my cell phone to call the airport, but the phone was dead. I checked it over, recalling I'd just charged the battery that morning. Frustrated, I shoved it back into my bag.

Jack returned a few minutes later. "There's a truckload of pigs jackknifed up at the other end of the bridge—they had some escapees, I was told," he explained, amused.

"What the hell are pigs doing in DC?" I asked.

Jack didn't miss a beat. "Running for Congress."

I looked at him, impatient, unamused.

He looked over the side of the bridge. "Can pigs swim?" he wondered aloud.

"Give me your cell, Goober," I ordered.

"Sure." He pulled it from his belt clip and tossed it to me. "What's wrong with yours?"

"Dead." I looked at the phone in my hand. "So's yours."

"You sure?" He took it from me. "That's funny. It was working ten minutes ago."

I looked up. There was a plane flying low, making its approach to the airport. As it passed over, I watched it for a moment, then turned to Jack.

"If I were a betting man—and I am—I'd say that's Flight 1103, right on schedule," he said.

"He's been flagged," I said. "He'll be detained in Customs."

"They said it was a satellite disruption," the Customs agent told me. "We lost phones, computers, the whole enchilada, for almost five minutes just before Flight 1103 landed. The place was in chaos."

"But it was back up before the plane was on the ground?" I asked.

The agent nodded. "He was on that plane. Not only that, he was given VIP clearance—they walked him through security to his connecting flight."

"His passport was flagged," I insisted.

"No."

"What do you mean, no?" I asked. "The FBI flagged him. *I'm* FBI."

"See for yourself." The Customs agent pulled it up on the monitor. I looked at the display. There was nothing to indicate he was to be detained upon entry. How had this happened?

Jack rejoined me. "I know where he's headed. His wife and son are at her family's home near St. Louis."

"Let's go."

"Let him go," Jack said in a quiet voice.

"We can't."

"Let him go," he repeated firmly. "Do you remember the things he told us in London?"

I rolled my eyes. "You didn't believe that crap, did you?"

"I didn't at the time," he said, "but look at everything that's happened today."

"Like what?" I challenged.

"The pigs. Our phones. The satellite disruption just before the plane landed that brought the whole place to a screeching halt. He's a wanted fugitive, but his passport's clean. Not only that, he was given a VIP escort through Customs. What would you call it?"

"Incompetence."

I started to walk away, but he grabbed my arm and spoke in a low voice. "Let him go. Please."

"Why do you care?" I demanded.

"He's got a kid, Blondie. I'd give anything if my old man had cared that much about me," he admitted.

102

CONNOR

The Harley Davidson roared along the open highway, headed southwest. It was early afternoon, and I had the interstate pretty much to myself. I stopped at a pancake house for lunch, but I barely touched the food. The server had tried to make conversation, but I found I wasn't hungry after all and had no interest in exchanging pleasantries. I was anxious to get back on the road as quickly as possible.

I'd waited long enough.

103

LYNNE

"Are you sure about this, Lynne?" Tim asked. I shoved my hands down into the pockets of my jeans. I wasn't sure about anything. "I can't live here. I thought I could, but I can't. I've decided to go back to New Zealand."

Tim, Isabella and I were in the front yard. The remnants of Kiwi's second birthday party were everywhere, and all the kids still wore party hats. Multicolored balloons were tied to the white picket fence. In the house, my mother and sisters were cleaning up the mess in the kitchen. My father and brothers-in-law had retreated to the church under the pretense of doing urgent work in the sanctuary. They'd do anything to get away from the wild bunch in the front yard.

Kiwi ran up the steps to the wraparound front porch and climbed into the porch swing. Two of the older kids gently pushed the swing, eliciting giggles from him.

"He needs me right now," I said with certainty. "We'll be joining you in Israel next summer. I promise. I wouldn't miss it. When he's a little older, I'll come back to full-time field work."

"He seems perfectly happy, all things considered," Isabella observed.

"He's never even had a cold," I said as we climbed the steps to the porch. I scooped Kiwi up in my arms and kissed his forehead. He gave me a hug.

Tim held the screen door open for Isabella and I as we entered the house, the rest of the kids darting in between us. "He's so much like Connor it's scary sometimes," I went on. "He walked and talked by six months, he started to read at fourteen months. On the downside, he got a head start on the Terrible Twos."

"I'll bet he's a real handful," Tim said.

"He is," I said with bittersweet pride. "He hates to sleep. He fights it every night. Connor never wanted to waste a minute. He slept only when he couldn't fight it any longer."

As we entered the house, Kiwi stroked my cheek affectionately. "Don't cry, Mummy. Daddy's coming."

Tim gave me a disapproving look. "Have you been telling him that?"

I shook my head. "I talk to him about his father, but I don't know where that comes from."

"I'll bet."

"I don't see anything of me in him, to be perfectly honest. I think I was just the incubator," I went on. Kiwi had his father's blue eyes and light brown hair. He'd also inherited Connor's mischievous smile. "He's going to be the worst nightmare of a lot of girls' fathers by the time he's sixteen," I predicted.

Isabella, always the photographer, noticed the large framed photograph I had placed on the mantle. It was Connor, standing in the desert with two ghostly figures, looking at something only he could see. "Darcy got an award for that one, didn't he?" Isabella asked.

I nodded. "I think he was being sarcastic when he titled it *The Deliverer*," I said. "I never thought I'd ever be grateful for Darcy's tenacity, but if it weren't for him, I wouldn't have even one photo of Connor to show his son."

"How'd he manage that, anyway?" Isabella asked. "Connor never let anyone photograph him."

"Darcy never quite made it into the twenty-first century," I said, pouring tea for us. "He still uses film. He had one roll in his bag and one in the camera."

"I wasn't sure I should even forward that package to you when Darcy sent it," Tim admitted, taking a drink.

"I'm glad you did," I said. "He's doing an exhibit in New York, you know."

"He is?" Isabella was interested. "Somehow that sort of thing never seemed to be Darcy's style."

"It surprised me, too," I said. "It's a collection from all the photos he took in Egypt and Israel. They're calling the exhibit *Images of Hope*."

Kiwi climbed down from my lap. "Call Daddy!" he repeated.

"He keeps saying that he spoke to Connor," I said. "He's got such a vivid imagination."

"What do you expect?" Tim asked. "You talk to him about Connor every day, you show him photos—"

"Kiwi is going to know his father," I insisted.

"Honey, it's been two years," he said gently. "You have to let it go. They probably killed him within the first twenty-four hours. If he were still alive, he would have contacted you long before now. And even if by some miracle he is alive, they've had him for the past two years. He may not be the same man anymore."

Isabella placed a hand on her husband's forearm. "Tim," she said softly.

"She needs to face facts, babe," he insisted. "This isn't healthy for either of them." He turned to me again. "How long do you plan to go on waiting for him?"

I took a deep breath. "I know he's gone, Tim, but I can't stop loving him."

"Still got the gun?" he asked.

I nodded. "My parents hate having it in the house, but I still can't completely let my guard down," she admitted. "There's a part of me that still panics if someone is driving behind me for more than a few blocks, or if a stranger comes to the door. The other day, there was a Hummer behind me. I drove twenty miles out of the way to keep it from following us home. When Kiwi starts school, I'll be a basket case. I worry every time he gets out of my sight."

"This isn't good for your son, Lynne," Tim warned. "You've got him waiting for a father who's never going to come. How do you think that's going to affect him when he's older? You know how tough it was for Connor, believing all those years his mother had abandoned him."

"His father didn't abandon him," I said, annoyed.

Kiwi, bored, climbed up into the window seat to watch a dove that had landed on the porch railing and his curiosity was piqued. He got down and went to the door. I never saw him go outside...

104

CONNOR

I saw him at the front door as I was getting off the bike. Even though I hadn't seen my son in almost two years, I recognized him immediately. He came out onto the porch and stood at the top of the steps.

"Hello, there," I called out to him.

"Mummy says I shouldn't talk to strangers," Kiwi told me.

"Your mummy is right, Daniel," I told him.

He cocked his head to one side. "You know my name."

"Yes, I do. I also know that today is your birthday, so I'm not really a stranger, am I?"

"I s'pose not." He lumbered down the steps and approached the gate hesitantly. "Do you know my mummy, too?" he asked.

"Quite well." I reached up and removed my helmet, and Kiwi smiled broadly.

"Daddy!"

105

LYNNE

I looked around. "Where's Kiwi?" I asked, suddenly alarmed.

"He's outside talking to that man," one of the kids told me.

"Man?" I panicked. I grabbed the handgun from the drawer and ran to the door, my heart racing. There was my son, in the arms of a stranger. I could only see the back of his head. I ran out the door, gun raised.

"Put him down or I'll blow your head off!" I shouted.

The man only laughed. "Not the welcome I was hoping for, but I suppose it's to be expected," he said as he turned to face me.

"Daddy's home, Mummy!" Kiwi laughed, hugging his father.

I couldn't believe it. It was Connor. He looked ten years older. There were deep lines around his eyes. "Oh, dear God!" I gasped—and burst into tears.

"Bloody hell, woman—you were crying when I left and you're still crying. Are you happy to see me or not?" he asked.

Tim grabbed the gun from my hand as I flew off the porch and ran to Connor, hugging him tightly. "What happened?" I asked. "Where have you been? I heard about Edward—I was afraid they'd killed you, too. Are you all right?"

"All valid questions, but I'm unable to answer them all at once," he said as we headed back to the house. He had one arm around me and held Kiwi in the other. "It took me weeks to locate you. I've been traveling for the better part of a week, darlin'. I could really use a hot bath and a bit of rest."

"Anything you want," I told him.

He grinned. "You haven't gone and remarried while I was away, have you?"

"You've been nothing but trouble since the day I met you," I teased. "Why on earth would I want to go through that with another man?"

He paused at the top of the steps and faced me. "You were right, love," he said softly.

I gave him a questioning look in response.

"About everything."

I didn't need to hear the words. I saw it in his eyes. He'd found the truth.

Dear reader,

We hope you enjoyed reading *Chasing The Wind*. Please take a moment to leave a review in Amazon, even if it's a short one. Your opinion is important to us.

Discover more books by Norma Beishir at https://www.nextchapter.pub/authors/norma-beishir

Want to know when one of our books is free or discounted for Kindle? Join the newsletter at http://eepurl.com/bqqB3H

Best regards,

Norma Beishir and the Next Chapter Team

ABOUT THE AUTHORS

Norma Beishir can't remember a time when she wanted to be anything other than a novelist. Growing up on a farm with mostly animals for companionship, she learned to use her imagination to entertain herself. In school, she often got into trouble for writing stories in class. When she went off to college, her mother encouraged her writing; her father advised her to have a backup plan in case "the writing thing" didn't work out—but she figured having a Plan B would make it too easy to give up, so there was no Plan B. While working at a large advertising agency (a clerical position—again, there could be no Plan B), she queried an agent, who took her on. Within a year, she'd sold three novels for a six-figure sum. Chasing the Wind is her fifteenth novel.

Collin Beishir didn't plan on becoming a novelist. He entertained a number of potential career paths, but this wasn't on the shortlist. He started out doing research for his mother. But geek that he is, he found himself contributing ideas, suggestions, and muffled laughter when she was going too far out there with an idea. He became her collaborator before he knew it. For the record, he would have liked the security of a Plan B. Working with her on Chasing the Wind made him start thinking of characters and plots of his own, which inspired a solo project for him, ELE—Extinction Level Event, which is taking him longer to complete than expected. He does have a Plan B of sorts. Somebody has to be thinking of the future.

You might also like

The Vienna Connection by Dick Rosano

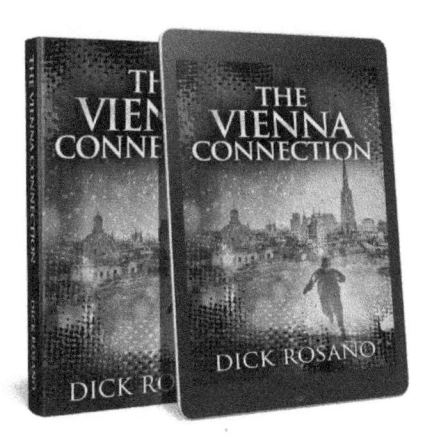

To read the first chapter for free go to:
https://www.nextchapter.pub/books/the-vienna-connection

Lightning Source UK Ltd.
Milton Keynes UK
UKHW040303310820
369008UK00013B/152